No time, no choice, Bolan realized

Sight, breathe deep, let it out. How many times had he dropped an enemy from a distance, an invisible shooter? So many killing fields, he briefly considered, since he was a Green Beret sniper in Southeast Asia.

Yesterday's victories and spilled enemy blood to save innocent lives didn't mean a damn thing, he knew, and never guaranteed success in the present. Dwelling on the glory days—believing reputation and prior success would carry a man through the day's trials—was best left for fools, wanna-bes and has-beens.

The future, Bolan thought, was now.

And in his hands.

D0724767

Don Pendleton's Mack Bolan®

Devil's Bargain

A GOLD EAGLE BOOK FROM

WORLDWIDE®

TORONTO • NEW YORK • LONDON
AMSTERDAM • PARIS • SYDNEY • HAMBURG
STOCKHOLM • ATHENS • TOKYO • MILAN
MADRID • WARSAW • BUDAPEST • AUCKLAND

First edition January 2005

ISBN 0-373-61503-5

Special thanks and acknowledgment to
Dan Schmidt for his contribution to this work.

DEVIL'S BARGAIN

Printed in U.S.A.

It is fatal to enter any war without the will to win.
—Douglas MacArthur,
1880–1964

However much enemy blood I need to spill,
whatever degree of pain is required to inflict
on the vipers and jackals, I will be part of this
war, without limit, without consequences. There will
be no concession. There will be no compromise.
—Mack Bolan

PROLOGUE

Jaric Muhdal was waiting for the miracle to happen.

Word of the alleged breakout had been written in Kurdish on a wadded note tossed into his lap five days ago by his Turk captor. Muhdal had been ordered to eat the missive once he'd read it. Or was it six days, a week since the encounter? And was this simply mental torture, taunting him with false hopes of escaping the hell on earth called Dyrik Prison? One last sadistic blow by his tormentors to break his spirit, and days, he believed, before he was marched out to the courtyard to be beheaded?

It was nearly impossible to track time or grasp insight into mind games played by his tormentors, he concluded as he hacked out a strand of gummy blood, wincing when his tongue ran over the craters inside his mouth. Rage building, he felt the slime ooze down over his bare chest and stomach, pool to a warm slither against exposed genitals. Time was frozen, but his hatred felt as if it could last an eternity.

How much more could he take? Daily he was hung upside down, pummeled by fists, flogged by a metal studded belt. A slice of moldy bread, a cup of tepid water a day—he was a withered sack of drooping flesh. For endless hours he sat naked and bleeding from his scalp to the soles of his feet in the blackness of a six-by-four concrete-block cell, breathing the stink of his own filth and fear; waiting for execution. Still, solitary confinement was respite from torture.

He knew plenty about deprivation, suffering, cruelty—his people, after all, had been savaged by the Turks for eighty years—but even those who believed they carried the heart of a lion could long for death under such brutal conditions.

Only they wouldn't break him, he determined. No begging to be spared when the time came, no crack in the armor of his will. He would take what he knew about his fellow PKK freedom fighters with him to the grave. As leader, there was no other way, the warrior's ego also dictating he stand an iron pillar, an example of unwavering defiance in the enemy's face. With the imprisonment of Abdullah Ocalan, the disappearance of his younger brother, Osman—previous heir to power—he hadn't climbed the ranks of the Workers Party of Kurdistan by showing mercy, either to friend or foe. Why expect anything now but the worst at the hands of a savage, hated enemy? He would die the way he had lived. At worst, he could take comfort not even his death would cripple the dream of a Kurdistan nation.

Muhdal felt the pain dig needles of fire through

every nerve ending. For some strange reason, agony seared to mind images of his wife and three children, murdered many years ago by Turk soldiers, leaving him to wonder how much they had suffered before they were beheaded, their bodies dumped in a mass grave with the other villagers. The ringing in his ears, his brain jellied and throbbing, smothered by darkness, and he found himself suddenly drifting away into warm darkness. Muffled by the steel door, the screams of other prisoners, whipped and beaten down the corridor, some of them, he knew, with testicles plugged into generators, echoing the cry of anger and hatred in his heart.

Pain was good, he decided. So was hate.

So was never forgetting.

Focus, he told himself, perhaps the Turk was being truthful. Hold on.

"Hope!" Escape first, then dip his hands in more enemy blood. Perhaps freedom was on the way, but at what price? he wondered. After all, the guards, like many Turks here, he knew, were Boz Kurt, members of a secret netherworld of militants, all of whom were hardly resigned to carry out the Ankara regime's wishes without personal gain. Their treachery and brutal ways were legendary, even by Turk standards. The Gray Wolves—or so went the mythical nonsense, he knew, fighting to pull thoughts together inside the crucible of his skull—believed the first Turk was suckled by a wolf on the Central Asian steppe. Whether or not the milk of a wild beast spawned a bloodline of ferocious warriors, Muhdal only knew all Turks were devils in human skin. As for the Boz Kurt, they weren't only considered terrorists by Ankara, but they were also drug traffickers.

Which was why he and fifteen of his fighters had been arrested in the first place.

Revolutions required money to purchase weapons, even loyalty. Briefly he thought back eight months, the Turks catching them asleep, but the question lingered as to how the Turks had found them, slipped so easily into the gorge. Of course, he never expected a trial, a just legal system all but an alien concept in Turkey. His crimes—so the Turks claimed—ranged from murder to drug trafficking, too many, in fact, to count.

Killing the enemy, he believed, was acceptable in the eyes of Allah. So was stealing from Turk thieves and murderers, a holy decree, spoken directly to him from God in dreams, God telling him the spoils of war were to be used to gain an edge against the enemy. How could he, in all good conscience, have stood idly by anyway, watch the Turks use the southeast corner of the country to fatten their own coffers with truck caravans of heroin funneled from Afghanistan, hashish from Lebanon. And when the Ankara regime, faceless butchers who marched their killers out to Anatolia, had declared a campaign of genocide against them generations ago, and soon after the treacherous Brits reneged on their promise to give the Kurds their own country...?

The groan echoing in his ears, he gnashed chipped, broken teeth, invisible flames racing down the long furrows in his back. It hurt to breathe.

The first of several rumbles sounded from a great distance, but it was next to impossible to judge direction, much less clearly absorb sound through the chiming in his ears, windowless walls and door a barrier to whatever the source. He strained his ears, heart racing, then shuddered to his feet, hand on wall to brace himself. Tremors rippled underfoot next, the thunder pealing closer, nearly on top of his cell. This region, he knew, was notorious for earthquakes, ground splitting open without warning, hills crumbling down to consume tens of thousands within minutes. Images of being buried alive were jumping through his mind, then the bedlam beyond the darkness broke through the bells in his ears.

Muhdal laughed, hope flaming as the racket of weapons fire, the screams of men being shot in the corridor seemed to pound the door, an invisible but living force shouting freedom was mere feet and seconds away.

The murderous din, he thought, oh, but it was the singing of angels.

Freedom! Salvation! Revenge!

He made out the rattling of a key being inserted. Laughing, so giddy with relief, he wasn't sure he could walk. But pain seemed to leak out of bruised and gashed flesh like water through a sieve right then. Waiting, he watched as the door swung out, light stabbing the dark, piercing his eyes, autofire and angry shouts blasting a wave of sense, shattering noise in his face.

Squinting, he made out the stocky figure of the Boz

Kurt guard. He was shoving himself off the wall when it happened.

There was a wink of light in the doorway, a shadow rolling up behind the man, an armed wraith clad in black, from hood to boots. Muhdal looked from the bayonet fixed to the assault rifle, believed he heard *tesekkurler,* the hooded one thanking the guard in Turk. Then a pistol flew up in a gloved hand, the shadow jamming the muzzle against the Turk's skull. Muhdal felt his knees buckle as the shot rang out and blood sprayed his lips.

THE UNIDENTIFIED BOGEY blipped onto the screen, dropping from the sky, out of nowhere, it seemed. By the time he calculated numbers scrolling on the digital readout—speed, distance and rate of descent—Colonel Mustafa Gobruz knew it was too late. The hell with his men assuring him there was no evidence of malfunction. Whatever the object, it was sailing a bullet straight course for the compound, less than one minute out, he figured, falling to slam right on top of their heads.

Gobruz felt the anxiety edge to panic in the room, his three-man radar team crunching numbers he already knew. "I can read!"

The colonel then barked orders to scramble all hands, man the antiaircraft batteries, shoot down the bogey on sight. But even as he punched on the Klaxon to throw the compound into full battle alert, Gobruz feared the worst, doomsday numbers ticking down now to mere seconds. The sprawling compound might survive a direct hit from a missile or a crash landing by a crippled aircraft. The dread concern, however, was for the ammunition depots fuel bins, choppers, motor pools, every machine in close proximity to the C and C, topped out with fuel and—

One explosion, pounding through ordnance and thousands of gallons of high-octane fuel, he knew, and the base would erupt, a conflagration leaving behind a smoking crater on the east Anatolia steppe.

Gobruz, snapping up field glasses, burst out the door, stared to the southeast. Baffling, frightening questions shot through his mind as he glanced at soldiers racing up behind the big guns, searchlights scissoring white beams over black sky, barracks spilling forth more troops.

This was no accident, he knew. A deliberate attack, no question, but who was manning the craft, plunging it to the base, perhaps using it as a flying bomb? Or was it one of those unmanned drones, maybe packed with high explosives? Again, who, why? The Kurds had no access to either surface-to-surface missiles or aircraft, much less high-tech unmanned aerial vehicles. Of course, Iran, Iraq and Syria bordered the nation, often providing weapons and fighters to the Kurds, hoping the primitive rabble could create its own independent nation, thus invite them in when the Ankara government collapsed.

Gobruz glanced at the antiaircraft guns, soldiers working with a fury to bring the cannons around and on-line. He was lifting the field glasses, but discovered there was no need.

The object was coming to them, hard, fast and low.

The searchlights framed the craft's bulk, not more than a hundred feet up and out, he saw, as it nose-dived for the cyclone fencing. It appeared a midsize cargo plane, lights out, but no transport bird he knew of carried what appeared to be missiles on its wings.

"Fire!" he shouted across the compound. "What are you waiting for?"

He heard the bark of small-arms fire—why weren't the big guns pounding?—glimpsed the fixed-wing plane clear the fenceline.

Then the world erupted in a flash of roaring fire. Blinded by a white sea of flames, eyeballs and face scorched by superheated wind, Gobruz caught the shrieks, his men torched by incendiary explosions he was sure. He was wheeling, about to launch himself through the doorway when he felt the flames sweep over him, his own screams added to the chorus of wailing demons as he was consumed by the wave of fire.

"LIVE OR DIE, your choice!"

Muhdal watched the faceless gunman, unsure of what was even real, senses warped, swollen by the din. Peering into the bright sheen, Muhdal saw the wraith flash white teeth, dark eyes burning with either laughter or anger. He strained to listen, his savior telling him he had ten seconds to strip the Turk and dress, or the door would slam shut.

Some choice, he thought. Outside, the price for freedom sounded more to him as if the gates of hell had opened to disgorge a legion of devils, there to devour every prisoner.

Men bellowed in agony, wailing from some distance. Muhdal nearly gagged as he sniffed the sickly sweet odor of roasting flesh. Were his men being burned alive, trapped in their cells, thrashing, craving for death to extinguish their misery? Were his rescuers Turks or Kurds? What was this madness?

His confusion deepened as the wraith snapped an order over his shoulder, switching to the Russian language. Another hooded shadow swept through the doorway and hurled what he assumed was water from a bucket. Muhdal took the liquid in the face and chest, then howled when he realized what doused him. The urine burned like acid, biting into countless open wounds.

"Bastards! You throw piss in my face?"

"Five seconds, or I shoot you dead!"

Was that laughter in his eyes? Muhdal wondered, the piss-thrower stepping back, kicking away the Turk's assault rifle, then melting into the corridor where the hellish noise reached a deafening crescendo. Cursing, with a bayoneted muzzle inches from his face, Muhdal nearly shredded the blouse and pants off the body, dressed, finally squeezing into boots a size too small. No weapon in his hands, but he felt the gun in his heart, cocked and ready with murderous wrath, the pain a scalding blaze, now that urine was smothered by clothing, soaking into fabric. He was tempted to lunge for the RPK-74 light machine gun, but the hardman grabbed him by the shoulder, snarled something in Russian, shoved him through the doorway.

"Move it!" Muhdal found more black hoods swarming the halls. Some were armed with the longer, heavier version of the AK-74, banana clips holding forty-five rounds, Muhdal noting holstered side arms, commando vests, webbing studded with grenades and spare clips, com links snugged over hoods. Two big machine guns, Squad Automatic Weapons with 200 round box magazines in the hands of giants. He figured eight invaders at first count, but with shooting converging from all directions it was impossible to say. The deeper he headed down the corridor, the more he feared his immediate future. Several of the invaders were emptying weapons into the cages, mowing down prisoners behind the iron bars, rats in a barrel. They were tossing something on the bodies. As he passed strewed bodies, he found playing cards, the ace of spades with a grinning death's-head resting on lifeless grimaces.

Muhdal wondered if they were murdering his own men, when, rounding the corner, thrust down the bisecting corridor that led to the north exit, he spotted Zeki and Balik being hustled outside by another squad of invaders manhandling the rest of his fighters for the open door, barking at them in a mix of Kurd and Russian the whole way. Whoever these hooded killers, they were professionals, he decided, wondering how they had taken down the prison so swiftly, no Turk resistance he could find anywhere. As long as they weren't Americans—who aided and abetted the Ankara regime—he figured he could live with the indignity of a piss shower for the moment, if salvation from Dyrik was guaranteed. Still, he wouldn't forget his shame.

Muhdal kept moving, saw several of the invaders spear bayonets through chests of downed Turks, gutting one or two like pigs, innards gushing to the floor. The vile stench was so strong now, bile wormed up his chest, hot slime rolling into his throat. And he spotted the smoke and flames leaping up through the grate in the floor of another wing, two fuel drums dumped on their sides. He picked up his pace, eager to put distance to the screams of men burning alive.

Muhdal hit the courtyard, grateful for fresh air, found the invaders ushering his men into the bellies of three Black Hawk gunships. The guard quarters had been reduced to flaming rubble, he saw, likewise the motor pool of Humvees and troop carriers, nothing but burning scrap. Forging into rotor wash, he gave the grounds and walls a quick search, spotted parachute canopies billowed out by heated wind. A look at the guard towers, he saw bodies draped over railings, the claws of four grappling hooks dug into the top edges of the wall.

Professionals, all right, he thought, aware the attack on the prison had been split down the middle between the invaders. Snipers, creeping in from the steppe, took out the guards, scaled the walls, the other half dropping square into the belly to blast and burn.

Nearing the Black Hawk, the Barking Hood on his heels urging speed, Muhdal looked to the distant northern sky. There, the sky strobed, blackness peppered to near daylight with brilliant white flashes. He knew there was a large Turk military base in that direction, thought he heard the rumbling of explosions, but the sound was muted by rotor wash.

He boarded the gunship, glanced at Balik before he was shoved to sit. He seethed, staring at the Barking Hood, another invader looking up from the green glow of a laptop monitor. White teeth flashed, a thumbs-up from the other invader, and the Barking Hood laughed.

Suddenly Muhdal felt as if he were quagmired in a nightmare, skin on fire, heart pumping with fury. Who were they? What did they want? They might have known who he was, but they didn't know that, make no mistake, he would return the favor for dousing him in his cell.

The Barking Hood turned, stripped off the com link as the gunship lifted off. As the man tugged off the hood, Muhdal stared up at a face, purpled and cratered around the eyes and jaws from past battle souvenirs, the whole grisly picture as sharp as the edge of a razor, it could have been the skull on the ace of spades.

The big commando chuckled. "Cheer up, Moody. We're here to help make you all rich men."

Muhdal felt his heart lurch, jaw drop. "Americans?"

The Skull laughed. "Yeah, well, they say even the Devil can speak in all tongues."

Speechless, anchored by fear, Muhdal wondered what horror lay in Kurd futures, staring into the Skull's laughing eyes.

"You do believe in the Devil, don't you, Moody? You damn well better—you're looking at him."

HE WAS CALLED Acheron, named for his resurrection after both the river of Greek mythology in Hades, and the demon who guarded the gates of Hell.

It was the sweetest thing, he thought, Judas bastards oblivious he was risen from the dead. Physically speaking, of course, it was impossible to breathe life into oneself, arise from ashes and dust, but the metaphor worked for him; he was alive and doing fine. Thanks to Big Brother, the old Michael Mitchell was long dead and gone, but Acheron was moving on into the night to settle that score, silence an unclean tongue.

And on national television, no less.

Acheron, he thought— he liked that, seeing himself as the living ghost of the charred bones of that skeleton body double from a forgotten covert war zone in Syria. Oh, he was back, all right, feeling good, strong, ready to grab center stage on the Josh Randall show, pull a dagger from the back of the operation of the ages.

With one final look over his shoulder, he found the Clairmont Studio lot clear of mortals, then keyed the guest door open. The kid at the gate had been easy, one shot through the forehead with the throwaway sound suppressed Walther M-6, but he had counted on the bogus *Washington Post* press pass to get him close enough to the booth, eliminate one problem, confiscate keys. That left two armed rental badges inside, he knew, certain his professional talent would drop a couple of overweight play babies who seemed more inclined to walk female employees to their cars after hours than patrol the premises between doughnuts and coffee. Nailing down the routine of the security detail—so much sloppiness and laziness, he stopped counting the errors of their ways thirty minutes into his first watch—his escape route was mapped out, dry run when he wasn't surveying the studio from his high-rise apartment directly across Connecticut Avenue. This, he figured, would prove so easy it was damn near criminal.

Snicking the door closed behind, he found the hall empty, focused on the lights and the chatter of fools at the end of the corridor. Snugging the dark sunglasses tight with a forefinger, his former Company boss wouldn't recognize him, he knew, not until he spoke the bastard's handle. Black wig, mustache and goatee pasted on, it was a shame, he considered, that other traitors may be watching the left-wing-circle jerk tonight and never know who made the special guest appearance. Well, what was fifteen minutes of fame anyway, when there were years of glory and pleasure at the end of the golden road, beyond his return from the dead?

Marching, he unzipped the loose-fitting windbreaker, pockets weighted down with two exit goodies, twin .50-Magnum Desert Eagles, the showstoppers. It was a bonus, he recalled, cozying up to the makeup girl at the neighborhood pub, plying her with drinks. She couldn't have drawn the setup any better. The stage then, would be off to the right, two cameramen, ten o'clock, rentals on standby, in case an unruly guest needed the hook. It happened, he knew, or so he heard, the punk star so extreme sometimes in left-wing diatribe, even the rational of viewpoint had taken a lunge at his mustache. By God, what he wouldn't give himself, he thought, to rip that mustache off his face, ram it down his gullet…

The coming statement would suffice.

A few paces from the studio, and he heard the loud-mouth in question—LIQ—snorting at something the kid said. "With all due respect," LIQ rebuked, "Josh, I was there. Your sources aren't quite on the money. I'm telling you there's a secret paramilitary infra-structure, of assassins and saboteurs working for the United States government."

No shit, Acheron thought. And why did the talking dickheads always soften the verbal blow "with all due respect?" Politicians were the worst of flimflam artists, he thought, all their "quite frankly" and "to be quite honest with you" spelling out they lied the rest of the time. Let that be him up there, he'd tell the punk, "With all due kiss my ass, here's the real fucking deal."

Stow the righteous anger, he told himself. This was business.

The canister, tossed and bouncing up in the heart of the staff, led the entrance, gas spewing a cloud of nox-ious fumes. Their reaction was typical, expected: cries of panic flayed the air, clipboards and cue cards fell, a mad scramble of bodies ricocheted off one another. He compounded the terror, the Desert Eagle out and pealing. Two heartbeats' worth of thunder blasting through the studio, he tagged the cameramen first, 250-grain boattails exploding through ribs, hurling them back, deadweight bowling down one of the rentals.

The act sticking to the script, he knew he was still live and in color, coast to coast. He was a star right then, and shine he would.

Another tap of the trigger, and he glimpsed a bright red cloud erupt out the back of the standing rental, bodies thrashing and hacking their way out of the tear gas. Tracking on, he dropped Rental Number Three as he staggered to his feet, a headshot, leaving no doubt. With only seconds to wrap it up, exit stage left, Acheron swung his aim stageward. The kid bleated out what sounded a plea, the star shrill next in demand his life be spared, silk-suited arms flapping. Acheron blew him out of his seat.

Rolling toward the raised platform, Acheron found the LIQ glued to his chair, hands raised. What the hell? Obviously the guy had gone soft, a civilian life of fame and small fortune dulling the edge of former killer instincts and battlefield reflex. Where he remembered the LIQ once lean and hard, Acheron saw a double decker chin, coiffed hair, pink manicured fingers, a goddamn walrus in Armani, he thought.

The former CIA assassin drew a bead between wide eyes, flipped the calling card on the table.

Fat quivered under the man's jowl as he looked up from the ace of spades with a death's-head. "You?"

"With all due kiss my ass—you're a dirty rat bastard, Captain Jack."

"Wait!"

"Waited more than ten years already," Acheron said, and squeezed the trigger.

FRAMED IN SOFT LIGHT, they stared back, a living malevolence, it felt, mocking sleepless nights, telling him they would come for a day of reckoning.

"The rebel angels have risen from the pit."

How could it be possible? he wondered. Another shot of whiskey, and the courage he chased kept running away, an evanescent ray of light in the shadows of his living room.

Over ten years had passed since he and several colleagues hatched the dread warning phrase they hoped none of them would ever need to pass on. Already one of them was dead, the national audience bearing witness to murder, and live on television, for God's sake.

It was happening.

Still, Timothy Balton wanted to believe it was some grotesque prank by former colleagues, perhaps envious of his early retirement, that he carved himself a slice of peace and quiet, or maybe angry he turned away from them after a life of service and dedication to national security. Unfortunately there was this blight—off the record—on his career, haunting them all for more than a decade.

Their deaths had been confirmed—sort of. After those two covert debacles, which never came to the attention of any Senate committee on intelligence or counterterrorism, even the President of the United States kept in the dark, the rumor mill churned, casting spectres of grave doubt and fear over the headshed in the loop. The best forensics teams the NSA and the CIA could marshal stated, off the record, they couldn't be one-hundred-percent certain the burned remains were those of Alpha Deep Six. Then there were the slush funds for black ops in secret numbered accounts, twenty million and change whisked into cyberspace following their supposed demise. Well, the horrible truth behind the vanishing act leaked out when the headshed's cover-up was launched in dark earnest. A few crumbs of intel, however, tossed their way, here and there, by followers deemed nonessential personnel and cheated by Alpha Deep Six of their own payday only magnified the enormity of the agenda. As former head of the DOD's Classified Military Aircraft-Classified Military Flights— CMA-CMF—he discovered, during a yearlong follow-up investigation, low- and high-tech jets, cargo planes and helicopters were vanishing from CIA, DIA and NSA bases and installations from Nevada to Afghanistan. The bodies of personnel responsible for guarding such aircraft began stacking up so fast, no witnesses, no clues, not a shred of evidence as to the identities of the assassins left behind, it struck him as if…

What? That all of them had been executed by murderous phantoms?

Trembling, he poured another dose from the half-empty bottle. Down the hatch, hands steady moments later, enough so he felt confident he could aim and fire the Taurus PT-58 with deadly accuracy. He pulled the CD-ROM from the desk drawer. Say they did come? What then? Hand Alpha Deep Six the gathered intelligence on all secrets known about them? Give up the details, hoping they would spare his life, about their disappearance and purported resurrection, what they had allegedly initiated as part of an agenda so horrific he now considered it the evil of the ages?

Evil, he knew, that he was, albeit indirectly, responsible for loosing on the world.

He stared at the picture on his desk. Choking back tears, he wondered if he would soon join his wife and only son.

He flinched, wind howling outside, pistol up as he pivoted toward the curtained windows, something banging off the wall. Shadows, it looked, danced in the night world. Could be, he thought, just moonlight shining through scudding clouds. Wind, he knew, often gusted over the plain, stirred south from the Badlands.

He hesitated, then laid down the weapon. One more shot, he told himself, he desperately needed sleep, if only for an hour. He was thinking he should check the alarm system one more time, recon the ranch and perimeter when—

"So I understand you want divine knowledge."

Balton froze. He felt them, no need to turn, he discovered, three shadows flickering over the wall. His hand shook as he reached for the pistol. He felt a strange urge to laugh, amazed and terrified at how easily they breached his security net, but knew they had the technology able to burn out the guts of a warning system, laser beams melting alarms and motion sensors to molten goo, no matter how complex. It was over, he knew; it was simply a question of how it would end, how soon, how much pain he would endure.

"Cramnon," he breathed.

"Richard Cramnon's dead, remember? I am Abbadon."

"What?"

"I have been raised up from the dead as Abbadon. That would be ancient Hebrew for 'destruction.' I am the bottomless pit, consuming the damned in eternal fire. I am the abyss that vomits forth the dark angel to spread plague and death across the earth."

"You're insane."

"No. I have never been more right."

Balton felt his heart skip a beat, a rumble of cold laughter striking his back.

"Don't look so puked out, Timothy. We just came by to say we love you." His laughter echoed by the others, Cramnon went on, "By the way, I was real sorry to hear about your wife. Breast cancer, huh. Pity about your boy, too. Heroin, was it?" He laughed.

"You rotten son of a—"

"Drugs, modern-day scourge, I always said, the invisible foreign invasion. Hey, they say it's a real heartbreaker, a father having to bury his own child. What do you think it was that pushed the little punk over the edge? Kid couldn't live up to your high standards?"

Balton squeezed his eyes shut, heard Cramnon laugh beyond the roaring in his ears.

"Too much pressure from the old man, not enough love and affection? Big shot that you were at DOD, too caught up in work, family always on the backburner. Bet you hated and blamed yourself when you stared into his coffin, huh? Wonder still how such a tragedy could happen? Wish to God you could have it back to do over. Thing about that, Timothy, human beings always wish they could do it over, make it right, the old 'if I knew then what I know now.' Being a little more

than human these days, well, I had a long chat with
God while I was away. He told me, among other things,
human beings would commit the same damn mistakes
even if they could turn back time. Oh, yeah, I was
thinking about you, asked God why even bother to
create your son if the punk was going to cause you such
grief. God, He tells me humans are always crying,
'why?' when they should ask 'how?' As in how to fix,
how to find a solution. That's why I'm here...the
disk?"

Shaking, Balton began to turn, aiming his rage toward their laughter. He hoped his body concealed the
Taurus, long enough where he could at least tag one,
two if he got lucky. He was in slow motion, dizzied by
shock, as he faced the three of them. The one he believed was Cramnon appeared to float across the room,
a tall shadow in a long black coat, rolling counter-
clockwise from the other two shadows peeling the
other way. Pistol coming around, trigger taking up
slack, he balked, shocked at how different they looked
than he remembered. Where they were once clean-cut
and fair-skinned, he found hair as black as a raven,
flowing to their shoulders. With prominent cheekbones
and hawk noses, complexions so dark or burnished by
sun, black eyes that were once blue, they appeared...

Semitic?

A shot cracked from the dark. He heard a sharp
grunt, pistol flying from his hand, then froze at the
sight of blood jetting from the stump where his thumb
was amputated. Balton slumped, clutched his hand,
gagged.

"Your boy, Gulliver, I made it last two days before he gave you up."

Balton heard his bitter chuckle, then felt tears welling as he looked at the picture. So this was how it would end, he thought, the world fading, the blood pumping out. So many mistakes, so much neglect dead-ending in too much pain and sorrow. It galled him, but Cramnon's cruel words rang true, ground deep. They—whoever they were, he thought—said a man's character was his destiny. Strange, he decided, he wasn't sure what was his own true character. Way beyond guilt and regret now—again, "they" claimed not even God could change the past, and, yes, that even the Devil knew the darkest corners of human hearts, the worst pain, the most atrocious of every man's thoughts and desires—he suddenly prayed to a divine being he hadn't thought about since his wife died. He heard the evil thing demand the disk. Brushing it to the edge of the desk, he heard, "And the password?"

Why not? "Agrippa."

He shut out the laughter, silently implored for a quick, merciful end he knew he didn't deserve. He prayed for forgiveness, his own sins too many, he thought, to even recall. He glimpsed one of the shadows falling beside him, slip the disk into the computer. A metallic click. Behind, smoke blew over his head, Cramnon laughing about the irony of the password. Something about how Agrippa was an ancient sorcerer's book, pages made of human skin, how it listed the names of every demon in Hell, how they could be summoned to earth to help the caller fulfill whatever desire and wish.

"We're in business," Barron heard the shadow say.

Then Cramnon asked, "You prefer it in the back?"

He straightened, offered up a last silent prayer this monstrous evil was soon, somehow, removed from the face of the earth, sent where it belonged, before it was too late.

Turning, he told Cramnon, "No."

CHAPTER ONE

If the nation's enemies pulled it off, Mack Bolan feared the United States of America would cease to exist as he knew it. Any number of apocalyptic nightmares charged through his mind, stoked a sense of dire urgency while inflaming a righteous anger he hadn't felt in some time. Martial law, he knew, would prove the least of the nation's woes. The shortlist of horrors spewed from the brewing caldron of this hell—looting, riots, interstates and highways parking lots as panicked civilians fled for the hills, murder in the streets by those left behind in the chaos and terror—was incomprehensible to rational human minds.

Unfortunately, he had walked this road many times in his War Everlasting. And he knew all about the cannibals unleashing death and destruction on free and not so free societies, consuming or oppressing the innocent, driven by whatever dark machinations churned in hearts pumping with the blood of the wicked.

Only this crisis defied any past experience Bolan had ever known.

Wedged in the doorway beside the M-60 gunner, the Black Hawk gunship sailing over the wooded country-side of Williamsburg, Bolan took in the command-and-control center. A quick head count, as the warbird descended, and he figured ten to fifteen special ops ringing the farmhouse perimeter. Four Black Hawks were grounded in the distance, fuel bladders, he found, already dropped off for quick topping out of tanks, one critical detail out of the way.

Slashed by midmorning sunshine, there were too many black sedans to bother counting—government-issue vehicles having delivered the best and brightest from the FBI, NSA, DIA and whoever else muscled their way into the game—he then noted the small armada of oversize vans in matching color. High-tech communications-surveillance-tracking centers on wheels, bristling with antennae, spouting sat dishes, they could garner intelligence at light speed. From past hands-on experience with war wagons, he knew they could mobilize and steer field operatives to the enemy's back door before they were aware the sky was falling.

Panning on, he saw satellite dishes staggered at various intervals, fanning away from the C-and-C center, cables hooked into generators mounted in the beds of Army transport trucks or Humvees. It appeared top-notch professional on the surface, but it was an operation marshaled in a few short hours, he knew, backed with the full blessing of an anxious White House and Pentagon. And the political-military powers had damn good reason to feel the collective knot in their belly.

Sometimes, though, haste, edging toward panic in this case, he thought, led to bad decisions. Warning bells told him there were too many chiefs in the act.

There was some good news, a ray of hope they could abort the enemy's twisted dream. The FBI had grabbed four of them—two in Richmond, two in Fredericksburg—Bolan learned during his initial briefing at the Justice Department. Under interrogation, the Feds had a general idea what was unfolding, but no clear fix on enemy numbers, where and when the big event—as the opposition called it—would happen. With their arrest, a nervous logic rippled down the chain of intelligence and military command, the former capital of Virginia chosen for strategic purposes, central command planted between what were believed intended strike points. Virginia Beach south, Richmond and Washington, D.C., due north, and Baltimore a short hop up the interstate from here, if the opposition was already on the move, if the enemy even partly succeeded....

Intelligence at this point, he knew, had to be on the money if he was to root out, crush the scourge before it unleashed its murderous agenda.

And hunting down the savages was the reason why he was here.

The Black Hawk touching down, Bolan bounded out the doorway, forged into rotor wash. Closing on the front porch, he found beefed-up security nearly invisible to the naked eye. Briefly he wondered how his sudden entrance into the hunt would be received, an unknown marching in with carte blanche to call the shots. On that score, all egos needed to take a back seat, he knew, as he glimpsed blacksuited men hunkered in the woods, Stoner 63 Light Machine Guns poking through brush, figures with FBI stenciled on windbreakers, Armalite AR-18 assault rifles slung around their shoulders, Feds scurrying in and out of the intel nerve center.

His orders were clear. And a presidential directive had cut through red tape, dropped him square in charge. If anybody had problems with that, there was a number to call, a direct line to the President. The Man in the Oval Office, and Hal Brognola, the big Fed at the Justice Department who gave him his marching orders, knew the credentials he was bringing here were bogus, but they were likewise aware this was no time for interagency backbiting and grandstanding.

It was the eleventh hour, time for decisive, swift and, hopefully, preemptive action.

Or else…

The grim thought trailed away as he saw the tall FBI man materialize in the doorway, venture a few steps across the porch, then appear to balk at what he saw.

"You Special Agent Matt Cooper?"

Of course, the FBI man knew that already, the coded message radioed ahead before his Black Hawk breached their airspace. "That would be me."

"Agent Michael James. ASAC, now that you're here."

"What do you have?"

"What we've got are definite major 'effing' problems."

"How about telling me something I don't know?"

He pulled up short, watching as ASAC James looked him up and down, the FBI man perhaps wondering more "what" he was than "who." No question, he looked military, specifically black ops, worlds apart from any G-man, he knew. Start with the dark aviator shades, for instance, then the combat blacksuit, his tried and proved lethal duo of side arms filling out the windbreaker. There was the Beretta 93-R in shoulder holster, the mammoth .44 Magnum Desert Eagle riding his hip, for killing starters. Just above the rubber-soled combat boots, a Ka-Bar fighting knife was sheathed around his shin, just in case all else failed. Combat vest, pouches slitted to house spare clips, webbing lined with a bevy of frag, tear gas, flash-stun and incendiary grenades, and whatever else he needed for battle, urban or otherwise, was bagged in nylon in the gunship.

"Come on, we're on the clock, Cooper."

Inside the nerve center, trailing James, Bolan felt the air of controlled frenzy, a hornet's nest of buzzing activity. Banks of computers, digital monitors and wall maps packing the room with inches to spare, he navigated through the web of cables strung across the floor. Above the electronic chitter and voices relaying intelligence over com links and secured sat phones, he heard James say, "We think there may be as many as six to ten cells, according to electronic intercepts, surveillance, what cooperation we've gotten from their own communities, informants, here and abroad, on our payroll, filling in a few particulars. In the plus column, we grabbed another of these assholes in Boston.

He appears willing to talk but I'm hearing he's second or third tier, meaning he was on need-to-know until the last minute before the big bang. We don't know if the cells are working in twos, threes or as independent operators, nor what their specific destinations of target."

James stopped by a bank of monitors tied into fax machines, sat phones. "Another sliver of sunlight— two more were snatched at Penn Station, while you were in the air. They were minutes from boarding the Number 90 and 93 trains. Two carry-ons per scumbag, four bags, all loaded with Semtex, the payload just inside Amtrak's fifty-pound limit. Military explosive. Begs the question how the hell they got their hands on it, where and from who in the first place. First-class tickets, one way, of course, they were booked two cars down from the driver's seat. That much wallop, we figure at least two cars trashed and gone up in flames, complete derailment, the works rolling up, one car after…"

"I've got the picture."

"Okay. We are on ThreatCon Delta, terrorist alert severe. If you could ratchet it up a notch the country would be under martial law. You can well imagine the panic already out there among John and Jane Q. Citizen, what with the media jamming mikes and cameras in the face of anybody who looks official. All local and state law enforcement have been scrambled to aid and assist the National Guard, the Army, Special Forces, Delta in the shutdowns, searches, sealing off perimeters of all terminals and depots, starting with the major cities, particularly the Eastern Seaboard, the West Coast. If we don't chop them off at the knees, and soon, well—"

"Airports?"

"Security personnel and procedures have been quadrupled, but we're reading this as a whole different ballgame than using jumbo jets as flying bombs. Just the same, the skies are swarming with every fighter jet we can put in the air. Incoming international air traffic, especially executive jets, will be intercepted and escorted to landing. No compliance, bye-bye, that's straight from the White House. Same thing with ships, large, small, pleasure or commercial. The Coast Guard and the Navy have formed a steel wall, up and down both shorelines, likewise the Gulf."

Was it enough? Bolan wondered. It was a task so monumental it boggled the mind. No amount of manpower, no matter how skilled or determined, could one-hundred-percent guarantee a few of the opposition didn't slip through the net. Then there were trains, buses, already rolling, loaded with unsuspecting passengers, potential conflagrations on wheels that could detonate any moment. He looked at the monitors, saw numbers scrolling as fast as personnel could scoop up sheafs of printed paper. Digital maps of Chicago, New York, Seattle, Los Angeles, Miami were yielding the locations of train and bus terminals, points of travel, layovers and final destinations, all flashing up in red.

"So far, we've sealed off and stopped all departures from Seattle's King Street Station. We're working on

Union Station in D.C. now," James said. "You have Metrorail, the VRE, MARC, and that's just Washington to worry about. The list is near endless as far as manpower is concerned, covering all bases. We're stopping trains and buses that are in transit—as we can get to them—board, clear them out, search all luggage, but it's going to take time, something we don't have. We've just alerted the Chicago Transit Authority. They are under presidential directive to shut down Union Station on Canal Street, but as you might know, Chicago is considered the railway center of the country. God only knows how many trains we're looking at, arriving or leaving in or within a hundred miles around the compass of Chicago alone. You're talking over two hundred trains, rolling anywhere along some twenty-four thousand miles of track at any given time. I don't even have the numbers crunched yet on how many Greyhound, Trailways and charter and tour-bus terminals and depots we have that may be in their crosshairs. There's more," he said, and paused. "The headsheds are thinking there could even be eighteen-wheelers, vans, U-Haul trucks out there, cab and limo drivers…you get the picture? If this thing blows up in our faces, the entire transportation network of the United States is shut down, end of story. Even if they set off one, two trains or buses, and you've got wreckage and dead bodies all over the highways and tracks. I don't even want to hazard a guess as to the chaos that would break out."

"I want everything you have in ten minutes."

"You've got it."

"I'm thinking we might be able to narrow our problems down in short order."

"How so?" James asked.

"Where are the prisoners?"

James grunted, jerked a nod to the deep corner of the room where an armed guard stood. "In the cellar. Problem is, we've already lost two of the four."

"What are you talking about?"

"I'm afraid the show's already started without you. I have to warn you, Cooper, it's messy down there. His name is Moctaw, or that's what he calls himself."

"What is he?"

"I don't know, but he was dumped in my lap, damn near a suitcase load of official DOD papers telling me I was to step aside—that is if I wanted to finish my career with the FBI. There was nothing I could do."

A sordid picture of what he was about to find downstairs already in mind, Bolan followed James across the room, the FBI man barking for the guard to step aside and open the door.

"I'll leave you to introduce yourself," James said, wheeled, then marched back for the nerve center.

Peering into the gloomy shadows below, he caught a whiff of the miasma, an invisible blow to his senses. It was a sickening mix of blood, cooked flesh, loosed body waste. He heard the sharp grunts, then a scream echoed up from the pit. He slipped off his shades, braced for the horror he knew was down there, waiting.

Then Mack Bolan, also known as the Executioner, began his descent.

HER NAME WAS Barbara Price, and it was rare when she left her post at Stony Man Farm. She was, after all, mission controller for the Justice Department's ultra-covert Sensitive Operations Group, her time and expertise on demand nearly around the clock. It was both her present role in covert operations at the Farm, however, and her past employment at the National Security Agency that now found her moments away from rendezvousing with a former colleague.

She watched the numbers on the doors fall, striding down the hallway, looked at a couple pass her by through sunglasses, her low-heeled slip-ons padding over wall-to-wall carpet. She couldn't shake the feeling something felt wrong about this setup. She hadn't survived, nor claimed her current position with the Sensitive Operations Group, by taking anything in the spook world at face value.

Since being informed by cutouts she often used to gather intelligence that Max Geller sounded desperate in his attempts to reach her, a dark nagging had hounded her for days. She hadn't seen, heard from or thought about the man in years, and there he was, hunting her down for undeclared reasons, popping up on the radar screen, out of nowhere.

Finally she returned his call through a series of back channels she arranged. It was the worst of times to leave the Farm, Able Team and Phoenix Force in the trenches, with Mack Bolan, the Farm's lone-wolf operative and a man she was, on occasion, intimate with, in the field. But Geller claimed to have critical information about what the Stony Man warriors were up against, likewise alluding to a threat so grave to national security the entire world could be changed forever. No, he didn't dare speak on any line, no matter how secure. They had to meet.

She had run it past Hal Brognola, the big Fed at the Justice Department who was director of the Farm and liaison to the President. He had given her three hours' leave, but she was to call the time and place for the meet, give him the particulars before she set out. The chopper had ferried her from the Shenandoah Valley to Reagan National, where the Justice Department maintained a small hangar, kept its own vehicles onsite for quick personal access, instead of using "invented" credit cards for rentals. From there in the GMC, a short drive to the hotel in Crystal City, where the feeling she was being followed intensified. It was nothing she could put her finger on, though. Crystal City swarmed with the work force that early-morning hour, a lone blond woman sure to grab the attention of men. Taking extra precautions, just the same, she sat in the hotel lot for fifteen minutes, her instincts flaring so bad she almost called off the meet. A short drive around Crystal City, then she parked in an underground garage, wondered if she was being paranoid. Follow through, she decided. She'd come this far, maybe Geller had something worth hearing. She was grateful, just the same, that the Browning Hi-Power with 13-shot clip was shouldered beneath the windbreaker, two backup clips leathered on her right side.

She found the door to the room where he'd registered under James Wilcox. It had been years since she had worked with the man, both of them gathering signals intelligence and human intelligence for the NSA in a classified program that often involved her directing wet work. Geller was the best at what he did. Tagged the Sphinx, he still was, she knew, the NSA's best code breaker.

She knocked, waited, glanced both ways down the empty hall, removed her sunglasses. The door opened so quickly that she wondered if he had X-ray eyes or had been standing on the foyer, waiting, listening.

"Thanks for coming."

The whiskey fumes swarmed her senses, the first red flag warning her again this felt all wrong. He wasn't the slim, sharply dressed, well-groomed man she remembered. He had aged terribly, gained weight, lost hair. But it was the eyes, sunken with dark circles, unable to focus on her, brimmed with so much anxiety she could smell the fear in the sweat soaked into the collar of his sports shirt. She almost turned, walked away, but he beckoned her to enter.

She did.

"AND JUST WHO the fuck might you be?"

Bolan looked at the ghoul, said, "I was just about to ask you the same thing."

The soldier found it was every bit as messy down there as James warned, and then some. Bolan felt a ball of cold anger lodge in his belly at what he saw in the bastard's torture chamber. It was gruesome devil's work to the extreme, and he couldn't even begin to tally how many laws the butcher had broken. He was fairly certain, though, whichever agency the man pledged allegiance to had given him the green light to do whatever it took to break the prisoners, that he was backed and covered by superiors who would, most likely, wash their hands of this horror show. Yes, Bolan knew the argument—extreme times demanding extreme measures and so forth—but torture in his mind only reduced a man to the same soulless animal level as the enemy. It sickened him to know Moctaw worked for the same government he did. Then again, it occurred to him Moctaw had bulled ahead, aware someone else was on the way to take the reins, the butcher running some personal agenda. Gain information, or threaten the prisoners about talking to the Feds? Every instinct Bolan had earned over the years—fighting every ilk of backstabbing homegrown traitor—warned him something didn't jibe with the man or his methods. Something else lurked behind the mask, he was sure. Any front Moctaw would put on that this was all done in the name of national security was a ruse. Whom was he protecting? What was he hiding? Or was this simply an extreme solution to the dilemma of fighting terrorism on American soil?

Bolan looked at the prisoners. Naked, they were strapped to thick wooden chairs, which were bolted down to the concrete floor. There were two bodies, a dark hole between their eyes. The soldier figured they were the lucky ones. The other two prisoners had some sort of steel vise holding their heads erect, clamps fastened to their eyebrows, their eyes bulging with terror, flicking around like pinballs at their tormentor. Whoever this Moctaw was, Bolan saw he was good with the Gestapo tactics. The black bag, opened on the table, had been emptied of a series of shiny surgical instruments, one of which was a bloody pair of shears. Tourniquets, Bolan saw, were wound around the wrists and ankles of the dead men, all of their fingers and toes strewed in the blood still pooling on the floor. At some point, the bastard had castrated his first two victims, genitals adding to the gory mess at the stumps of their feet. It was obvious where the cigar in the butcher's hand would have gone next. One glance at Moctaw, and Bolan pegged him as little more than a thug. Six-six at least, the muscled Goliath swelled out the black leather apron, blood speckling his craggy features, red drops still falling from a dark mane of disheveled hair. In the tight confines of mildewed brick the stench alone was damn near enough to make even a battle-hardened soldier like Bolan gag. Then he saw the series of oozing burn holes running up the torsos, necks, cheeks, the bastard working his way up, letting them know they were seconds away from having their eyes seared out.

Bolan produced his credentials, thrust them in Moctaw's face. The butcher grunted, unimpressed, or disappointed, the soldier couldn't tell. "Your fun's over."

"Special Agent Matt Cooper, uh-huh. I heard about you."

"Then you heard I'm in charge. That's straight from the White House. You're out of it."

"Out of it? This one here," he snarled, shoving the

glowing end of the cigar toward the prisoner at the far end, "was just about to talk."

"I'll handle it from here."

"You'll handle it? What—you going to bring them some cookies and milk? Sweet-talk 'em? Maybe offer them some all-expenses-paid deal if they sing?"

Bolan stepped around the table, saw the Beretta 92-F within easy reach of the butcher. "Give me the cigar."

It was a dangerous moment, Bolan watching as Moctaw wrestled with some decision, the soldier braced for the butcher to make a grab for the weapon. Moctaw bared his teeth, dumped the cigar on the table.

"It's your party, G-boy. I hope you're not just some six-pack of asskick, all show, no go, since you're the man of the hour now. Maybe you don't know it, but this country's entire transportation system is on the verge of being shut down, I'm talking 9/11 five, maybe ten times over, depending on how many of these scumbags are out there. This is no time for 'pretty please.'"

Bolan made his own decision right then, picked up the cigar. "I'm aware of what's at stake."

"Really? These Red Crescent terrorists pull off their big event, shit, we're going to need Iraqi oil revenue ourselves to help put it all back together. This country will never be the same, they light up even one train or a couple of Greyhounds."

"Besides your gift for stating the obvious, exactly what have you learned?"

Moctaw hesitated, then picked up one of four small square black boxes from the table. The clips-on gave

Bolan a good idea of what they were, then Moctaw confirmed it, saying, "These are satellite-relay pagers. Far as we know, only the Russians and the Israelis, and maybe the Chinese and North Koreans, have this sort of technology."

"And the NSA and the CIA."

Moctaw hesitated. "Right. There are no markings, no serial numbers on these. I couldn't tell you where they came from. They house computer chips that can tie into military communications satellites. Punch in your personal code, hooks you into the principal user, you can beep or be beeped, send or be sent a vibrating signal anywhere from three to five thousand miles. That's how they knew to move."

"Which means whoever's running the operation is still out there."

"That would be a good assumption. We've learned they were communicating by courier when they set up shop, or used P.O. boxes. Basic, keep it simple. For the most part they stayed off the phone, e-mail, Internet, but a couple of them got antsy, even made some overseas calls back home to their loved ones to say goodbye and they were on their way to Paradise. Not real smart. We were able to intercept—"

"I know all that."

Moctaw scowled, then continued, "The usual bogus passports, only they come to America as Europeans, dyed hair, clean-shaved, perfect English. Never know they were camel jockeys. Two of them," he said, nodding at the corpses, "were Iraqis, former fedayeen, to be exact. Made a point of letting me know they were going to blow up some buses and trains, jihad for Gulf II, standard Muslim-fanatic tirade. The two still breathing are Moroccan, recruited, they tell me, in Casablanca by Red Crescent about a year ago." Moctaw pulled the Greyhound tickets from his bag, slapped them on the table. "Four one-way tickets. Two heading north, Port Authority. The other two were westbound, final stop Houston. I've got their ordnance upstairs. Three hundred pounds of Semtex between them, wired and ready to be activated by radio remote."

Bolan looked at the tickets. "Richmond," he said, noting the gate numbers and times of departure. Checking his watch, he found they were due to leave in an hour, give or take. It stood to reason they had been en route to link up with another cell, in Richmond or beyond. He stuffed the tickets into a pocket.

"You have a plan, or are you here to profile, Cooper?"

"What are their names?" Bolan asked, produced a lighter, then put the flame to the end of the cigar.

"I was calling them Ali Baba, one through four."

Bolan puffed on the cigar until the tip glowed. "I could have you arrested."

"Not if you're about to do what I think you are."

"I still might cuff and stuff you."

"You could try."

"Telling me whoever you work for has clout."

"This thing isn't being run by the White House. You could have the President arrest me himself, and

I'd be out and free in less than an hour. And, no, I won't tell you who I work for. You do your own homework."

Bolan blew smoke in Moctaw's face. There was no time for the hassle of arresting the man, get mired in a pissing contest. Besides, the more he heard from Moctaw, the more the bells and whistles rang and blew louder. If he let the man remain at large, he decided, he might end up using him to churn the waters.

Bolan turned his attention to the prisoners. Sometimes, he knew, the threat of torture, especially if a man faced permanent mutilation, worked better than the act itself. One look at the terror bugging out the eyes, bodies quaking, limbs straining to break their bounds, and he knew Moctaw had brought them to the breaking point. They just needed another shove.

The Executioner showed them the glowing tip, then puffed, working the eye to cherry red, let the smoke drift over their faces, choking them. "What are your names?"

"Khariq…"

"Mah…moud…"

"You have two choices," Bolan said. "Tell me everything you know about your end of the operation. If you do that, and we find you're just foot soldiers, no previous track record of terrorism, no blood on your hands, there's a chance you eventually will be sent home to your families. I have the power to be able to make your freedom happen."

"Cooper, you do not have—"

"Shut up," the Executioner growled over his shoulder. He put menace in his eyes and voice that would have even made Moctaw flinch, he believed, leaning closer to their faces, holding the end of the cigar inches from a bulging orb. He saw tears break from the eye as it felt the heat. "One eye at a time." He flicked his lighter, waved the flame around. "While I work on your eyes, I'll put this to your balls. This is not good cop-bad cop."

"We talk…we talk…."

And they did. Bolan stepped back, listening as they babbled so fast he had to slow them down, one at a time. They were to meet three more Red Crescent operatives in Richmond. Bolan got a description of both their attire and the duffel bags with custom designs. Two would be attached to each half of the four-man cell, then they would split off at other depots along the way. The lone operative out was the question mark; they didn't know what his role was. Bolan figured the odd terrorist out for the cell leader. Then the clincher. Enough explosives were going to be left behind in lockers it would be enough to bring down the building.

The Executioner had a critical call to make, but decided to do it in the air while choppering to Richmond. He ground the cigar out on the table. "I'll have James take these prisoners off your hands. He'll take their passports and secure the ordnance."

"That's it? I'm dismissed?"

"No. For your sake you better hope I never lay eyes on you again."

Moctaw made some spitting noise, an expression hardening his face Bolan read as "We'll see." The Executioner put the ghoul out of mind, bounding up the steps. The doomsday clock, he feared, was ticking down to maybe a handful of minutes.

CHAPTER TWO

Barbara Price took the couch. Her back to the wall, she could watch the foyer, the main hall leading to the bedroom, alert to any sound the two of them weren't alone. The Stony Man mission controller caught Geller throwing her a funny look, then the code breaker shrugged, claimed the chair he obviously arranged for his guest directly across the coffee table. Before he turned around his laptop and aluminum briefcase, Price spotted the Beretta 92-F resting on folders stamped Classified. That a lifelong deskbound super-cryptographer—who, to her knowledge, had never heard a shot fired in anger—would arm himself, tossed more fuel onto the fire of nagging suspicion. Was he afraid for his own life, trailed by shadow gunmen ready to silence him, aware of his meeting a former NSA mission controller to which he was prepared to divulge classified intelligence? If that was the case, she knew she had just been tossed into the equation.

Aware it could go to hell at any moment, she

watched her former colleague pour a drink from the bottle of Dewar's, the cigarettes a new vice, ashtray overflowing with gnawed butts. Impatient, she waited while he swallowed his tranquilizer, topped up another round, fired up a cigarette with a silver lighter. Clearly, whatever was eating Geller, the booze and chain-smoking weren't calming the storm. Professional that he was, though, she was grateful he skipped any trip down memory lane, awkward questions about what she'd been doing since leaving the agency. Or did he suspect something in regard to her missing years? she wondered. Was this a fishing expedition? If so, why? She might have worked for the most supersecret, high-tech, intelligence-gathering, black-ops group on the planet, but there was one absolute truth she knew existed in all the covert world. Only death—or the threat of death—ever truly kept a secret. And the longer she sat in Geller's sweat and agitation, the more disturbed she grew.

If he didn't know about the existence of Stony Man Farm outright, did he think he knew something about the Sensitive Operations Group? Then again, he could be clueless. She told herself to keep an open mind but proceed with all due caution. Truth number two—only those individuals with iron principles, she knew, feet planted in a solid base of integrity, never really changed, no matter how many years down the road. Max Geller, in her mind, had always been a question mark, and he had changed, for the worse, she suspected. Genius he might be, but she was aware of his duplicitous streak. Word around the agency had been that

Geller was responsible for the careers of several prom-
ising cryptographers ending abruptly as he backstabbed
his way up the pecking order. Now, like then, Price kept
up her guard.

Down to business, rifling through a Classified
packet, Geller fanned out six eight-by-eleven black-
and-white pictures, rattled off each name. "Alpha Deep
Six. What do you know about them?"

"Deep-cover black ops. I heard they were the best
wet work specialists the CIA and the NSA ever cut
loose," Price told him. "Beyond that, I confess to having very little idea what they were actually involved
in—other than rumor."

"Such as?"

"They went renegade. And I heard they were dead."

"What do you know about 'slush funds'?"

"Ready cash for black ops."

Geller worked on his smoke, bit his lip, appeared
to dredge up the courage to continue or choose his
words carefully. "Numbered accounts. They were created by the Department of Defense, which—very few
people know—own entire banks, just to keep these
slush funds secret from both the public and Congress.
Manhattan, Switzerland, Frankfurt, Qatar, Tokyo, the
numbers special ops could access in these banks
were—are—staggering, so I've heard. In order to by-
pass normal channels, à la DOD going before a Senate subcommittee with its hand out, the slush funds
were originally dollars siphoned from inflated military
contracts. They were created for special or black ops
to purchase arms, large and small, buy informants,

even create and mobilize small paramilitary armies in whichever country our side felt should be working with a little more fervor toward our own interests—'them' doing what 'we' want—but that's not all the money was used for. Anyway, I'll get to that.

"Okay, altogether, between the CIA and the agency, the slush funds totaled about twenty million, U.S. value, with a conversion system in place to switch to whatever currency was required. Of course, there were firewalls built into the system. An operative could only withdraw up to a hundred thousand in any six-month period, and the directors had to know in advance how much, and what it was being used for. Each time a withdrawal was made, access codes were changed in an attempt to circumvent repeated withdrawals or outright theft. They failed, miserably."

Geller had a way of lapsing into stretched silences that struck Price as dramatic, irritating, but she waited him out.

"Alpha Deep Six found a hacker. Before DOD, the CIA or the NSA knew it, they cleaned out the bank. It was a theft so embarrassing that only a few people knew about it, and they were sworn to secrecy, mind you, under the penalty of termination—and I don't mean a pink slip on your desk at the end of the day's business. Conventional wisdom at the time thought this heist was supposed to be Alpha's retirement fund, but it turned out they had no intention of whiling away their golden years on a beach in Tahiti. Shortly after the cyber-heist, they were allegedly killed, supposedly in a doublecross by field commanders who knew about the heist ahead of time—and what they were intending to do following the electronic bank job."

Geller shook his head. "Who knows, maybe a few of them grew a patriotic conscience, I couldn't say. Those in charge of handling ADS, I do know, ran for cover, basically denied everything, but the firestorm was already sweeping through the ranks on both sides of the tracks, bodies of CIA and NSA agents who had them smelled out turning up all over the globe, even here at home. As for Alpha, allegedly their remains were found in burned-out compounds, one outside Damascus, one in northern Sudan, during two ostensibly botched raids on Muslim terrorist strongholds. And the hacker? He was found in a Zurich hotel suite, two months later, sans legs and arms, and a few other body parts, one of which was shoved in his mouth. Supposedly what remained of Alpha Deep Six was identified by CIA and NSA forensics teams. Question is, how could they use DNA testing on dust?"

Price had a feeling where Geller was headed. "A cover-up."

"So one would gather."

"You keep saying 'allegedly,' 'supposedly.' You're not implying..."

Geller took a deep drag from his smoke. "Alpha Deep Six is back from the dead."

Price narrowed her gaze at Geller. "How's that?"

"Their violent demise was carefully orchestrated, and by their own hand. They knew the end was coming, so they arranged their deaths, and their resurrections. I'm surprised you never heard even a rumor about this."

Price saw another red flag. Geller, she sensed, was doing an end run before getting to the point. Was he acting? Digging to try to discover what she knew about Alpha Deep Six? She decided it best to listen, no matter how much Geller blathered on, danced before dropping whatever his bomb.

"Well?"

"If I did," she said, "I shrugged them off as wild gossip by lower-tier operatives with more time and imagination on their hands than substantive work to perform. Geller, what does all this have to do with the current threat to our nation's transportation network by Red Crescent terrorists?"

"I'm getting there, bear with me. By the way, is the smoke bothering you?"

"I'll manage."

Another shot down the hatch. He glanced at the bottle, showed Price a weak smile. "Oh, please, forgive me my bad manners. Would you care for something to drink?"

"No. Go on."

He smoked, coughed, drank, then laid the ace of spades with death's-head on the coffee table. "That was their calling card back then, a mock tribute to their victims, or a warning to future casualties," Geller said. "This was taken by NSA operatives last night from the crime scene at Clairmont Studios. They were there before the D.C. police arrived. Advance knowledge, but, I'm assuming, not until the play was in motion, the signature card left behind expressly for them, a middle finger to the agency and everyone else in the intelligence community, but I really couldn't say."

Couldn't or wouldn't? Price wondered. Whichever it was, though, if he was being truthful about the death's-head ace of spades, then the agency knew about their meeting.

"Alpha is back, and they're letting their former employers know their heads are on the chopping block. Do you watch the Josh Randall show?"

"I heard about the murders," Price answered. "I know a former CIA paramilitary operative with more ego than good sense had his head blown off last night."

"Live and in color, before a national audience. Now, if you watch the replay carefully there's no mistaking, despite the hokey disguise, the killer was this one," he said, stabbing a picture, third man in line.

Price looked at the grizzled face, bald dome, eyes hidden by shades, but she was struck by the ridges of bone hung over the sunglasses like some birth defect or grotesque plastic surgery. She looked at the other members of Alpha Deep Six, Geller remarking how the group apparently had no race problems, equal-opportunity brigands, two of them black. Price read their cold, pitiless eyes. She knew the type, men blinded to all but their own animal instincts and passions.

Sociopaths.

"Michael Mitchell was the shooter. He vanished without a trace, dumped two grenades on his way out of the studio to seal his exit. Like the others, he can kill, and is a veritable ghost in the night. Three tours of duty in Vietnam, like Richard Cramnon and Ryan Ramses, they were Special Forces. The stories about their roots are too many, too atrocious to bother repeating. They say you have to be a borderline psychopath to want to have done three tours in Vietnam to begin with. The others—Delta, Marine recon—saw action in Panama, Gulf I. The word is they maybe even had a hand in smuggling out a few top Iraqi officials and some WMD into Syria during Gulf II. All of them, no wife, no kids, no ties. With no past, no roots, no one who cares for them or they care about, they could have futures that would never exist be created to further the interests of certain parties who were reading the future of the world, and decades ago. They were the perfect deniable expendables. They were chosen to become the perfect assassination machines."

"I suppose it wouldn't do me any good to ask how you know all of this?"

Geller snorted, as if she'd asked a stupid question. "You know as well as I do how it works. In our business, information is bought or bartered. If not, you beg, borrow or steal. In Alpha's case they had more extreme methods. Last night was payback on the Josh Randall show, a grandstand moment for Alpha to announce they've risen from the grave. The word I get from my sources is the late Captain Jack got cold feet at the last minute way back when over the real agenda behind the staged deaths of ADS. Either way, you could say he signed his own death warrant, promoting himself all over the cable talk shows, shooting off his mouth about things he had no business revealing for civilian consumption. I'm thinking if Acheron didn't get him, the CIA or the NSA eventually would have yanked his ticket."

"Acheron?"

She watched as Geller looked away, focused attention on the bottle, his hand trembling as he filled the glass. There was enough of a flicker in his eyes that told her Geller wished he could kick himself. He'd slipped. Accident, though, or act?

"It's believed they have chosen handles—from Greek mythology, ancient Hebrew, various playwrights and mystics—all in reference to Hell, the gates of Hell, eternal damnation, beasts from the pit who unleash death and destruction on the earth. It's gathered that's their warped idea of dark humor." He waved a hand. "I know, you want me to get to the point."

She shrugged, no hurry, not willing to concede she was on any clock. Geller bobbed his head, sucked down another shot, Price watching as some intense, near fanatic fire lit his eyes.

"Bottom line, these men not only helped create the global arms race, they were the global arms race. They were the original shadow merchants of death, the negotiators for the United States military-industrial complex, the real movers and shakers who sold far more than just fighter jets to Saudi Arabia. Allow me to run some numbers by you. Out of the 169 countries on Earth, fifty are presently at war."

"And you're telling me Alpha Deep Six is responsible for all these conflicts?"

"The United States is the number-one arms exporter

to Third World countries, but that's a drop in the bucket compared to where the rest of the hardware goes. Someone has to do the legwork, make the deals happen with countries with leaders most rational, civilized people find detestable but who are willing to spend the cash. Are you aware 130 billion in weapons and military assistance has been shipped to 125 countries in the past decade alone by the United States, and the numbers are going up every year? America's yearly arms export sales eclipse the GNP of Russia. It's easy enough to verify, if you care to."

"The enemy is us?"

Geller ignored the remark, working on his smoke with renewed fury. "I always believed you were something of the altruistic sort, a lady of principle. I admired that in you when we worked together, but I always admire the virtue in others I know I can never possess."

"Careful, Max. Whatever you've heard about flattery does not apply here."

"Sure, sorry." He took a moment with his smoke. "You want to know how much of an upside-down world we live in? Just look at what the World Bank and the International Monetary Fund say about loans they are practically forced by the United States to make to African dictators, what the international community has called 'the crocodile rulers.' Broken down to basics the price of one helicopter equals twelve thousand schoolteachers in Africa, a one-million-dollar modern tank the equivalent of a thousand classrooms for thirty thousand children. In terms of comparing the gross dis-

crepancy between arms to food, the numbers are beyond astronomical. In a perfect world I suppose there
wouldn't be this immoral madness, but it's a madness
that is man-made. I'm telling you this nation is involved
in the deliberate worldwide proliferation of arms. You
see, what the voting public does not know is that the
military-industrial complex of this country—or rather
a shadow group that have knighted themselves the in-
heritors of the Earth—is seeking to create wars, unleash
whole campaigns of genocide, perhaps even drive the
human race into World War III. Three reasons. One, the
military contractors need to keep the plants running, or,
simply put, there would be a lot of people out of work,
likewise some heavy brass at the Pentagon. Two, since
Vietnam, there are certain circles within the intelligence
and military communities who saw the creation of future conflicts around the globe as a means to justify their
existence, gain personal glory in history, albeit a
shadow note."

"And they would get rich in the process."

"Obscenely rich. Three, by 2020 it's believed by our
top scientists there will be fifteen to eighteen billion
mouths on this planet to feed. Simply stated, these
powers want the strong—themselves—to survive,
whatever masses crawl out of the rubble and the ashes
of a holocaust to serve them. They believe if something
isn't done to contain the swelling numbers on this
planet, there'll be mass starvation, natural resources
depleted, nations swept up in anarchy with the collapse
of the global economy. Plague, famine, pestilence,
death, they're seeking to accelerate what they see as

the natural process of evolution to weed out the weak before they devour the strong."

"The lions eating the lambs."

"Precisely. That's why Alpha Deep Six was created in the first place."

"To bring on Armageddon."

"That's one way to put it."

Price had listened with a neutral expression, suspected there was a lot more Geller wished to tell her, but wouldn't. He was dangling bait, but why? She knew no institution was above corruption, and she could accept what the man said about the military-industrial conspiracy, up to a point. True, there were bad seeds in the U.S. military and intelligence communities, but she knew the rot wasn't endemic. Still, she knew enough about the grim realities of the world to be wary once the genie of power and greed was let out of the bottle.

"You want one example of what Alpha Deep Six has done?" Geller said. "Right before Gulf I the former Iraqi regime nearly got its hands on krytons, or nuclear weapon triggers, along with 'skull furnaces,' which are used to melt plutonium for nuclear bomb cores. ADS arranged the deal with the Iraqis, but again, someone got nervous at DOD, probably saw far worse than just their careers circling the bowl. Before the ship sailed out of the Delaware River it was boarded and seized. A cover-up ensued, generated by the same people who don't want anyone to know 1.5 billion in dual-use technology was sold and delivered to Baghdad right up to the eve of Gulf I. Alpha Deep Six created that regime, kept it in power, I kid you not. You want maraging steel for making centrifuges? Alpha delivered tons of it among weapons-grade uranium and plutonium, fuel rods, light water reactors, the whole sorcerer nuke package to the Pakistanis, thus insuring their nuclear weapons program. Same thing with the North Koreans. Likewise they have kept the Khartoum government flourishing in guns and money, fomenting the unrest on the Horn of Africa, were even in the process of helping Khartoum go nuclear before their purported end. Further, they were involved in training and arming the mujahideen in Afghanistan, and they were instrumental in creating both the Taliban and al-Qaeda during that ten-year conflict."

"Busy boys."

"This isn't funny, Barbara. Do you hear me laughing?"

"And you have proof of all this?"

"Nothing in writing. If you don't trust my word, I can send you to sources who can back me up, men so high up in the intelligence and military communities they're the next closest thing to talking to God. They'll also tell you that Alpha Deep Six is responsible for creating and landing the Red Crescent in this country, that they trained, funded and armed them for what could be the biggest catastrophe to ever hit American soil. One from which this country may never recover."

She stiffened, braced to grab her Browning as he suddenly reached into his briefcase. She stayed on edge, even as Geller produced a CD-ROM.

"It's all here," he said, placing the disk on the table.

"All what?"

"Dates, places, times, people, the entire alphabet, the who's who on Alpha Deep Six and the shadow world that created them There are decoded messages, intercepts about who they know, what they've done and what they are doing. Red Crescent is their creation, their vision of the gates of Hell unleashed. Do you know anything about them?"

"Only what I've heard on CNN," she lied.

"Well, here are a few facts you won't get from the media. Al-Qaeda, Hezbollah, a few other marquee terror groups were, so to speak, read the tea leaves by ADS in the late eighties, but it took until the early nineties until they became believers in the ADS infidels and their vision of the future. Osama and his top lieutenants knew that if the United States declared all-out war against them, they would go down hard, disfigured, dismantled, captured or killed. They knew their money would be the first target. Thus Alpha mapped out a contingency plan to keep their jihad afloat, but it was only a small part to their own big event.

"Before our government froze the first million, the major terror orgs were cleaning out their banks, transferring every asset they could get their hands on into ready cash. They began buying up diamonds from West Africa, precious gemstones from India, Myanmar, Indonesia. They invested heavily in narcotics, aligning themselves with the South American drug cartels, but most of their investing went with heroin to the east. Financially, able to remain solvent with gemstones and dope, if all else fails, they are far from bankrupt. And they would have no problem getting funds, from what we've learned, if the well began to dry. Every radical sheikh, imam and mullah from Algeria to Indonesia gave the Red Crescent their blessing during what we know was the Grand Islamic Council just before the outbreak of Gulf II.

"As for Alpha, they personally recruited RC operatives, before and after their 'demise.' After Afghanistan and Gulf II we know there was a huge influx into RC of al-Qaeda and Taliban and the former Iraqi regime's fedayeen who were willing to come under the new umbrella, even if it was hung over them by infidels. The Red Crescent received help principally from Jordan, Syria and Turkey. But, when Syria fell onto the radar screen for helping Iraq, our supposed allies, the Turks and Jordanians held out their hands—for a price. Now, from various methods of surveillance and intercepts of chatter between Red Crescent operatives and other terror orgs, we believe but cannot verify that somewhere in the neighborhood of one to two billion dollars—hard currency, jewels, diamonds, narcotics—is stashed in underground armed fortresses they call the Bank of Islam. We believe Alpha Deep Six marshaled a small army of fanatics to invade and wreak death and destruction on this country's ground-transportation networks for payback, and to take all intelligence eyes off their violent resurrection, and vanishing act two."

Price watched Geller nod at the disk. The list of questions she could put to him was too long, an instinctive fear mounting, warning her to get out of here. He pushed the disk across the coffee table.

"Take it."

Price picked up the subtle note of insistence. If she took the disk, it might confirm whatever suspicions he had that she was still actively involved in covert work. If she didn't, the Farm and its warriors might lose out on invaluable intelligence.

"I told you, Max, I'm retired."

"Really? Is that why I had to go through about six cutouts from every intelligence and law-enforcement agency we know of? Then you finally get back to me, using about four different back channels not even the almighty NSA know exist?"

"Say I take it. What is it you expect me to do with the information?"

"It would appear you still have friends and sources in very high places. Pass it on. You still believe in freedom, truth and justice, don't you?"

Clever, she thought, how he'd boxed her in. She was damned if she did, damned if she didn't. She picked up the disk.

"The password," Geller said, "is 'Resurrection.'"

ACTION, IN BOLAN'S experience, cured fear. From the warrior perspective it most certainly excised the cancer of evil. The hesitant or the paralyzed in the face of mortal danger sometimes died from the strangehold of fear. But the warrior, he knew, acted on fear, used it to motivate, propel him to new heights—in this case—to violence of action. The enormity of the task before the nation might be so daunting, funded and planned for nobody knew how long by unknown financiers— the lurking notion in his mind they had inside help from homegrown traitors—with fanatics prepared to commit suicide if only to unleash mass murder, the Executioner knew only one answer would wipe out the evil ready to consume the country, slaughter countless innocents.

Identify and strike down the enemy, lightning fast and hard. No mercy, no hesitation, no exceptions.

To the credit of the man on the other end of the sat phone, Bolan knew Hal Brognola was more than up to the grim job, bloody as it would prove, lives in the balance, perhaps an entire nation on the verge of collapsing into anarchy. After all, he and the big Fed had known each other since mile one of what was the genesis of the Executioner. Those days were light-years distant now, when Brognola once hunted a young soldier during his war against the Mafia, but they were of like mind, immutable in principle and commitment when it came to solving the problem of dealing with the enemies of national security.

No sooner was Bolan in the air, the Black Hawk soaring now over I-64 at top speed, than he had raised Brognola at his Justice Department office. A quick sit-rep, Bolan printing out the grid map of the blocks surrounding the Greyhound terminal in Richmond, and Brognola filled him in.

"They what?" Bolan said, forced to nearly shout above the rotor wash pounding through the fuselage.

There had been a few minutes' lag time between

them, during which Brognola had contacted the FBI SAC in Richmond. Bolan now feared the problems had just begun to compound, as he listened to Brognola.

"The order came straight from the Office of Homeland Security, who received their orders from the President and who just passed it on to this office. Before your intro to this butcher—Moctaw—and believe me, the President will hear about this, and I will move mountains to find out who this son of a bitch is—it was already believed the bastards intended to pack lockers with plastic explosives before they boarded their respective buses. Every terminal from Miami to Maine, New York to Los Angeles, is being locked down by local and federal authorities. Buses are being emptied of passengers, luggage searched, same thing with all trains, national and local rail service. It's a logistical nightmare, I'm sure you can imagine, but we tackle the major cities first, take it from there—and hope."

Bolan didn't like it, FBI agents already inside the Richmond terminal, forcing open lockers, their presence alerting the Red Crescent operatives there the game was over for them. But the soldier knew he couldn't be everywhere at once. The threat was so grave, so public now, no telling how far and wide or how many operatives were out there, human resources stretched so thin as it stood....

"The descriptions you passed on, Striker, match up. They're being watched as we speak."

"Pull those agents back, Hal, discreetly. Don't let them approach those three. If that happens..."

"Understood. The bastards might panic and just go

ahead and light up whatever they have. I've alerted Special Agent Wilkinson you will be landing shortly and that you are in charge."

Bolan moved into the cockpit hatchway. The interstate in both directions was gridlocked, he found, a vast parking lot east to west, the state police having erected checkpoints, roadblocks, staggered every other exit. With national alert, all civilians were ordered to stay home, get off all buses and trains at the next stop if they were traveling, but Bolan wondered if it was too little too late.

The skyline of Richmond looming ahead, Bolan spotted the Black Hawks soaring above the city, ready to report to him any suspicious vehicles, specifically buses that might have pulled out of the terminal before the FBI descended.

"There's a stadium, directly across from the terminal," Bolan told the flight crew, both of which were Farm blacksuits. "Set it down in the lot."

When they copied, Bolan went and opened one of three war bags. He opted against going in loaded to the gills, even though once he was spotted by the terrorists, they would know he wasn't any late-arriving passenger.

The Executioner decided to march right through the front door, mark the position of Red Crescent operatives from agents inside. He hoped to do it quickly, with as little mess as possible. There would be panic, chaos, of course, but a hard charge into the terminal, wielding the HK MP-5, could prove disastrous. One clean quick head shot each, then, with the Beretta would have to do it.

Bolan stood by the door gunner. Roughly two hundred feet below lay the interstate, groups of civilians standing outside their cars. Arguments appeared to break out in pockets, stranded motorists flailing their arms. It didn't take a mind reader, he knew, to imagine those thoughts swarming with panic and terror. Then, recalling the omen of ASAC James, he looked at the smattering of eighteen-wheelers, spotted a U-Haul, several cabs.

And he wondered.

One crisis, one terrorist at a time, he told himself.

"Striker?"

Bolan caught the grim note ratchet up in Brognola's voice.

"Nail these bastards, Striker."

"Count on it."

"Get back to me when it's done there."

Not "if," he thought, but "when." There was no other option, no margin for a half victory, the soldier aware that if one rolling bomb was right then on the highway...

The thought was echoed by Brognola.

"If only one of them is out there, Hal," the Executioner vowed, "then I'll make damn sure he is on a highway to Hell."

BEYOND GRATEFUL for fresh air, Price felt relief as she slipped away from Geller, no dramatic goodbyes or promises to get in touch. So why did that bother her? On the way out the door, she expected the man to press her for some callback, update him on whatever progress he believed she might deliver.

Nothing.

She wondered if she was being unduly paranoid, scanning the bowels of the garage, an itch going down her spine, her heart racing. It was empty of human or vehicular traffic, no sound anywhere—too quiet, too still—her surveillance working down the gauntlet of parked vehicles as she hastened her strides. She spotted her GMC, backed in against the wall, and she was anxious to get in and drive off. She wanted to play back the entire meeting with Geller, hash over all the questions he left hanging, but the nagging instinct was back, stronger than ever, warning her to get out of the garage.

She reached her vehicle, hesitated, looking over her shoulder. Keying open the door, she heard a thud, scoured the garage, unable to determine where the sound originated, but aware someone had just stepped out of a vehicle. Was that a shadow at the far end? she wondered, opening her door. Two shadows, easing in her direction, trying to move, swift and silent?

Hopping in, she shut the door, slipped the key into the ignition. Staring down the garage, she saw the dancing silhouettes, but no bodies. It was almost, she determined, as if they were using cars for concealment. And the shadows were indeed, she saw, advancing her way.

She was about to twist the key when she spotted it out of the corner of her eye.

Price froze at the sight of the signature card on the shotgun seat, then she glimpsed the shadow rise up in the rearview mirror, the weapon aimed at the back of her head.

Silently she cursed Geller, heard the ghoul chuckle as she threw her shoulder into the door.

CHAPTER THREE

"All passengers inside the terminal are asked to remain seated or standing where you are. Those passengers at boarding gates are asked to step back to the center of the terminal. Passengers are asked to leave or place all bags on the ground. This includes purses, or any item that can be carried."

And Qasi Alzhad saw the dream vanishing before his eyes, felt the slow fuse of anger sizzle toward simmering wrath. Silently he cursed the sudden injustice of it all, the seat trembling beneath him from fury, ears ringing, sweat breaking out beneath the bill of his cap. Glancing at the other two in the row of seats ahead and to his right, he found them, eyes wide and darting around the terminal, cornered animals perhaps, but still dangerous enough, he knew, despite the falling net. Contingency plan locked in place, though, the three of them were ready to martyr themselves, even if they couldn't fulfill their final role in the big event. So it was written during their correspondence by hand-delivered mail.

So it was spoken by God.

It was easy enough, he thought, to read between the lines of the voice issuing commands over the loudspeaker, telling passengers to remain calm, exit buses, leave carry-ons behind, apologies once again for the delays. Something had indeed gone terribly wrong, the glory of jihad about to be derailed, he feared, and when they were so close. The logical conclusion was that one of the cells had been captured, talked, betrayed the operation.

It was a gross miscalculation, he now discovered, killing time in the terminal, waiting for the others to arrive before he packed the locker with what the letter—delivered two days ago by courier to his motel room near Richmond's airport—called divine retribution. Two of them stood at the ticket-information counter, he saw, huddled with Greyhound employees, three more breaking open lockers with small drills, working with methodical grim purpose. No FBI stenciled on the backs of windbreakers, but he noted bulges beneath their shoulders betraying concealed side arms, earpieces the glaring tip-off the building was about to come under siege by American law enforcement. Yes, perhaps they were surrounded, outgunned, he thought, but before the infidels began searching baggage and they were staring down weapons, he would take decisive action.

The run to Chicago would never bear sweet fruit, but there was hope yet. Or was there? he wondered, catching the eye of a windbreaker by the lockers. The infidel looked away, watching him without watching, he sensed. Was the FBI man—if that's what he was—taking special interest in the three of them? Perhaps, he thought, their attire and nylon bags were more errors in planning, marking them, pearls in a sea of infidel swine. He knew next to nothing about the Great Satan's Arena Football League, but their jackets, caps and bags were emblazoned with individual team emblems, meant to identify them to their brothers-in-jihad. Instinct for survival long since honed in Iraq, twice over, he knew all the signals warning when the end was coming.

The babble of infidels swarming his ears, he shut his eyes. And the past drifted back to him from a dark corner of bitter memory. Beyond the rage and hatred he forced himself to lapse into a soothing trance, wishing to use visions of years waded through in anger and grief to fuel the fires of courage and resolve.

In the beginning it seemed the impossible dream, but the miracle of bringing holy war to the land of the Great Satan had already been mapped out by Syrian sympathizers, well in advance of his fleeing Baghdad the second time around. Before that moment of hope in Damascus, more than a decade since what the enemy called Gulf I, there was unimaginable horror, the foreign devils destroying all that he cherished in his heart. The death and destruction he had witnessed on the way back home from Kuwait had been terrifying enough, the American vultures slaughtering thousands of his Republican Guard brothers on that highway. The unholy ones, he recalled, dropped their bombs, safe in their flying cocoons of death, thousands of feet above the column of vehicles, decimating their numbers, a cowardly act, to be sure, but the worst was yet to come. With his own eyes he had seen many of his brothers burned alive, trapped in the wreckage of tanks, transport trucks, luxury cars rightfully taken from the treacherous, self-indulgent, obscenely rich Kuwaitis.

He could still hear their screams of agony, the stench of cooking flesh something he could so vividly remember. Somehow—call it divine intervention, or a special destiny reserved for him by God—he had escaped the conflagration, wounded, crawling off into the desert, praying all the way back to Baghdad that someday he would return the favor to those faceless cowards who murdered from the skies. He discovered the enemy had robbed him of what life he hoped to return to, a blow so cruel it would have been better to have burned alive on the highway of death. The murder of his wife and two sons, massacred along with many innocent Iraqis during a bombing run on the city, had been grief enough to bear. Only the dagger, he discovered, plunged deeper, twisted harder. Shuddering, he saw in his mind's eye his daughter—or what remained of her. He found it especially tormenting he couldn't even recall what she had looked like in all her innocent, youthful beauty, then or now. On his return and discovery, it had taken several weeks of agonizing before he made the decision, praying for the answer, the strength to do the thing he most dreaded. Certain it was God's will he finally acted. And how couldn't he? How, as a loving father and true believer of the Islamic faith, could he stand idly by, allow her to suffer her horror and shame of living on like that? How could he, in all clean conscience and purity of soul, let a child languish in perpetual horror and pain, no arms, no eyes, half of her face sheared away to the bone from a coward's bomb? Small comfort she never saw it coming, but...

He jolted, eyelids flying open, the crack of the pistol swept away to the deep caverns of memory. Oh, but there was now fuel, determination enough to proceed, the fearless holy warrior, carrying out the will of God.

Let there be vengeance. Let there be blood. Let the horror descend, the wrath of God, on the enemy.

He found commotion in all bays beyond the doors on both sides, passengers ushered from buses, large gaggles herded near the gates, Greyhound employees and armed security guards trying to soothe nerves, hands waving down the battery of questions. A quick tally of the anticipated body count, and he figured that between the three of them they could bring the building down while consuming, at the pitiful minimum, three, four hundred in God's divine retribution.

He looked to the others, held their stares. He didn't know these men, the names or their Arab country of origin. That the three of them were of like mind and spirit, nurtured the hearts of lions, was enough to succeed in Pyrrhic victory. No choice, no turning back. How it had all been arranged, though, was a miracle by itself, their destinies about to be fulfilled, divine warriors blessed by God. Tactics changed, naturally, to circumvent the enemy's high-tech countersurveillance, but the ends of retribution always justified the means.

Qasi Alzhad unzipped one of the two bags, granting him easy access to the Ingram MAC-10.

It was time.

He rose with his brothers aware, too, he would see them shortly in Paradise.

KHELID AMNAN LAUGHED. For him it was over, but the brilliance of foresight would preempt the problem. He wouldn't be denied.

They were swarming the terminal from every possible entrance, he saw, FBI or SWAT or whoever, armed with submachine guns, full body armor and helmets, creating a ruckus as they began searching carry-ons down the line. Other armed enemy began surging into both men's and women's restrooms to clear them out. The building was sealed, then locked down. So be it. The more, he believed the Americans said, the merrier.

Fear not, he told himself. Let them come, let them search his bags. He was prepared, expected them, in fact, to have arrived well before now.

Close to two hours, and no bus arrived or departed, repeated messages over the loudspeaker regretting all delays, instructing all passengers to remain calm, stand where they were. Since the first announcement the knot in his gut warned him he wouldn't leave Washington, never make it to the Port Authority, the dry run and reconnaissance in vain. A lesser man, he decided, would have felt defeat, but initiative shielded him against failure.

He ignored the strange looks several infidels threw him, chuckling again. They looked confused, fear bordering terror, questions hurled between them, but he would soon enough shed light on their ignorance. There was some irony in the moment, he thought, unable to decide what it was, but there was most certainly truth and justice ready to be delivered by his hand. He was a holy warrior, an instrument of the will of God, after all, there to fulfill the promise he'd made to fellow Iraqis he'd left behind in his homeland of Syria. They would remember what he had done here. Someday soon they would sing his praises, glorify his martyrdom. From Karachi to Casablanca, they would pen his name in stories, splash his heroics all over Arab satellite television, his face wreathed on banners as they marched the streets, torching American flags and effigies of the Great Satan President. But this was about far more than a few dozen fedayeen and Iraqi officials smuggled over the border, seeking safe haven in his country, crying out for personal revenge. And more than his own glory.

Then he fathomed his mood, a bolt of lightning between the eyes, telling him why he felt so strong, amused even. The American barbarian law enforcement, representative now of those occupiers of Arab land, those destroyers and oppressors of all Muslim peoples, he saw, were marching toward his departure gate. Just a few more moments, he told himself, reflecting on the source of his sense of invincibility.

"Sir? Are these your bags?"

Amnan lost the smile, but enjoyed the cold touch of the small box in his coat pocket as he wrapped his hand around it. "Yes, they are, sir," he told the FBI man in perfect English, thumbed the switch to the On position, forced confusion and anxiety onto his face as he glanced at the armed phalanx around the gate. He listened to the angry bleat of infidels demanding to know why they were searching their bags, one of them snarling something about a police state. Amnan watched, riding out the moment, his heart thundering in his ears. Without asking, the FBI man unzipped his bag—and froze.

"What the—?"

It was a moment carved into all eternity, the sweet second he had been searching for, perhaps since even before birth to the end of his nineteen years. Confusion and horror etched on his face, the FBI man appeared torn between pulling away the T-shirt emblazoned with Osama's face, sweeping the submachine gun his way or shout a warning.

Amnan allowed the infidel to snatch up the T-shirt, discover what lay beneath. It was reckless impulse, he knew, pulling out the detonator box, displaying it for a heartbeat, risk a barrage of bullets that would tear into him, defeat the moment. He skipped any jihad eulogy or war cry and thumbed the button.

He believed he was still smiling as the explosion lifted him off his feet, hurling him into the air. He was blinded by the light from the blast, deafened by the roar, but not until he thought he glimpsed bodies sailing through the firestorm, caught the evanescence of their screams.

FROM THE ENEMY'S twisted perspective, the Executioner knew bombs on wheels was the next logical phase in their unholy war. Make no mistake, trains and buses were soft targets, he thought, but they had long since drawn the grim concern of every intelligence and federal law-enforcement agency in the nation. Airport security might have been nailed down, all bases covered as well as humanly possible, but the task—between available human resources, public outcry over inconvenience and government funding— would prove so monumental it was next to impossible to protect America's ground-transportation network. Consider the enormity of checking every bag or purse, he thought, running a metal detector over each passenger, choked webs of stalled, impatient travelers. Consider the vast nationwide system of countless trains, subways, buses. Consider every moving company, every eighteen-wheeler or van, cab or car on the road, in the cities, at any given time. Unless the country locked itself down, declared martial law....

Well, all it would take to perhaps push America to the edge of a police state, he knew, was one or two rolling bombs lighting up an interstate, a major highway or taking down an entire terminal or depot, a few hundred bodies buried under the rubble. Every overt and covert intelligence agency may know about Red Crescent, that it was created from the shattered or disgruntled remnants of al-Qaeda and a host of other known terrorist organizations impatient to unleash another 9/11 on America....

They were here, and it was happening, as Bolan heard the shooting inside the terminal.

Blueprints of the Richmond facility and perimeter

committed to memory, having handed out the orders
to Brognola's people along with descriptions of the
three operatives, the Executioner gathered steam, closing on the Norfolk bay Beretta 93-R leading his
charge, he shouldered his way through passengers bolting for the lot. It was just as he feared, the RC operatives panicking at the sight of agents inside the
terminal, now going for broke. There wasn't a second
to spare on "what ifs," the inside of the terminal
Bolan's turf to nail it down—or get blown into a thousand grisly pieces if they lit up the terminal.

Clinging to hope, propelled up the side of the bus
by racing adrenaline and dire urgency, the Executioner
spotted the first terrorist and drew target acquisition.
Just inside the door, the enemy swept the MAC-10
around the terminal, the doomsday bag bouncing off
his shoulder, screams rising to ear-piercing decibels as
he fired on with indiscriminate bursts. For whatever
reason—perhaps due to his murderous outburst—
Bolan found a clean field of fire behind the savage. No
chance of an innocent victim taking a projectile, tumbling on after a fatal exit wound to the head, so Bolan
went to grim work.

The Red Crescent operative whirled, ready to barrel through the door, when Bolan squeezed the trigger.
The 9 mm subsonic round blasted through glass, cored
smack between the would-be martyr's eyes, a dark
cloud of blood and brain matter jetting out the back of
his shattered skull, the Dallas Stars cap flying. Lurching back, the Red Crescent butcher then wobbled, eyes
bulging in shock, nerve spasms shooting through his

arms, the package of mass murder slipping off his shoulder. The Executioner advanced, pumped two more rounds into the enemy's forehead, dropped him.

One down, the soldier thought as he threw wide the door and waded into the bedlam. He was aware the doomsday clock had ticked down to zero, that quite possibly he was marching to his own death.

PRICE THOUGHT the bastard laughed as she hit the ground on her shoulders, rolling up between two SUVs one row down, her sunglasses flying. Digging out the Browning Hi-Power, she thumbed off the safety, sprung to her feet. Mitchell-Acheron, she found, hadn't budged, the killer grinning, laughing to himself. Was he winking at her, blowing a kiss with his weapon? It occurred to her this psychopath could have already killed her, but given his track record she wasn't taking any chances. And she was certain he hadn't come here alone. There would be time enough later to track down Geller, make him spill the truth—whatever it took—why he'd set her up, assuming, of course, she made it out of the garage alive.

He was still enjoying his belly ripper when she framed the laughing face in her sights, squeezed the trigger. Even before the first 9 mm round blasted out the window he was gone, melting to the seat, anticipating her preemptive strike. A combination of adrenaline and fear coursing through her veins, she cracked out two more rounds, ventilating the far window, shuffling for deeper cover. Hunched, she searched the garage, thrusting the weapon around each corner as she surged down the line of parked vehicles, in the direction of the exit ramp. If there were in fact more gunmen on the prowl, then she had to believe they had all escape routes covered. No choice, she knew, other than a fighting evacuation.

She stopped, listened to the silence. Popping up, she saw the back passenger door open, the bald dome emerge. She capped off two more rounds, Acheron ducking as bullets tattooed metal. If she could draw him deeper into the garage, then double back for the GMC...

Two peals of thunder, and she saw the GMC's tires flatten out, Acheron's laughter flung away by the booming reverberation of gunfire. Worst case, she could hope the attendant or some civic-minded individual heard the racket of weapons fire, dialed 911. Then what? Was the bastard crazy enough to commit suicide by cop, if it came down to that?

"Might as well come to Daddy, Babs," Acheron called. "I promise I'll break it to you gently. Max—I know you didn't have to worry about that sorry little sack of shit hurting anything. Me, well, you're looking at a man-size pre-dic-a-ment. What the hell, consider me your incubus, baby-cakes."

Where was the psycho freak now? she wondered. He moved like a ghost, there one second, gone the next, laughing as he taunted her, circling her, she was certain.

Keep moving, then.

She was darting across open ground, saw the exit sign that marked the service stairs when she spotted two more gunmen in black. Without warning, they opened fire with MP-5 subguns, chasing her to cover, ricochets screaming off the concrete behind her, spanging metal. Running on, she flinched as twin streams of subgun fire blew out a line of SUV windows behind her, glass slashing her back, bullets drumming metal. Shooting only to chase her? she wondered. Forcing her to run toward the service stairs? They had her out in the open seconds ago, dead to rights, could have dropped her easily. No, they wanted her prisoner, she decided. But why? If that was the case, they had given her something of an edge.

She was free to shoot to kill. No problem, she would live or die by that.

A pall of silence descended behind her as she stopped, peered around the corner of a Jaguar. It was as if they had vanished, no sight or sound of them. They were close; she could feel them, probably moving to outflank her. She looked to the service stairs, maybe a dozen yards or so away, but it might as well have been the dark side of Jupiter. She looked back, glimpsed a shadow about six cars down, the Browning jumping in her hand as she rode the recoil, blasting out two rounds, vandalizing a Mercedes.

Price was ready to bolt for the service stairs, looking back at the gap she would have to sprint across, when three more of them materialized, black leather trench coats flowing behind them as they marched through the door, MP-5s leading the way. She peered at the tall dark one in the middle, wondering where she'd seen him before. Then it hit her. Despite the long black hair, swarthy complexion, figure some plastic surgery, it was Cramnon.

And they had a hostage, she saw, tossing still more critical mass into the equation. The woman was honey-blond, slim, the one on Cramnon's right flank holding her to his chest, hand over her mouth, muffling her cries. Had they snatched what could pass as her twin on purpose, or was it just a fluke?

"I know who you are, cupcake," Cramnon said. "Make it easy on yourself. Hey, I promise, Babs, I won't let my men savage you. I'm a gentleman when it comes to the fairer sex."

She was torn between watching her six, Cramnon and his goons, when she heard the woman scream. A short burst of subgun fire, and Price saw the victim flung to the ground from the burst up her back.

Oh, God, Price thought, squeezing her eyes shut for a dangerous second, sickened at the sight of cold-blooded murder, as she slumped back against her SUV cover. The sound of Cramnon's laughter echoed through the garage, as she heard the monster warn her he still had a few more victims on tap.

THE EXECUTIONER KNEW he couldn't spare a second in-dulging anger or grief over the carnage he found inside the terminal. He discovered two of Brognola's people were down by the lockers, blood pooling around their skulls. The killer opted for head shots, bypassing body armor.

"Clear the building! I want a perimeter, no less than three blocks out!" Bolan shouted at the Justice agent kneeling beside the bodies of fallen comrades. "You copy?"

The agent looked at Bolan, eyes burning with rage, nodded past him. "I heard you. The last son of a bitch went in the men's room!"

"Get out of here!" Bolan said, then wheeled, got his bearings as he marched for the men's room. A quick sweep of the terminal, and he figured ten, fifteen civilians cut down. Where they weren't surging out the nearest door, a stampede of flailing bodies, the soldier found walking wounded limping for exits, the air pierced by screams and shouts of terror and panic. The last one? he thought, then spied the heap near the westbound gates, the New York Dragons cap beside his tattered carcass with doomsday bags. Two helmeted, armored FBI agents toed the body, secured the ordnance. That left Grand Rapids Rampage, he knew.

Bolan made the opening to the restroom, hugging the wall. Framing the layout from memory, he heard the scuffling sounds, someone cursing around the corner. One deep breath, Beretta up, and the soldier whipped his weapon around the corner as—

The Red Crescent thug triggered a burst into the back of a guy Bolan figured for no more than twenty. He read the situation, Grand Rapids having attempted to grab a human shield to cover his suicide demolition. Difficult to manage, since the terrorist lugged two nylon bags Bolan figured weighed in the neighborhood of a hundred-plus pounds, wielding the compact subgun while trying to grab a hostage. The victim kicked forward, Bolan tried to sight around the tumbling body, a scarlet mist hitting the air, when the butcher held back on the MAC-10's trigger. The spray and pray, as the leadstorm ate up tile and flayed his face and neck with stone shrapnel, bought the killer a critical second. Bolan saw him bull into a stall. This was it, the soldier knew, time up.

Braced for sudden incineration, the Executioner hauled out the mammoth Magnum .44 Desert Eagle, charged around the corner. No telling how thick the stall's metal barrier, but he knew he had to wax the jihad butcher with the first shot, opting for the ultimate stopping power of the Desert Eagle.

The would-be mass murderer was scrambling behind the door, thrashing against the tight confines of the stall, feet dancing in panic when Bolan tapped the hand cannon's trigger, aiming for a bull's-eye midway up. Ears spiked by the booming retort, Bolan thought he heard a sharp grunt, a thud against the wall, but it was impossible to say, senses jolted by the thunder. Two more peals and Bolan watched, waiting for the world to blow up in his face. The .44 slugs blasted the door off its hinges, the ruined slab banging down on the body crumpling to the toilet. Bolan drilled another .44 round between the killer's eyes, splashed the wall with a gruesome mosaic that left no doubt.

Weapons holstered, Bolan raised Wilkinson on his tactical radio. Nearly deafened by his own hand, the warrior was forced to shout he was clear and coming out. A quick check of the ordnance next, ordering Wilkinson to get some people in there to secure the explosives, and he spotted the detonator box on the floor, thumbed off the red light.

The Executioner felt the urgency ratchet up to another level, unable to hold down cold rage as Wilkinson filled him in. They had done it, the soldier thought. From the sound of it, he pictured where the Greyhound terminal in Washington once stood there was now nothing but a smoking crater. Complete destruction, a triple-digit body count, Wilkinson speculated. The future, Bolan feared, was in grave doubt.

"We may have another situation, Cooper, and I'm afraid it's already on the highway."

"What?"

"We may have a rolling bomb on the way to Norfolk!"

"THERE'S NOTHING LIKE a broken heart, huh? What do you think, Little Miss Independent? Seems you don't have too much luck with men, and I'm not talking about the fruitcake, Max."

They were moving her, tightening the noose, she knew. Other than Cramnon taunting her, that damn bellow of laughter in her ears, the only sound she heard was the hammer of her heartbeat. She spun in all directions, glimpsed two shadows one row over, triggered two lightning rounds. If she scored anything other than car windows, she couldn't tell. It was as if, she thought, they could feel the bullets coming before they left the barrel. Sliding between vehicles, she saw the two goons peeling away from Cramnon, then hit the Browning's trigger, only the bastard moved so quick he appeared—

To what? she wondered. Float? Walk on air? No, that was impossible. She figured the fear and adrenaline warped her senses.

"Referring to your former husband, Babs. Kevvy, the defense lawyer? Understand he liked to wave his little flag around outside the marital bed. Piece of shit, huh? I mean, how could he fuck around on something that looks as good as you? Bet that hurt, stung the old pride. Hey, you still need a little comforting? Nursing a broken heart, are we? I'm here for you, cupcake."

She ignored the taunting, tried to focus on any sound beyond the voice and that damn laughter, meant, she was sure, to distract her. She risked stopping, stretched out to look under the chassis of an SUV. There! Not a second too soon, she thrust the Browning out, sighted on the pair of legs on the other side and blew the bastard off at the ankle.

Price was up and running, weaving between vehicles, the exit ramp at twelve o'clock. Whoever she dropped screamed and called her every name he could think of, vicious but creative in his agony. She gathered steam, darting across open ground, then angled for another row of metallic cover when she heard the brief stutter of subgun fire. The cursing ended, the abrupt silence chilling her. She looked back, straining her ears. Nothing but another vanishing act.

She reached inside her windbreaker to unbutton and ready another clip, up and bolting between cars when he seemed to rise up out of nowhere. She was sweeping the pistol around to blow the smug look off Cramnon's face when he buried a fist in her gut. A slap lashed her face next, her head exploding from the blow, lights threatening to wink out as she toppled into a car. Price felt her knees buckle, instinctively knew she was empty-handed. She sucked air, paralyzed by the blow to her gut, a picture of pure evil floating into blurry vision. Before she could gather her senses, fight back, they were all over her, someone throwing her to the ground. She felt her arms wrenched behind her, plastic cuffs fastened around her wrists.

Cramnon grabbed her by the hair, jerking her head up. "Handsome, aren't I, Babs. But they say even the Devil was in love with his own beauty. Welcome to my world. Looks like I'm your destiny, after all, cupcake." He laughed. "You can call me Mr. Wonderful."

CHAPTER FOUR

When he called on the spirit of the supernatural beast to help unleash jihad, a mental picture of al-Jassaca rose to life. Eyes shut, he could see the monster of Islamic folklore clearly now, sitting, utterly still and quiet in his seat, the thunder of wheels over track somehow soothing taut nerves. Legend or myth, he decided, usually bore a scintilla of truth, no matter how exaggerated, fantastic or frightening. That in mind, feeling the full weight of his final moments on Earth before ascending to Paradise, he was a believer in the power and righteous fury of the creature with its head of a bull, body of a lion, legs of a camel.

Smiling to himself, Harim Tabizi imagined al-Jassaca place the flaming sword in his hand, heard the creature urge him to go forth among the infidels, burn into their souls the sacred seal of those condemned to eternal damnation in the fires of Hell. Where, he believed, every infidel, including Arabs who betrayed Islam to become minions of the Great Satan, belonged.

If there was doubt over the justice of his mission, the glory of the operation as a whole, eight months, two days and six hours in this wicked land cured the ills of waffling, guilt, regret. And divine guidance from the next world was surely granted those faithful, he thought, who helped themselves, acted on the teachings of Islam, lived to avenge the blood of martyrs already gone to Paradise.

It had proved clever, indeed, albeit disturbing, staying on the move, traversing hostile country in the car provided him for the operation, living in seedy motels—no more than two weeks at a time, paying his way in cash—while gaining insight into the enemy, shoring up the fury and hatred. There was reconnoitering, of course, the dry run from Seattle to Los Angeles on the Coast Starlight to choose time and place, hammer out details, search for holes in security and boarding procedures, all of which, he discovered, were flimsy at best, negligent at worst. Beyond surveillance, the plan itself and waiting final orders he wished to understand—for holy justification—why he believed the infidel an abomination in the eyes of God.

And the truth came to him, a blinding light shone forth from the darkness of the land.

Between their television and movies, media bombast slanted against other countries they didn't like, understand or agree with, wandering streets choked with prostitutes and drug addicts, it took two days for prior conviction to become a living fire in his heart. Better still, the resolve to proceed became far more incendiary than he could have imagined during the flight from Frankfurt to New York.

He was more than ready now.

Opening his eyes, he caught his shadowy reflection on the monitor of his laptop, the dyed-blond hair lending his sharp features a ghostly sheen. Planning, intelligence, faith were critical components of the operation, equal to courage and commitment to decisive action. And the operation, he thought, had fallen into place, as if orchestrated by divine will, the dream of jihad about to become reality. But where there was faith there was always resolve to perform the seemingly impossible. What the infidels thought they destroyed in Afghanistan and Iraq had risen up as Red Crescent. No mistake, they were united, regrouped, learning from the hard lessons of the past. Consider the passport declaring him Peter Dietrich, German national in America on business, getting him in-country, where he melted into the general population. Then the post-office boxes, established before his arrival in three cities on the way to Seattle, keeping him on target, informed and moving. Last, but hardly least, armed with secured pager and cell phone detonator, on board with the weapon and explosives, picked up days ago, exactly where he was informed by letter they would be found in the Tacoma storage bin. The new organization had refined its strategy, he knew, always searching for new methods to stay one step ahead of the American authorities. Use smaller cells. Appear Western in every way. Keep it simple to primitive with communications. Do not integrate in Arab communities, for fear of informants. Remain alone, quiet, patient. Obey their laws, keep moving.

It worked.

The rest now, as his enemies might say, was up to him.

Tabizi looked out the window at the passing countryside, clouds shrouding snowcapped peaks he viewed. He found he was still alone at his table, but he'd positioned his laptop and briefcase to discourage company, hogging every available inch. Glancing into the open briefcase, aware the Taurus Model PT-58 was hidden beneath papers and folders, he looked around the car, wondering when the moment arrived if he would be forced to use the weapon, should one of them wish to play hero. They slept, read or watched the morning news, he saw. But something began to bother him, as he felt a cold stirring in his gut. He wanted to dismiss the feeling as mounting desire to get on with it.

Staring back out the window, he wondered over the gnawing unease, thinking perhaps failure spared no man. He wasn't alone in this operation, he knew, unsure how many brothers-in-jihad were out there, waiting for the signal to vibrate the pager attached to his hip—

The pager—that was it! A check of his watch, and he discovered it should have begun, twenty-two minutes ago. Why did the delay trouble him? Why did he feel a tight fist clenched in his chest?

Don't panic, he told himself. According to his map, he was south of Portland, north of Oregon City. He found they were crossing the steel bridge spanning the Willamette River. Exact detonation point didn't matter, as long as he fulfilled his role, ignited the payload, derailed the train. Ahead were suburbs, the train cutting its path between the Cascades and Coast Range. So many targets, he thought, between Seattle and San Francisco alone, so little plastic explosive. Oh, he could have done so much, even if he was only one. There was the Space Needle back in Seattle for starters. Six to twelve martyrs, he figured, wrapped in high explosive, two or three truck bombs—that could do the job, the payloads erupting in sync, say along the base of the building. Then there were countless restaurants, art galleries, markets, waterfronts, packed with unsuspecting infidels out for a day of leisure until a bomb blew among them. There was the Trojan Nuclear Energy Plant he had passed, just inside the Oregon border. Unable to hold off the visions, he saw how an attack on the plant would succeed. Take four twin-engined private aircraft—no, better yet, use faster executive jets. Equip them with radar jamming, wings topped off with fuel. Stuff the fuselage, floor to ceiling, stem to stern with primed plastique. Swoop down, thumb on the detonator, blast into the radioactive guts, one of four streaking jets sure to make it through any antiaircraft battery.

Slow down. He was distracting himself, he knew, with fantasy, trying to ignore the nagging that now cut from belly to spine. Suddenly he felt terribly alone. How many holy warriors were out there? What were their targets? Were they working alone, in twos or more? What were their weapons? How much payload did they carry? Had it started without him?

Surely, the one regret was he hadn't been handed over enough Semtex to pack a locker back at King Station. Forced to tote just enough weight below the 150-pound maximum, two check-ons, one in the overhead, he hoped it proved enough. Pull the trigger now? What if he'd been found out by American law enforcement or their intelligence operatives? Say one of them had been captured, talked? He ordered himself to stay calm, conjured up in his mind's eye glory of the final act, steeling himself. If only his car in first-class disintegrated in the fireball, a domino effect would derail the trailing cars. He envisioned the cars, a rending string of giant tin cans, crushing on top of one another, hurtled off the tracks. Bodies would be tossed through the air, shredded, crushed in the pounding whirlwind, limbs amputated by jagged metal sheared apart by imploding wreckage. Any survivors would be so mangled, broken bones jutting out of them like pin cushions, they would cry out for death to relieve their misery. The body count, he hoped, should reach well into triple digits, total destruction of the Coast Starlight.

The vision faded, the beast of al-Jassaca boiling to life, frothing, snarling. A strange angry voice hidden in the cavern of thought and fantasy warned him he couldn't wait much longer. He took the cell phone from his coat pocket, began punching the series of numbers. He felt the fire of anticipation swell his chest, his hands trembling now the decision was final, senses electric with adrenaline. Instinct shouted something had gone wrong.

He was on his own.

Do it!

Tabizi punched in the last two numbers, looked at the miniscreen—and nearly shrieked.

"Access Denied."

"Oh, God, no!" Tabizi felt sweat break out on his forehead, his heart pound, the cell phone visibly shaking in his hand. Voices cracked the buzz in his ears, ahead and behind, believing he heard questions flung through the car. Looking up, he found two porters ushering passengers from their seats, one of the redcaps walking straight for him, telling everyone to remain calm. That they were getting off at the next stop. Leave all luggage and personal possessions behind.

Tabizi shot a look out the window and felt his heart skip a beat.

He spotted one, then two Black Hawk gunships, fearfully aware of their power, having hidden from them during his flight from the training camp in Afghanistan. They still appeared sleek aerial sharks, a door gunner manning the M-50 machine gun, only now they knifed out of the mist, dropping nearly on top of the train.

They knew!

"Sir, please put down the cell—"

Tabizi found the porter, nearly on top of him, something too aggressive in face and tone igniting another blast of panic. Furious and afraid, he began punching in the numbers again, certain in his excitement he'd reversed the last two digits.

"Sir?"

The porter, closer now, mere feet away. Focus! he heard his mind shout, slamming in the last two digits. It felt an eternity as he waited, stared at the screen, imploring God—

"Access Granted."

Tabizi glimpsed the porter reach out, the expression on the infidel's face warning him he was perhaps ready to get physical. Not a nanosecond to wonder if the porter would snatch the detonator from his hand, Tabizi snaked out the pistol. He was surprised how swiftly he reacted to the threat, grateful now for three years of brutal training at the camps. Raw instinct took over, allowing no margin for hesitation, regret, no mercy. The Taurus pistol seemed to have a life of its own, leaping up in his hand, cracking a round. He scored a bull's eye between the porter's eyes, the body pitching back, screams and shouts flaying the air. He felt the hysteria, then sensed anger and desperation. Out of the corner of his eye he spotted a big infidel charging him. Tabizi stole a microsecond to smile at the would-be hero, then pressed Enter.

BOLAN WASTED no time pondering, with all the Black Hawks, state and local police helicopters swarming the skies, how the Grand Charter Tour slipped the aerial net. There was no such thing as a perfect world in the war business, he knew, especially when dealing with rabid enemies bent on mass murder, and at the expense of their own lives. Which meant improvising, experience and making judgment calls on the spot that more often than not spelled the difference between victory and failure, life and death. Supertech surveillance and countersurveillance gadgets, all the hot intelligence received from intercepts or informants could never replace the skill and guts of the operator in the field. Killing the enemy before he succeeded with his agenda was the only acceptable result.

In minutes flat, soaring due southeast over I-64 at top speed, the Black Hawk streaked up on the big gold coach, dead stern. Despite the state of emergency declared by the White House, Bolan found the interstate heavy with traffic in both directions. Now that word of another terrorist attack was launched, targeting the nation's ground transportation, the panic below was evidence enough to Bolan that the terrormongers had achieved part of their goal, fear and chaos. Vehicles darted back and forth across the lanes, Bolan spotting stark terror etched on faces below. They pounded steering wheels, mouths vented to bellow silent screams and curses, many of them playing a dangerous game of bumper cars, jockeying for position, while other vehicles flew off exit ramps. Sure, he understood their fear, but he was watching human nature in a tailspin.

It was every man for himself.

Bolan figured they were fleeing cities and suburbs for the relative safety of deep countryside, or racing home to be with loved ones Either way, with congested roads thickening closer to Hampton, scores of innocents smack in the middle of a potential rolling battlefield...

It made his task that much more difficult, but not impossible for the strike he intended.

Standing in the fuselage doorway, high-powered field glasses ready, the Executioner weighed the dilemma as the pilot cut back on the throttle, as ordered, veered off the highway to fly parallel to the coach's port. With one hand, Bolan grasped the harness, looked into the glasses, adjusting the focus.

There was no positive confirmation of a Red Crescent cell on board the charter, as he recalled the sitrep from ASAC James. There was, however, a warning flag raised by one rider in particular. Aware the Feds could move mountains when they wanted, James had gotten a copy of the bus manifest and itinerary as soon as the charter was spotted, square between Williamsburg and Newport News, rolling for Virginia Beach. Apparently a group of students from the University of Syracuse were on a week-long break, the Ramada Hotel in Virginia Beach its final destination. According to James, the group had reservations, which would swell the Ramada near capacity when the students arrived. That in mind, Bolan believed there were two possible targets. On the inbound-to-Norfolk side, the Hampton Roads Bridge-Tunnel, James told him, was blocked off by state and local police. If the bus was in fact a rolling bomb, contingency plans were in place. Steel spikes were stretched across the highway, enough distance from the tunnel's entrance to slow the steel beast, Delta Force snipers in Black Hawks ready to blast the engine housing to smoking junk, medevac choppers and paramedic crews on standby. If the bus, Bolan thought, plowed through the barricade, a massive explosion touched off by an operative probably wouldn't bring the tunnel walls down, the waters of Chesapeake Bay rushing in to drown everyone down there, but why risk it? The other target could be the Ramada itself. Say the coach parked in front of the hotel entrance, a series of enormous blasts could obliterate the lobby and take out half the building, grim shades of Oklahoma City. Including the bus passengers, Bolan feared the body count could reach well into triple digits, if that worst-case scenario played out.

Sixty-four aboard, the soldier knew, including driver and two professors, but it was the passenger with the Spanish passport and student visa who grabbed Justice's concern. The same twenty-six-year-old student who, Bolan was informed, hadn't attended a single class or even signed up for one in two semesters, lived alone off campus. Questioning the director of INS, James was informed the department had intended to investigate the person of interest, suspicious the passport was bogus, confirming he'd recently made two overseas phone calls to Damascus.

Far too damn little, too late, the soldier fearing yet another INS snafu....

Stow it, he told himself, the blame game wasn't his baggage.

Good fortune, Bolan found, appeared on the side of the good guys, at least for the moment—the bus windows were plain glass instead of tinted. Problem was, no one had a clue what the passenger in question looked like. But the Executioner was betting—if he was a Red Crescent operative—the panic factor would force him to make a move.

And yet another dread concern. There was no weight limit for luggage on this chartered ride. The enemy could be ready to detonate a few hundred pounds of plastique any second.

Bolan lowered the glasses and saw a Black Hawk shadow the coach, order and strategy already passed on to that crew by his pilot. The gunship then shot over the coach, stuck to a low soar, nearly skimming rooftops of other vehicles, in full view of driver and passengers. North, the soldier spotted a state police cruiser racing down the left lane, lights flashing. It was the trooper's job, Bolan knew, to pull the bus over—or attempt the stop.

Beyond that, if it was going to happen, Bolan figured any moment now.

The soldier framed young faces aimed to the front, anxious stares fixed on the black warbird. He was searching for one nervous rider, believing instinct would let him single out a Red Crescent operative ready to pull the trigger on his mission.

The Executioner found him.

Midway down, port side, and Bolan focused on the swarthy face, saw his expression torn between agitation and anger. He looked out the window, frenzy in his eyes, then rubbed his face, mouthing what appeared to Bolan a curse. Whoever he really was, the soldier knew a savage cornered animal when he saw one. The hostile made his move, nearly walked all over his female seatmate, bulling his way into the aisle, reaching for the overhead.

The Executioner tossed the binocs aside, delved into the war bag, shouting at his flight crew, "We're on!"

"WHAT IS WRONG with you!"

Jabal Owhali, aka Enrique Cordoba, ignored the woman. She sickened him, this vile creature, he thought, who boasted about her sexual exploits, as if he were supposed to be impressed that she fancied herself a connoisseur of many cultures and races. He had often wondered what her father would think of a daughter who spread her legs for any swinging package of rainbow flavor. How could any man who called himself a man feel special with such a despicable person? In his country she would be whipped, publicly, within an inch of her life, then cast out of the home to wander the streets, whore that she was, doing what she did best, just feed herself. Beyond satisfying his own urges, or allowing her to show off her Spanish trophy to girlfriends—some of whom he'd sampled behind her back—she served no purpose on earth he could see.

Until now.

Somehow the enemy knew about him, but he anticipated this problem before leaving Syracuse. Two bags were below in the storage compartment, one in the overhead. He hoped the combined blast from two hundred pounds of Semtex could take out at least a hundred-yard stretch of interstate. If he went for the glory now, he could see battered vehicles, lifted by the firestorm and shock wave, pulped garbage cans on wheels, sailing off the road. A chain reaction of speeding, out-of-control vehicles slamming into one another was sure to follow, the holocaust piling up wreckage for a great distance behind, the dead and dying strewed all over the highway. The payload was primed, ready to blow, but first he had to punch in the numbers on his cell phone, activate the signal.

Briefly he thought it sad he would never reach the principal target, unable to blow the bus in front of the hotel, enough ordnance, he believed, to turn the face of the building into a giant smoking hole, the lobby vaporized. Option two was the Hampton Roads Bridge-Tunnel. Though his sponsors and instructors at the training camp in Syria didn't think he could punch a hole large enough in the wall to open a floodgate to Chesapeake Bay, they were certain he could spread carnage victorious enough through the tunnel with the explosion. If he was lucky, they stated, the blasts might crack a fissure, so that the pressure of the bay would eventually force its waters into the tunnel.

For the holy warrior, he thought, hope lived forever.

He took a moment, breathing deep, one last prayer for courage. Their voices raised in fear around him, he heard the whore bleating on, shrill, demanding. She would serve him now, in ways far greater than the service of her tainted body.

The swirl of light catching his eye, he spotted the state police cruiser, barreling up the side, then unzipped his bag. Certain the trooper would wave the driver over—or try—he dug out the cell phone and Beretta 92-F, then heard one of the American kids scream he had a gun.

Option two then, he thought, calculating distance to tunnel.

He grabbed his "girlfriend" by the hair and hauled her out of the seat.

CHAPTER FIVE

The Executioner intended to play out a deadly hand, his ace in the hole on reserve but ready to fly.

SOS. Shoot On Sight.

For surgical removal of hostile—confirmed now, as he saw the commotion break out and spotted the pistol in the target's hand—Bolan opted for the Heckler & Koch MSG-90 A-1. The latest state-of-the-art sniper rifle had been recently adopted by U.S. Marine Corps marksmen, and specs included adjustable iron sights for windage and elevation up to 1200 meters, cartridge casing deflector, adjustable buttstock, threaded muzzle for sound or flash suppression. Lighter by over three pounds than the MSG's predecessor, the PSG-1, the killing masterpiece fired the 7.62 1mm NATO—.308 Winchester—round. The most critical feature in Bolan's estimation, though, was the mounted Hensoldt ZF 10 x 42 telescopic sight. With a range of 1000 meters, the Executioner found he could frame his target in the thin black crosshairs, as near perfect a reach-out-and-touch shoot as he could desire. This improved version could be fitted with a 50-round drum, or a 20 or 5-round detachable box. Bolan went with the 5-shot clip, aware if he didn't nail the hostile with the first shot, nothing else would matter.

For sixty-three innocents, and God only knew how many occupants in nearby vehicles, any failure on his part to deliver could render the interstate a vast slaughterhouse.

Unacceptable.

And not on his watch.

Secured in a sturdy canvas harness, the Executioner took a knee in the fuselage hatchway, weighed factors that could make the grim job one of the most difficult sniping kills he could recall in recent or distant memory. Dropping a stationary or walking enemy, as he had countless times, seemed as easy as breathing air compared to the task at hand. Distance to target wasn't the problem—two hundred yards and change, no sweat under different circumstances, given his track record and skill. The Black Hawk holding steady to port of the coach, Bolan took into account downrange grade, figured just over fifty yards. Two out, fifty up, flying smooth and parallel to target, but factor in rotor wash whipping in his face and potentially threatening to throw his aim, tack on wind shear maybe jostling the gunship. Then there was the glass itself, impact perhaps altering the projectile's trajectory. Add in the coach rolling down the highway, somewhere around fifty-five miles per hour, the terrorist now in possession of human body armor, spinning down the aisle, mouth working overtime to shout or curse down any threat...

No time, no choice, Bolan knew.

OWHALI SPARED a moment to laugh at their terror. Arm locked around the whore's throat, he spun, side to side, backpedaling up the aisle. He whirled forward, the whore crying out as he whipped her around in his grip, then swung back again to watch his rear. Beretta thrust out, he hoped one of the fools would lunge for the weapon.

He cursed them all out loud, soft and stupid Americans, briefly recalling how they looked at him back on campus, rage and contempt fanning the fire inside. In his mind, they were naive, weak, knew nothing about the real world, safe as they were in the cocoon of so-called higher education. Beyond that they were indifferent, he believed, to the suffering and misery that smothered the planet beyond America, wondering if any of them could survive one day in Syria on their own wits. Doubtful. There were those, he thought, who did pay lip service to various horrendous plights, but only in Africa, South America or Southeast Asia, countries their politicians, professors and movie stars deemed sacred to rail about before a captive audience they knew wouldn't disagree with them. He'd been to several such human rights rallies on campus. All of it seemed empty grandstanding to him, meant to make the infidels feel less guilty about privileged lives, their slaughter of innocent Muslim women and children. How he despised these unholy infidels.

He laughed at their terror and rising panic again, feeling more superior by the moment. Many of them drove expensive cars, bragged about their wealth, luxury and privilege, all of which, he knew, wasn't earned by their own hands. Well, their parents' money and status, he thought, wouldn't save them now. He was a lion among the sheep, and he would eat them all. He would rob them of their futures, whatever their hopes and dreams. Better yet, he would abort their bloodline, slay their spawn before they were even born.

"Enrique—"

"Shut your mouth, you stupid whore!" He turned his attention on the driver, the old man, he found, tapping the brake, the sudden lurch nearly knocking him off his feet.

"There's a cop—"

"I can see him, old fool!" he shouted at the driver, spittle flying from his mouth as he jammed the pistol's muzzle in his ear. "Drive over him!"

"What? Are you—?"

"Floor the gas now or I will kill you! I will drive myself and kill everyone on this bus! Do it!" he screamed, pulled the weapon back and cracked a round through the window beside the driver's head.

Owhali watched the driver's expression shift from terror and grief to panic and despair. One more bellow in his ear, and the driver let out what sounded to Owhali like a whimper, but floored the gas. He felt the whore struggle with more desperation in his grasp, wailing. Owhali put pressure on her throat, cursing her, laughing at the wicked creature, shouting in her ear who he really was. He was then forced to split attention between passengers and the armed helicopter, found the gunship hovering directly above and maybe a quarter mile down the highway. Waiting in ambush? Certain the door gunner would open fire with the machine gun, Owhali sidled down the aisle, away from the windshield. He knew there wasn't much time, perhaps the door gunner prepared to shoot out the tires. Option three then, he decided, angry that traffic ahead was slowing, all lanes a choked barricade that would prevent him from reaching the tunnel. Somehow he had to watch enemies, outside and in, hold on to the whore as a shield, while fumbling with the cell phone, punching in the numbers to bring life to his jihad.

Senses adrenalized, Owhali locked on to sudden movement behind, certain the floorboard trembled from more than the driver slamming the bus into the cruiser.

Owhali found the black student, some football star on athletic scholarship, he believed, rushing him. Without hesitation, stepping back to give himself enough room, he shot him in the face.

One wish granted, he thought, cursing into their screams and shouts of anger and outrage.

WITH THE STUDENT as a barrier between them and the target's frenzy of movement, Bolan couldn't trigger a clean shot. The Executioner was bringing him into the crosshairs once more, then the enemy wheeled, pulling back, covered by the driver's partition as the soldier began to take up slack on the trigger. Bolan saw the pistol jump in his hand, witnessed the body topple down the aisle.

It was going to hell, he knew, pure rage and panic now seizing the target. He needed to get closer, lower, so shouted new orders to the flight crew. The only plus Bolan found was the construction of the bus itself. Built for comfort, the coach was oversize, windows larger vertically than commercial rides, with overhead compartments high enough so the target's head could be framed in the crosshairs. Had the enemy stood several inches taller, though...

Being born short was about to kill him, Bolan decided.

Above, the soldier heard the familiar shriek of turbofans, aware the tidewater peninsula was on red alert with every available fighter jet in one of the nation's key military towns scrambled. Sure, he was in charge of the operation, but knew the situation could spiral into complete anarchy any second. Panic could ripple through the chain of sitting military powers in the area, someone pulling the trigger and the plug on his authority, giving the order to their fighter jets to blow the bus off the highway.

It could happen, he knew, and the bastard would get a Pyrrhic victory.

As Bolan rode out agonizing seconds, the Black Hawk dropping, cutting hard to starboard, he saw the bus gather speed, then plow into the cruiser. Cursing, Bolan knew where the enemy was headed with the strategy, aware he had to end it, one way or another, within the next few moments. The enemy suspected he'd never reach the tunnel, most likely now craving to hit the bottleneck at Hampton, set the bus off in the crush of stalled traffic. Bolan knew the bastard wanted a fat body count, however and wherever he could get it.

The gunship settling into position, the soldier watched the cruiser become the first casualty of sudden demolition chaos. For a heartbeat, the cruiser seemed glued to the coach's nose, then jerked forward, either from impact or acceleration, Bolan couldn't say.

The bus picked up even more steam next, smashing into the bumper. Sheer brute force of impact appeared to lift the cruiser's back end, holding it suspended. Thrown ahead, the cruiser went into a half spin before it was bulldozed off the road. It slammed down on its roof, glass spraying, then flipped across the shoulder, top to wheels and back again, burrowing into thick brush.

The Executioner refocused the optics, finger curling tighter around the trigger. Urging the gods of war to grant him one microsecond for a clean head shot, he discovered the girl had gone limp in the enemy's hold. He saw the whites of her eyes, mouth gaping, tongue out, head lolling.

The bastard, Bolan knew, had accidentally, in his mindless bent on murder and mayhem, choked her to death.

"FASTER! UP THE SHOULDER—now, or I'll kill you!"

The driver looked about to weep, shaking his head, lips flapping in some unintelligible noise or plea. Owhali decided he needed more incentive, drilled another round through the window beside his head, blasting out the rest of the spiderwebbed sheet. He heard a horn blare, a Klaxon wail that mingled with wind gusting over the driver. The rumbling eighteen-wheeler, he saw, loomed, back end to their nose.

"Drive up the shoulder! Now!"

Owhali braced himself as best he could, as the driver shot the bus up the shoulder. Whether accident, panic or the narrow gate of passage the shoulder allowed, Owhali saw the front left side clip the starboard tail of the eighteen-wheeled leviathan. The bus rocked, Owhali fighting to stay on his feet. The passengers' screams rising to ear-shattering decibels, Owhali spun, shouting, "Shut up!"

The bus shuddered even more violently next, Owhali afraid it was going to tip over, as running impact shaved off a whole section of the eighteen-wheeler's side. Wall flapping open like a skinned animal, Owhali saw boxes and crates spill out, the guts of the rig's merchandise a tumbling wall of debris, hammering off the windshield, pounding the side of the coach.

"Faster! Go!"

BOLAN MOUTHED a curse, froze his trigger finger. The bastard was either blessed by some evil charm or suicidal recklessness that kept winning him points, staving off his sudden death.

Whichever it was the carnage began in horrific earnest.

There was no doubt in Bolan's mind the driver had gone berserk, terrified under threat of being shot dead in his seat, perhaps hopeful that by doing the SOB's mad bidding there was a chance he could save his passengers.

That hope suddenly became even slimmer, fading fast.

The eighteen-wheeler fishtailed as the bus slashed its rear, back end snaking out to punch an SUV trailing one lane over. Bolan watched, helpless and enraged, aware the horror show had just begun. A chain reaction, Bolan feared, was inevitable. The SUV whiplashed, starboard to port, wobbling, shotgun side jacked up, before the vehicle crashed down on its side. A van riding the doomed SUV's bumper plowed into the downed vehicle, the collision exploding glass, sheared metallic trash flying. Trailing vehicles began to slam on brakes, horns wailing, Bolan gnashing his teeth at the eruption of shrieking rubber and rending metal. There would be wholesale death down there now, he knew, broken bodies strewed all over the highway, untold misery, shattered lives.

The Executioner couldn't spare a second to watch, grieve or pray some of them survived, as the churning line of death machines banged into and off each other, metallic whirling dervishes hurtled in all directions, blurs of vehicular objects ramming then sailing over downed fellow travelers in the corner of Bolan's angry eye.

"Son of a…"

Somehow the soldier found the bus clear the front end of the tractor trailer, angle hard back onto the highway, just as the behemoth hammered down on its port wall, the cargo hull breaking apart, spewing contents in volcanic eruption.

"Get parallel, then hold it steady!" Bolan shouted at his flight crew.

"DRIVE INTO THEM! Now!"

"I can't!"

"Do it!"

Owhali cursed the driver's cowardice, screaming in his ear, waving the pistol in his face. Whimpering, the driver appeared on the verge of collapsing from terror and panic but did as Owhali ordered. With a roar of either anger of despair, the driver threw the wheel left, barreled through the tight gap between two SUVs about to stop as traffic began to bottle up. The collision, as Owhali felt the terrible impact with one of the SUVs kicked into the air and dumped on a car in the next lane, almost bowled him down.

"Go! Floor the gas!"

"I can't!"

"Go!"

The driver kept on bellowing. With the bus as his personal battering ram, Owhali shimmied and shook with each metallic explosion, the nose plowing through three, four cars, tossing them aside like so much crumpled tin, glass jetting from shattered windows, bodies thrown side to side in those vehicles.

Not much time left, he knew, down to mere seconds perhaps. The bus would either lose momentum with each hit, come to a forced standstill as the wreckage piled up and traffic snarled altogether, the gunship's shooter would unload on the bus or the driver might faint at the wheel.

Owhali hung on, saw infidels ahead jump from vehicles, darting for cover off the highway. Their horror was a beautiful sight to behold, he decided, but he wouldn't let them off that easy. Suddenly, then, he noticed the whore had gone limp in his arms. Adrenaline and focusing solely on the urgency of his mission, he figured, had kept him from becoming aware she was deadweight. One look into her lifeless eyes and he realized he'd crushed her throat. He tossed her to the floor, just as he spotted two male students charging him. They were screaming at him, eyes wild with berserk rage. Owhali triggered two quick rounds, one each to the chest, dropping the heroes to heap on his former hostage. He found one of the professors, a middle-aged guy with salt-and-pepper goatee and permed hair, imploring him to put the weapon down, ask why he was doing this. Owhali laughed. The imbecile libertine was professor of some philosophy class, he knew. Rumor, according to the dead whore, was that his female students had a knack for passing his course with flying colors, even if they skipped half the sessions, chose not to spend their money on the required books. She had said that with a wink and a grin. Owhali was certain she had likewise been blessed with an A from this professor of more than just philosophy.

"You would not understand!" Owhali told him, shuddering into the space between the partition and the first row of seats.

"Please…"

Owhali aimed his pistol at the professor, who sunk in his seat, hands raised, the infidel looking set to shriek in terror. He should have shot him, but he—all of them—would be dead in the next few seconds. Pulling the cell phone from his belt, he punched in the first set of numbers, the bus slowing, but jolted with each grinding thud through vehicles. He was down to five numbers when he felt an itch between his shoulder blades, his chest tightening as he found two of the students staring out the window, pointing at something. Two more digits tapped in, but he froze, turned to look out the window. He caught a brief glimpse of the dark-clad figure kneeling in the gunship, webbed in the doorway, rifle in hand. How did he miss him?

Owhali heard his mind scream, the gunship so close, nearly skimming the treetops on the other side of the highway....

Owhali mouthed a curse, would have sworn he saw the rifle buck. Less than a nanosecond later, Owhali thought he saw glass shatter, feeling the impact against his forehead, but the lights had already snapped off.

BOLAN TURNED AWAY from the highway of death, depositing the sniper rifle in the war bag. Anarchy had been unleashed with the final bulldoze phase of the bus. The skies swarming with choppers, military and medevac, the soldier knew he could do nothing for victims down there, forced to leave the gory cleanup to others. In both directions, he found the interstate a stalled line of vehicles as the Black Hawk turned to fly north. One last look at the charter coach and Bolan saw the survivors filing off the bus. They would have memories of this day, nightmares even, grieve for their dead friends, but they were alive. He couldn't begin to count the crushed vehicles, the numbers of maimed or even dead inside metallic coffins, or laid out on the road. Small comfort, but he knew it could have been worse. He didn't question the sudden twist of fate, as the terrorist had presented him a perfect bull's-eye, working with a fury to punch in the numbers on the cell phone that would detonate smuggled explosives.

One head shot, end of game.

How many more were out there? he wondered, taking his cell phone, tapping in the numbers on the secured line to Brognola. If they stuck to past numbers, he had to believe, between killed and captured, the enemy had to be down to under half strength. That was still too many.

No answer on Brognola's end, Bolan then discovering the big Fed had switched the line to secured voice mail. Strange, Bolan thought. With the ongoing crisis, even if he was speaking with the Man on the red line, or in war conference with agents...

Brognola always picked up a call from him, no matter what, how busy, even to put him on brief hold. It shouldn't bother him, considering what was happening. He thought about calling the Farm to get a sitrep, then tried Brognola once more. No answer. Why did that bother him?

Aware he needed to track down the next killing field, the Executioner put Brognola's AWOL status out of mind, went to the radio and dialed up ASAC James.

HAL BROGNOLA FELT a cold, almost paralyzing fear he hadn't known in a long time, perhaps ever. If it was true...

God, he raged in silence and grief, it couldn't be possible.

Showing two Arlington County patrolmen his Justice Department credentials, the big Fed lifted the yellow crime-scene tape, somehow moved on wooden legs deeper into the bowels of the garage. Forensics teams and detectives, he found, were hard at it, shooting photos, talking to witnesses huddled in the shadows near the exit sign, examining shell casings. Brognola saw the plastic sheets draped over two bodies, groaned to himself. He stopped, afraid to venture any farther, but he had to know. After hearing about the shootout on local news in his office, he choppered straight to Crystal City, his stomach so knotted it was all he could do to keep moving, breathing. The whole time he wanted to kick himself, a dozen or so "should haves" and "what ifs" flaming to mind. Fearing the worst, he turned off all channels of communication to the Farm and Bolan until he was positive.

Brognola found a big plainclothes detective moving toward him. He showed the cop his ID.

"Detective Mahorn. She's over here," he said, leading Brognola toward a covered heap near the exit.

Brognola listened with one ear as the cop ran down what he believed happened. The big Fed spotted her GMC, shot to hell, piecing together his own scenario. Judging the line of vehicles with battered windows, frames scarred by bullet holes, he could see she put up a hell of a fight, running while being shot at, returning fire. There were two bodies, Brognola heard, one male, one female, no ID on either victim. Brognola thought he was going to be sick as the detective knelt beside the body. He waited, sucked in a long breath, looked at the cop, nodded. When he pulled the sheet back, Brognola felt his heart skip a beat, staring down at the mane of honey-blond hair, afraid to even breathe. Her face was turned away, but something told Brognola it wasn't Price. Bending for a closer look, he felt his face flush with shame when he discovered he was right—this was, after all, somebody's girlfriend, wife or mother or sister who had been gunned down.

"Is that your undercover agent?"

Brognola shook his head at Mahorn. This was no

hit, it dawned on him—it was a straight kidnap. Why? Who? Oh, he knew where to start the Q and A, and Max Geller would talk, make no mistake. There was no hole deep enough for the treacherous SOB to hide, no safe haven far enough where he could run for cover. Barring the bastard's suicide, Brognola would get his hands on him. If he didn't talk, if he danced, if he lied, Brognola entertained a number of ideas that would allow the truth to set Geller free.

Brognola looked toward the other body. "I'm sending in my own team to help you with your investigation. You have any problems with that?"

"None at all. I understand this is a federal case, since it looks like your agent was snatched."

"How many of them were there?" Brognola asked.

"We're hearing six, including the dead guy. Submachine guns—probably military issue—big guys, black leather trenchcoats, that's about all the description we've gotten. Looks to me your agent capped that one over there through his ankle, nearly tore his foot off. Way I read it, the others didn't care to haul the baggage."

"The attendant see anything?"

"No."

"No?"

"Heard the shooting, called it in. Laid low in his cubbyhole during the fireworks. Can't say I blame him."

"They just drive out of here?"

"Witnesses said they flew off the roof."

Brognola unwrapped a cigar and stuck it in his mouth. "Flew? As in birds? Hanggliders, what?"

"They choppered off the roof. By the time we could

scramble our own bird, they were long gone. I regret to tell you we can't even say in which direction they vanished."

Brognola grunted. This was orchestrated, he knew, with the utmost planning, with someone high up in the shadows of the intelligence, military or black-ops community pulling the strings. Again, why grab Price? He believed he already had some clues, and he didn't like where his line of thinking was headed. Someone knew, or thought they knew about the Farm's existence. It had happened before. Was Price, then, going to be used as some blackmail chip? Or was it something else more sinister?

"Keep me posted," Brognola told Mahorn, then turned away.

With the country going up in flames, he thought, under siege by an undetermined number of terrorists, the President on the edge of dumping the nation under martial law…

Now this. Coincidence? Planned in advance? The Farm would have to know, and soon. Then…

There was Bolan, he thought, aware of the history between the Executioner and the Farm's mission controller, both personal and professional. It would be, he knew, one of the most dreaded phone calls he would ever have to make. Wherever Bolan was, whatever fight he was engaged in at the moment, Brognola would hit him with the next-to-worst of all possible news.

And he knew the Executioner would move mountains to get Price back. May God have mercy, he thought, on these sons of bitches, if they so much as ruffled her hair, because Bolan would certainly show no mercy.

The kidnappers didn't know it yet, but they were in a world of hurt they couldn't even begin to imagine in their worst nightmare.

CHAPTER SIX

"That's it? Six bags of dung? The man said ten, Artie, we needed at least ten. This is not good. This is where I start to get a little pucker...."

Artemus Dawson dragged the last body bag over the gunship's floor. Braced for a dressing down, he slid the bundled and squirming heap out the hatchway of the Black Hawk, dumped the bag on rocky earth, the cargo inside thrashing to break free. Shucking the AK-47 higher up his shoulder, his six-man team piling out around him, Dawson showed Ryan Ramses a big smile, then bobbed his bald black dome at the line of body bags. Despite short-changing an important detail of the operation, he was still pleased with the outcome. The good news was he hadn't lost a single man, not a scratch or a ding to show for their trouble. That left them about twenty strong at present, while they waited on the other half of Lazarus to rise up.

Ramses, aka Adamus Exul—tagged so after a seventeenth-century Latin play, the theme of which being nonexistence was preferable to eternal damnation, and that the Devil's only revenge on God would be robbing Him of as many souls as possible—knew what a tough chore he'd been handed out. Dawson—his own handle was Apollyon. after the dark angel who ruled Abbadon—caught Ramses scowling, running his hand over the white bristles on scalp and jaw, getting worked up. Letting the man think about the grim feat he'd pulled off, Dawson was never sure what might spew out of AE's mouth, but he was certain a few choice racial epithets were buzzing the man's thoughts. Fine by him; he'd heard it all before, to his face, no less, but he wasn't the sensitive type. No, sir, there wasn't any race prejudice on this team, he thought, to a man they held the entire human race in utter contempt and disdain, equal-opportunity haters all around. Well, he could appreciate, respect that, being a farm boy from Alabama when the old South was grinding through civil-rights changes but where he still had to fear a daily lynching.

Dawson caught the muffled grunting, drilled a boot into the package by his feet as the merchandise inside kept worming around. "We had twelve," he told Ramses, then loosed a deep chuckle, Ramses shooting him a look. "I reckon them seeing a big angry Negro boil up out of the dark, cocked and locked first thing before dawn, well, they got a little shitty, boss."

They spoke in Spanish, just in case any Kurd eavesdroppers were tucked away in some cave or deep fissure that sliced the walls of the gorge, and on up. He knew Ramses preferred Russian, but Dawson's grasp of barking machine-gun Russian was woeful, at best.

"All right, six it is. We'll live with it," Ramses said, then kicked at a writhing bag, snarling in Arabic for the human cargo to shut up and lie still or get shot.

Figuring that was as close to a job well done as he'd get, Dawson looked up the gorge, found the others marching out of the mist. He exchanged greetings with a few of them he'd served with in Special Forces or black ops in the lower Americas, some backslapping, vigorous handshakes before Ramses got down to business. As Ramses barked the order to haul the merchandise to their cave, the black commando stole a few moments to breathe cold, clean mountain air. He was damn grateful to cool off after sucking on the grit and dust of Iran, sweltering in hundred-degree heat. It had been a hard and nerve-racking chopper ride, he recalled, just to get to target in the deep northwest edge of the country. Intel was on the money, and for that Dawson had been thankful the right wheels were clearly greased.

So bag Iraqi fedayeen, still in hiding from coalition forces, snap up six, dropped by tranquilizer guns. Cuff 'em and stuff 'em, cross the border, homed into the beacon Ramses's tech team lit up their Hawk's screen with. He knew he didn't need to detail the blow by blow to Ramses, how he and his men were forced to mow down a half dozen who chose to stand and fight. Six would have to do. Shit happened, and he'd be damned before he crossed the border again, just to scrounge up a few more fedayeen, who were walking dead men anyway.

Beyond six, it could get real nasty, if what he'd heard was true, and fedayeen were biting the worm out of the gate.

Breathing deeply, Dawson looked up the towering, broken cliff face. About a thousand yards in the air, the plateau was an ideal spot to hole up, he decided. Clouds shrouded them from any Turk military fly-overs, but few in their right mind, armed or not, ventured into wild frontier country controlled by Kurd rebels who blew away outsiders on general principles of hostility and distrust. Somewhere up there in the clouds swathing the snowcapped peaks of Mount Ararat, he thought, Noah's Ark was parked, or so went the legend. With what he knew lay ahead for all of them, there were going to be more than a few who wished to God they had their own oversize lifeboat to save their bacon, any faint of heart crying out to drift away to calm waters when it hit the fan. For better or worse it was going to be a really big show. Whatever he might think of Ramses or the others, all of them shared a few virtues in common. They hadn't dropped off the radar screen all those years just to return and embrace humankind. Yes, there was, however, plenty of love in their hearts. Start with themselves, their love of and commitment to the operation. Finally the golden glory ride into individual futures, waving a middle-finger salute to more than a few treacherous and spineless former employers in the States.

"I hope it wasn't wasted effort, me and the boys hanging it out there to get you this fedayeen shit," Dawson said, torching a cigarette with the flick of his lighter.

"Nothing about any of this is wasted effort."

"Do tell. So how you plan on explainin' the facts of life to them, Cap'n?"

Ramses chuckled, helped himself to one of Dawson's smokes. "I've got a few ideas."

"Promise 'em a slice of pie?"

"That has some definite appeal."

Dawson stared at the scarred face, thinking the man's own mother would have considered abortion, if she could see him now. "How about our Kurd comrades? They gonna pledge allegiance?"

"I'm still working on it."

"Sounds like problems."

"The chief, Muddy, I call him," Ramses said as he lit his smoke. "Shitbird didn't move fast enough for me when we broke them out. So I hit him with a piss shower to get his ass in gear. He's still looking kind of steamed and surly, having evil thoughts about yours truly, if you get my meaning."

Dawson laughed. "But they'll play ball?"

"Oh, they'll dance, trust me. It's all in those facts of life you mentioned, Artie. Or should I be calling you Apollyon?"

Dawson flashed the man his winning smile. "Whatever works for you, boss. Just don't call me late for this gig."

THE RED WHITE and Blue Cab Company was a stroke of genius in his opinion. For one fact, the percentage of Arab immigrants driving cabs was high enough they were nearly invisible to the average American, as long as they were behind the wheel. A step further, and they were viewed by the infidel, for the most part, as ignorant lackeys, fit only to chaffeur, a nonentity, a nonthreat. Best of all, there were the almighty vehicles themselves.

Since being recruited as this cell's operational director in Syria, he had the utmost faith he would succeed in this glorious endeavor. There was training, naturally, both physical and technical, parameters established involving infiltration, the safe passage of ordnance, among other strict guidelines on how to live, invisible, among the enemy. Passing himself off as a Lebanese Christian—under, of course, an assumed name and bogus passport—skillful fine tuning of details had brought him the vengeance he and his chosen six drivers so craved for so long. Take the three thousand pounds of plastic explosive, for instance, shipped, piecemeal, to his garage during the past year, concealed in engine parts, among new tires, inside paneling. All of it primed with detonator cord, homed in to radio signals, the payloads were now divided between the six. Packed in their trunks, topped-out fuel tanks would ignite additional fireballs to the primary explosions.

He had to smile, laugh at the beauty, the simplicity of it all. Six years since launching the small business, keeping a low profile, obeying their laws, drawing no attention to himself while raising a family of four, and the sleeping lion finally roared to life.

Iqbhal Mohammed felt so good he considered humming the "Star Spangled Banner." Why not? he decided, and began purring the tune. After all, he lived in the city where their Francis Scott Key penned what the infidels thought of as their freedom anthem, a screechy, annoying song they played before all of their sporting events. How they worshiped their own, indeed, aware of some of the history here, in what was the second-largest port city next to New York. These fools, he thought, honored a fat dead baseball player, this Babe something or other, known as much for his gross self-indulgence as for his heroics on the field. Here, they still lauded a dead, drug-addicted writer of horror stories and bad poems, the local rumor being an unknown idolater placed roses and a glass of champagne on this Poe's grave every year, commemorating his death. They boasted about native state sons who signed their so-called Declaration of Independence, a piece of paper they had to feel gave them some supreme authority to invade and oppress sovereign Muslim nations.

By the blessing and divine will of God, though, their glory days would turn to bitter memories, their idolatry about to leave ashes and bile on screaming tongues. This day, he knew, was the beginning of much wailing and gnashing of teeth, very soon to be heard and seen around the Arab world. Oh, his people would surely dance in the streets, he thought, the young perhaps inspired to march out, create immortal history themselves. Warriors, after all, led by example.

Leaning back in his swivel chair, working on a cigarette, he split attention between the television mounted on the wall of his office, the dispatch radio and the frequency monitoring all local and state police bands. Laughing, he savored the panic, anger and outrage he heard from infidels sworn to enforce law and order.

Baltimore was going up in the cleansing holocaust of jihad. It was happening, he chuckled, all over their city, across their land.

The reports of mayhem were coming in so fast it was all he could do to focus, assess situations in progress. Standing, he went to the war map, stuck a black pin into the area known as Canton, replacing the red flag. It was a fashionable neighborhood, well-known to his drivers, choked with restaurants, art galleries, a veritable smorgasbord of ripe targets. Due to the outbreak of jihad, the chaos in their streets was shaping up even better than he had envisioned. Panic had fanned the flames of simmering anger, the poor and oppressed seizing the opportunity to lash back, vent rage and frustration at the wealthy, the power structure they felt kept them pinned under its boot heel. Riots and looting were sweeping across the city, mobs embroiled in hand-to-hand combat with National Guard troops, police officers, state troopers. They ransacked stores, smashed windows, vandalized whatever stood in their rampage. Like wild beasts, they were overturning and setting fires to cars, torching shops, invading private homes. As of yet, there was no clear fix on dead and wounded, the reporter simply stating casualties were in the hundreds.

More good news, as he looked at two other black pins, stabbed on I-95 and 83. Two of his drivers, slipping into stalled traffic, as the infidel masses attempted to flee the city or return home, had touched off their five-hundred pound payloads. Aerial news shots revealed to him what he believed was at least several hundred feet of roadkill, infidels kneeling by victims, pulling at their hair, silent shrieks caught on film. Whoever was out there on the highways was trapped, he knew, thrashing in panic, no doubt, wondering if the vehicle next to them would blow up.

The beauty of it all, indeed.

That left three, he knew, smiling at the red flags impaled on their respective strike zones. Any second now, he hoped to change them to black.

The killing, he knew, wouldn't end with the last car bomb. Two green flags marked current positions of his snipers, both of whom also toted RPG-7s in nylon bags to their rooftop firepoints. Eight warheads between them, and he figured they could knock out half a city block. At worst, as instructed, they were to gut a small apartment building, or attempt to topple one to smoking rubble. That feat depended on size, structure, of course, some flammable material or substance ignited in the explosions. God willing, they would succeed before martyred by police. In that event, wrapped in plastic explosives, their final act would be charging American authorities when they ran out of bullets and warheads.

From the reported massive blast and derailment of the Coast Starlight on the West Coast, to the utter destruction of the Greyhound Terminal in Washington, D.C., it was proving a day of immortality for Muslim freedom fighters the world over. Dreams, he thought, did come true.

The only glitch, as far as larger body counts went, was the infidels had, seemingly, received some advance warning about the attacks. From the news reports he discovered all ground and air transportation had ceased nationwide. No trains, planes or buses allowed to move, every terminal was an armed fortress. So be it. What they didn't destroy today, however many infidels they didn't kill in this epic event...

There was always tomorrow.

He looked up, just in time to find another reporter, standing in a new location looking aghast, flailing at smoke and balls of fire behind her. Turning up the volume, he discovered Number Four had erupted on Pratt Street, the explosion so devastating it had taken out a chain of restaurants. According to the visibly shaken female reporter many workers in the area, unable to leave downtown due to the attacks, traffic jams and the shutdown of public transportation, had sought refuge in restaurants and sports bars, the woman rattling off the names of the establishments.

"Yes! Praise God!" Iqbal Mohammed laughed, shaking a clenched fist at the scene of carnage. Hearing initial reports of casualties, he lowered the volume, satisfied they were making good progress.

It would be clear to the authorities, he knew, who was responsible, but he was prepared for when they surrounded his garage and office, burst inside, weapons searching for him. One of his finest soldiers, his sixteen-year-old nephew, positioned at one of the only two ways in, was weighted down with fifty pounds of plastic explosive. He had his own vest, laid out on his desk, but decided he could wait until his nephew went to Paradise before shrugging it on. He had no deep, consuming desire to martyr himself, at least not until he was certain the operation was a stunning victory.

Say he allowed himself to be captured, there would be a trial, national and international media coverage. Yet another way to get the message out, an Islamic hero, taking on the Great Satan in the infidels' own courts. They would parade him before their cameras, speaking his hated name every night on the news, their cable talk shows. Young Arabs, the future of jihad, the salvation of Islam, would hear of his sacrifice and determination. Angered by his suffering, a captive of the infidels, humiliated by their barbaric ways, they would emulate his path, pick up the sword where he left off. That struck him as a much more noble alternative to suicide.

He was dialing up the volume on the police radio when he thought he heard a heavy thud, somewhere outside in the corridor leading to the garage. Alarmed, he grabbed up the HK 33 assault rifle canted against the wall.

"Sayyid?"

No answer. Heart racing, he wondered why—if intruders had breached the building—the security buzzer hadn't sounded. Checking the small bank of monitors, he found nothing but white fuzz dancing in his eyes.

"Sayyid! Answer me!"

Torn between watching the door and hauling up the

vest, he didn't see the black-clad invader until it was too late. He swung the assault rifle toward the figure crouched in the doorway, but the M-16 was already spitting lead. His screams lanced his ears, a nanosecond after the raking burst blew his legs out from under him, his arm going numb for some reason. Nearly passing out from agony, he found himself on his back, wondered why he couldn't move his hand to pick up the assault rifle.

Then he saw the ragged lump of gristle and meat, blood jetting from the stump where half of his hand was blasted away, along with the weapon. Iqbhal Mohammed choked on rising bile.

"How many are out there?"

He couldn't die like this, he heard his mind scream, wishing the pain in his shattered legs and ruined hand would end. If the invader wanted him dead, however, he wouldn't have simply shot to cripple. There was hope, then.

Looking up, he stared into the big commando's icy blue eyes, fear rippling through his bowels at what he found. They were pitiless, the eyes of a man who had seen and dealt out plenty of death, eyes of retribution. He feared his misery had only just begun at the invader's hands. The commando repeated his question, his voice sounding as if it echoed from out of a crypt. Strange, no one else entered the office behind the invader. No sounds of an armed force stampeding the hall, swarming the garage. Only one man?

Iqbhal Mohammed heard his own laugh, strangled by greasy vomit and white-hot agony. "You cannot stop it. So arrest me." He lay there, bleeding, clutching his arm, the invader kicking away the HK, then looking over at the war map. This was America, he thought, felt confidence swelling, erasing some of the pain. They had laws, rules of engagement here. They had a constitution, something called Miranda their authorities had to honor. He was down, shot, perhaps bleeding to death. He needed medical attention. He had rights—the right to counsel, the right to remain silent—even if he was a terrorist, a mass murderer by the enemy's standards.

He was smiling at the commando, then saw something darken his face as he examined the war map another moment.

"Looks like I don't need you," he heard the commando tell him.

And Iqbhal Mohammed knew what was coming, the M-16 aimed at his chest. He was about to scream for those rights, when he heard the stutter and felt the bullets tear through his flesh.

THE EXECUTIONER SEETHED as he watched the madness ripping apart the heart of Baltimore.

He knew about the Coast Starlight from ASAC James, as did the rest of a terrified, panicked nation. The body count was rising with every slab of wreckage removed, every hunk of rubble lifted. Would this day of horror ever end? he wondered. Were the attacks over? Winding down now to death throes, nothing left but to tally dead and wounded? Was the anarchy he found from his bird's-eye view, harnessed in the hatchway of the Black Hawk, all that remained to deal with? Even if that was the case, he knew the fallout would sting bitter poison into the nation, perhaps for years to come. No telling, he knew, how the ripple effect of the day's mayhem so far would shake up the country's entire infrastructure, or if martial law would be declared to restore law and order in the streets. Yes, there would be public hue and cry, outrage over how this could have happened. There would be scapegoats, fall guys throughout the bureaucratic maze, in-house cleanings from the Pentagon to Langley. There would be blame enough, real or perceived to go around until a sufficient number of official heads were lopped, displayed for the public by those too high up the pecking order to be touched. None of it, he knew, would prove near enough to take the bite out of the nightmare of this day.

America, Bolan thought, had changed forever, once again.

Whether or not he'd done everything he could was moot. Call it hot intel, luck or fate, but his one-man blitz on the cab company may have saved lives. It helped his cause that an informant had stepped forward at the last moment, relaying to the FBI information about shipments of plastic explosive to Red White and Blue from a Brooklyn dock. Granted, the cooperation from ASAC James and the man's tireless effort to keep him moving to the next flash point carved another bloody slice off the Red Crescent Hydra. Certainly, dropping the human bomb in the garage—a kid, no more than sixteen, he figured— with one head shot from his sound-suppressed Beretta had eliminated the potential for more tragedy. Yes, the Black Hawk's state-of-the-art heat sensors pinned numbers and location of targets, laser-guided jammer knocking out the security web, allowing him swift and invisible penetration to crush the terrorists in their command center.

Why, then, did he feel so angry, shortchanged by his own effort? So many lives lost, perhaps, with chaos spiraling across the nation, entire families left to grieve their dead and maimed. Spreading terror, he knew, gave the enemy joy, left them believing they had branded the invisible cancer of fear on America, nearly as good in their minds as the body count itself.

He wasn't sure how he knew it, but Bolan suspected the savages had help from inside America's borders. If that were true, the Executioner would fuel more grim determination, ratchet up his lethal skills to another level, leave no doubt to his victims there was such a thing as Hell on Earth.

Cradling the sniper rifle, the soldier took in the bedlam as they soared over the inner harbor, veering into downtown Baltimore. The skies were choked, Bolan found, with military and police helicopters, the streets packed with emergency medical vehicles, police cruisers, fire trucks, National Guard transports. Tear-gas clouds boiled over the mobs, chasing looters away from stores and shops. Other antlike figures scurried down surrounding blocks, whatever their howls whipped away by the frenzy, the combined Klaxons of official sirens. Fires engulfed brownstone buildings, helmeted police and Guardsmen rolling in waves....

Was this the beginning of the real horror and bloodshed? Was this the end of America as he, as freedom-loving, right-living people across the land knew it?

The intercom buzzed, Bolan hearing the crew chief inform him the last of the snipers had been taken out, but not before he dumped an RPG round into a police cruiser. Turning toward the small bolted-down metal table, the Executioner stared at the war map. No sooner had Bolan cashiered out the cell's leader than he raised his crew chief. As he suspected, the red-and-green flags proved to mark the target sites for operators still at large, black pins signifying opposition victory.

Instinct told Bolan it was over, at least in Baltimore.

What next? he wondered, then Bolan saw the red light flash on his satlink. That would be Brognola, he knew, and switched the big Fed on the secured frequency. He took a second to gather his thoughts, clearing his throat, feeling adrenaline meltdown, but aware another crisis demanded his full attention.

"Striker?"

"I'm here."

There was a moment of silence. Bolan sensed the big Fed was composing his own thoughts, how to unload yet more bad news.

"We have a very serious situation," Brognola said, then fell silent again.

Bolan, feeling his own strain, knowing already something was terribly wrong on the big Fed's end, caught the edge in his voice as he said, "I'm listening."

"Mack...it's Barbara."

PRICE HEARD TWO VOICES, aware she was coming back to life. They were evanescent, at first, but as she groped her way up from the black hole, cracked open heavy eyelids, the sound of men talking in low tones filtered through the sludge in her brain.

"I damn well hope the picture you've painted is nothing short of perfect."

Recognizing Cramnon's voice, she wondered where they had taken her, strained to pinpoint the direction of the only sound nearby. Vision blurred, her senses numb and tingling still from whatever it was they shot into her arm, she recalled the lights being doused when they dumped her into the chopper for the rooftop get-away. She breathed slowly, deeply, quietly. How long had she been out? Why did they sound right on top of her, or speaking around her as if she were invisible? It was the dope, she knew, her senses warped with its thick residue, reality fogged.

"My friend, I have told you. I have been there, many times. I was their courier, a cutout to both sides."

"That much I already know."

"I have left out no detail, no matter how small. I know every inch, I can count the number of stones. The picture, my friend, is as perfect as a Rembrandt."

The second voice was thick with accent, Eastern European, perhaps Arab, she thought. Then Cramnon chuckled, the bastard loving the sound of his own voice, she thought.

"Fear not? Trust me? Is that what you were going to say?"

"I would assume," she heard the foreigner state, "if

there was no trust on your part, if there was fear or
doubt in your heart about this, you would have already
sought out an alternative"

"I always have alternatives."

"What are you saying?"

"Think about it. If it goes bad for us—"

"Ah, listen. You do your job, I do mine. We are professionals. Everything will fall perfectly into place. It
will be classic. I see the exquisite beauty of it all as we
speak."

"Like looking at a Rembrandt."

"Precisely."

"And we all live happily ever after?"

"Paradise."

A few more seconds of steady breathing, and she
brought the world into focus. She found herself in a
cushy high-backed seat, her hands and feet now cuffed
with steel. The back of Cramnon's head aimed her
way, he sat one row up, two o'clock. She looked at the
low ceiling, squinted against the soft light, her eyes dry
and stung raw, but her brain felt as if it were solidify-
ing. Shimmied in her seat by an unseen force, and with
the narrow dimensions of the curved fuselage she saw
ahead and above, Price knew she was in an aircraft.
Leather seats built for comfort, bulkhead paneled with
mahogany polished to mirror sheen, she figured the
ride for an executive jet. Peering around the edge of
the next seat, she found two new additions to Cramnon's crew. Togged in black, big pistols in shoulder
holsters, they sat in what she assumed was a small
communications module. The partition blocked her

view of their monitors, but she bet they were tracking air traffic, plotting whatever the course, gathering intel. Assume they had access to state-of-the-art surveillance and countersurveillance, figure they could jam radar, throw out ghost signals and frequencies to divert any pursuit, and Price believed they would make it to their destination. She noted several palls of cigarette smoke hanging above heads in more seats forward, legs sticking out in the aisle. Cramnon had beefed up his force, but she couldn't be positive from where she sat how many additional guns were on board. There was something far more insidious to this game, she was certain, than just her abduction. By now, with police sure to have responded to the mayhem behind her, not checking in as promised...

Brognola, the Farm and Bolan knew she had vanished by force. They would take action, instead of hitting panic buttons. And if she believed in nothing else in life, she knew Bolan, the man and the warrior. Whether for personal or professional reasons or some of each, Bolan would move heaven and hell to track her down. She was one hundred percent confident about that.

Several pressing questions right now, though, consumed her anxious thoughts. What did they want with her? What were they going to do to her, how far would they go to get whatever it was they wanted out of her? Information? Was she a bargaining piece on their chessboard for whatever their end game?

She saw Cramnon rise, turning toward her in that slow-motion float. As he smiled and took the seat across the aisle from her, Price was certain of one fact.

She was looking at the face of pure evil.

Cramnon struck a thinking man's pose. "Not going to fire off a bunch of questions?"

"I'm sure you'll tell me only what you want, when you want."

Cramnon chuckled. "Oh, you are a player, Babs. I like that. No *Cosmo* girl here, flying into hysterics. But from what Max told me about you, and from what I've learned on my own time, I'd be heartbroken if you turned out any other way."

Price determined she wouldn't be goaded, held his eye.

"I'm thinking, cupcake, maybe you're wishing life had worked out a little different. Basic female nature, all that nurturing instinct telling you should be a wife and mother instead of Miss Independent, out there all those years in the shadows where I and my kind dwell. Could have had a nice home in the suburbs. Married to an honorable man who loves his wife, respects his wedding vows. Soccer mom. Cook Thanksgiving dinner. Christmas shopping. Kitchen, bed and home the order of your day, simple but sweet and safe. Do I sound a trifle politically incorrect?" He laughed.

She thought of the cold-blooded murder of the woman in the garage, anger burning in her heart. This monster had robbed not only her of life, but also turned some loved ones' present and future into a hell of grieving, a crime so senseless whoever she left behind would cry in their souls, wanting justice, wondering why.

Since Price doubted he could read minds, he had to have caught something in her eyes as he said, "Thinking about that woman? I had to do something, Babs, smoke you out, end a nasty little standoff. Cops showing up next, and then it would have turned real ugly. You want to talk about an unnecessary body count? But, hey, let's put our shaky beginning behind. Let's look toward the future."

She watched as the laughter died in his look, a darker shade of evil hardening his expression.

"As a former President once said, 'Let me be perfectly clear.' You are going to give me what I want, make no mistake, and I'm not talking about some sport fucking." Cramnon paused, stood, the laughter back in the eyes and voice. "I'm going to have a drink. You want one?"

"That's very generous of you, but I'll pass."

"We'll talk again."

As he walked away, the words "Laugh now, bleed later" almost came out of her mouth.

Price decided to let the future do the talking.

CHAPTER SEVEN

The decision was simple, starting point logical, the course of action clear. As far as Bolan was concerned, there never was an option.

The Executioner was going straight to the well. Or, rather, in this instance, he thought, down into the abyss, where the demons who had the answers he needed dwelled, those beasts whose blood he intended to shed.

Crouched behind a thicket of brush, the soldier took in the lay of the land, assessing enemy setup, weighing the situation as far as he knew it. The Beretta 93-R, threaded with sound suppressor, was the weapon of choice to lead his penetration of the grounds. Once inside the split-level home, the HK MP-5 subgun with fixed laser and commando flashlight, snug for the moment around his shoulder, would take care of upping the ante. According to both the Black Hawk's sensors and his own infrared heat-seeking handheld device, the targets totaled four. One hostile—the pilot of the Bell JetRanger, he assumed—looked oblivious to everything but his cigarette. Displaying a pistol in shoulder rigging, he puffed, as content as a newborn, shuffling around from foot to foot. Standing amidships on the starboard side, the pilot was hidden from any watching eyes in the target's house, as if he feared being caught goldbricking instead of guarding the perimeter. Aware of who was inside, Bolan doubted the others would prove as nonchalant as their flyboy. In fact, he was sure of it.

Bolan ran back the aerial shots committed to memory of grounds and targets in question. When learning the grim news, several agonizing hours were lost—between the brief with Brognola and trying to pin down Max Geller's trail and present whereabouts—before the Black Hawk dropped him off, two klicks north, where he hoofed it to his present roost. Considering what was at stake—the abduction of Stony Man's mission controller, with several dire scenarios attached to the crisis—Brognola had marshaled every available resource, called in markers, one of which was an associate of Geller's at the NSA. Geller was AWOL. No surprise to Bolan.

Combined good fortune, dogged backtracking and investigation by Brognola into Geller's life, along with aerial surveillance, had finally turned the corner. The door was now cracked enough for Bolan to smash through and get answers, whatever it took.

Less than an hour ago, flying eyes in the sky, the soldier knew, spotted the NSA intel-gathering wizard disembarking from the now grounded chopper. And he was accompanied by Bolan's favorite butcher. The Executioner could venture a good guess at what was going down here, but he would get the whole truth soon enough.

Make no mistake, the Executioner determined there would be an answer. He wasn't in the torture business, but he'd do what needed to be done.

He surveyed Geller's spread, gauging the real estate he'd need to cover before hitting a breach point into the split-level. Manicured lawn, he observed, fanning away to walled-in pool and brick patio leading to French double doors. Gazebo, swathed by neatly trimmed azaleas, a rose garden, vineyards on the other side of a tennis court. The NSA intel wizard had snapped up prime turf in historic Annapolis, the wood-and-stone split-level perched on a hill, providing its owner with a scenic view of the Severn River. Bolan's Black Hawk crew was watching Geller's sixty-foot cabin cruiser, the *Doll Baby,* just in case the enemy bailed, forced to use escape hatch B when he crashed the butcher's fun and games. All things considered, it was impressive real estate, he decided. Not too shabby for a government employee who probably brought down all of a midrange five-figure salary.

Greed, Bolan thought, knew only two words: "Give me." Geller, though, was about to reveal his generous side.

The Executioner decided to play it right down Broadway. He'd worry about home invasion after dropping the pilot.

With twilight draping shadows over the grounds, the skies buzzing with roving choppers in the distance, the soldier felt he owned an edge as far as his opening advance went. Weapon and stare locked on the pilot, Bolan slid forward into open ground. Adrenaline, coupled with urgency and anger over why he was there, seemed to propel him ahead, as if a strong wind were at his back, carrying him to target.

He was less than ten yards from the smoker when the hardman had to have sensed the presence on his six. The guy was cobra fast—Bolan gave him that—smoke glued to his lip, the pilot holding the relaxed pose before he made his move. Mr. Nonchalant wheeled, a lightning-fast one-eighty, the pistol out and tracking. Bolan punched his lights out, with one 9 mm subsonic round drilled between the eyes.

One last surveillance of the bastard's homestead, satisfied he was alone right then with only the dead, and Bolan sheathed the Beretta. Why bother with stealth? Why worry about alarms and sensors? The country was going up in flames, though no more attacks had been unleashed since the Red White and Blue Cab Company was put out of business. Recovering Barbara Price, safe and unmolested, was now his sole, grim focus. The clock on Price, he knew, was running.

Taking the HK subgun off his shoulder, the Executioner recalled his last words to Brognola.

"I'll take care of it."

Bolan bolted across open ground.

WILLIAM BAINES TOOK enormous professional pride in his work. He considered himself not only a master craftsman, but a student of human nature. Over the course of several decades learning his trade from the CIA in Vietnam, he had come to know each and every one of his subjects. He could recall every delicious moment spent with them, from introduction to farewell, so intimate, it fell just shy of sexual intimacy. In fact, when he was finished with them, he knew their likes and dislikes, fears, hopes and dreams, their failures, foibles and follies so well it felt as if he were taking their souls with him to bed at night. Sometimes, truth be told, he might even tuck a souvenir under the pillow.

With all his experience finding inner truth inside a subject he usually knew—before the first cut, slice, electric jolt or burn—in which classification of human nature they belonged. There were three categories of subjects, he thought, zipping open the tool bag settled on Geller's desk.

Snivelers, shitters and sharks.

He had a personal favorite, but already knew Max Geller was no shark.

He began the ritual, slipping into his black leather apron, taking his time getting fastened in, breathing in the fear he smelled oozing out with Geller's sweat. Gloves next, wiggle fingers, crack knuckles, a master piano player about to claim his seat before a captive audience. Baines then indulged a moment to smile at Geller. Warm him up, he thought, show him a nice, easy smile, hey, they were long-lost buddies, getting reacquainted. He ran a look over Geller's naked, flabby body, bobbing his head, serious now, as if examining an exotic insect he was about to dissect. Stripping a subject was the first step to breaking him or her down, though he'd allowed Geller to keep the Gucci loafers, the guy looking especially silly with only shoes on. He was always searching to improve his game of psych-spirit debasing.

Displaying steel instruments of various sizes and shapes was the next order of business. Let them see the devices meant to slice, dice, mutilate and skin. Try to catch some light glinting off the mirror polish, always a nice dramatic touch. That really got the fear juices boiling, he knew, their little imaginations burning with visions of dismemberment, the snivelers and the shitters helpless to do anything but whimper for mercy.

Baines went still, smiling to himself, feeling the moment. They were in the subject's study, Geller strapped to the metal chair brought in for the occasion, the legs already bolted down from the small drill gun. Gorman, as ordered, he saw, was busy stripping walls of paintings, flinging the man's art to the floor, in search of a safe.

While he listened to Geller whimpering, Baines strolled to the wet bar. Again, he took his time, building a whiskey, swirling cubes around the glass. Sipping, he oohed and aahed on the way back to his subject, glass and bottle in hand, making a production of how delicious the whiskey was, thrilled with the moment. He considered asking Max if he wanted one, then decided to just leave it in his sight, tempt him to beg for one. During the session of slicing and dicing,

Baines decided he'd take a time out. Why rush his pleasure?

Baines was ready now, warm and fuzzy, turning to Geller. The subject, he saw, trembled, a pissed-on leaf, sweat already coursing down his face, bleating about to rise to octave levels, a lamb to the slaughter. A sniveler, no question, but Baines never had any doubt.

"Please, I only did what Crannon—"

Baines put a finger to his lips. "Shh. Relax. It's gonna be fine. I'll walk you through this. Shucks, I'll be as gentle as if you were a virgin, Max, I promise, sweetheart." He pinned the crotch area, putting on a grim face, then dug the white filter mask from his bag. "Please tell me you're not a shitter, Max."

"A wh-what…"

Baines waved the mask, then flipped it on the desk. Chuckling, loving how the sound seemed to echo through the study, he picked up the propane wand, flicked on the blue-orange flame. It was going to get messy, he knew, Max already blowing gas, bowels ready to burst, a tear breaking from the corner of his eye.

Shaking his head, Baines heaved a sigh, sickened by the sight of Geller. The past few years it seemed all he'd taken to class were snivelers and shitters. When was the last time he'd looked and broken a shark? Why was it there were so few subjects these days who could truly resist, even enjoy or use pain, could turn their fear into defiance? Was it a sign of the times? Where had all the sharks gone, that rare fearless breed angry to turn a session into a contest of wills? Had the days of wooden ships and iron men gone the way of the dinosaur? What kind of world was he living in anyway, where pain and suffering were to be dreaded, avoided at all cost?

"Oh, God, please… I don't know anything…I told your guy when he grabbed me at the hotel…please…."

Baines put down the wand, took up and examined the prod. Battery fully charged, he could crank up the juice from five to ten to maximum twenty-five thousand volts with a twist of the dial. Slowly, chuckling, he walked up to Geller, aimed the wand at his shriveled crotch. "Did you know George Washington called it quits as commander in chief in Annapolis, Max? Did you know Congress signed the treaty here to end the Revolutionary War?"

"Listen, for the love of God, look—"

"God isn't here in the room, Max. God doesn't care about you." Baines paused, let Geller suck on his terror. "I was just thinking, Max, I'll bet the only thing you know about Annapolis is that it's home to the United States Naval Academy. By the way, you ever do a midshipman, Max?"

"I've got it."

Baines glanced over his shoulder at Gorman, then turned back to Geller, smiling. A few more inches of sizzling juice lowered toward his joy-boy, and Geller blubbered out the combination. Baines was disappointed he gave it up so quick.

"Whatever I had on Cramnon and a few of the others, it's all on the disks."

"You're lying, Max."

"I swear to you, I'm not!"

"You gave copies to someone—I'm sure of it. Guy like you, always covering his six."

"No."

"You worked with the woman."

"Cramnon had me arrange the meeting."

"You know something about who and what she is, Max."

"She didn't tell me anything…she said she was retired…."

"Then you failed."

"I did what Cramnon wanted!"

"You're holding back, Max."

Geller became hysterical. "Anything I knew about the Middle East connection anything about Red Crescent and Alpha, it's all—"

"Calm down, Max. Damn, son, I haven't burned or snipped off anything yet. Show a little courage, huh?"

Geller wept. "No one knows but me."

"If you say so," Baines said, an edge to his voice. He slapped Geller in the face. "Look at me! I've been doing this a long time, Max. I've seen and broken every bullshitter, con man, filthy liar and hardcase who thought he could never be cracked. I've done women. When I tell you I know when someone's lying to me it might as well be carved in stone. I can smell a lie like the fart you just ripped. And you're a goddamn liar, Max." Swiftly, he went to the desk, dropped the prod, snapped up his Beretta. "You think you can keep on lying to me, asshole?"

"Oh, God! Don't do it!"

"Love the Gucci loafers, Max," Baines snarled as he rolled toward his subject and aimed the Beretta at Geller's foot.

"No!"

JARIC MUHDAL LISTENED to the scarred, ax-faced commando, while grappling to keep his expression free of true feelings.

It was the second time now Ax Face laid out what was expected of the Kurds, the same condescending voice and look telling Muhdal the American thought he was dealing with a bunch of ignorant peasants. If he didn't carefully consider the bottom line of the strange offer, Muhdal knew he would have swept up his AK-47, shot the commando for his disrespectful attitude, take his chances with the rest. Muhdal looked at the big black hovering close to Ax Face, glaring down at him like a bug to be stepped on, and thought he should kill them anyway. Their obvious contempt enraged him.

At the moment, there were only ten of them against his sixteen, the American commandos who spoke many tongues fanned out, hugging the rocky wall on each side of the cave. Most of them appeared more concerned about staying warm, dancing from foot to foot, attention split between briefing, the fire and dark maw that led to the gorge. The other commandos were outside, he knew, sentries posted to watch their gunships, perhaps looking to the night skies for Turk aircraft. Beyond not trusting these arrogant Americans, Muhdal plain despised them. What they proposed, however, was indeed tempting, staving off his urge to cut loose with autofire. He could wait. Besides, the others would come running at the first shot fired. With only one way out, it could prove suicide.

Muhdal stared back, deep into the scarred commando's dark eyes. They mirrored the flames, dancing from the fire between them, but those eyes couldn't hide a madness Muhdal found, alive and seething, in this one's soul. This man, he knew, enjoyed killing and causing others pain, lived to murder and maim, a hungry shark always in search of a fresh meal. He could only imagine all the suffering and horror he'd left behind him, perhaps in countries he'd never even heard of. They were eyes betraying the soul of a man who took what he wanted, indifferent to who or how many were ground up beneath his boot heel. Whoever the commando, Muhdal knew when he was in the presence of evil.

Muhdal remained still, kept a grip on withering patience, felt the anxious temperature rising from his men grouped behind. Gauging the depth of their excited murmurs, Muhdal knew most of his men were willing to go along with the insane scheme. He had reservations, but he was their leader. It was his right to question motives, weigh risk against gain, make the final decision.

He lifted a hand to silence his men, nodded at the commando to continue. He watched Ax Face stab the map with his stick, outline the road they would travel, by military transport, to Ankara. The commando's grasp of the Kurdish language was excellent, Muhdal wondering when and how he'd learned it so well. Was he CIA, he wondered, working for the Turkish intelligence, the dread MIT, an assassin playing a deadly game of double cross? If so, why break them out, only to kill them in some elaborate trap? The more he listened to what was expected of the Kurds, the deeper his suspicions grew, fueling the raw anger he felt still burning over the man throwing piss in his face. Recalling the incident yet again, it had taken hours, scrubbing the deep furrows in his chest, shoulders and back with ice and snow. Using Russian vodka for disinfectant, he cursed the Turks and the American, teeth gritted the whole time against the fire eating up his body. The burning gradually gave way to a slithering itch, making him now feel as if he had snakes crawling all over.

The commando peered at him, Muhdal wondering if he could read the look—or his mind—then went on. First, he stated he had enough room only for the men gathered in the cave. All of them would be heavily armed with assault rifles, RPGs, grenades. The commando then pulled a small handheld radio from a bulky nylon bag. Each Kurd would carry a radio, tied in to his frequency. He would raise them when necessary, but otherwise maintain radio silence. The way he explained the journey to Ankara, full of assurances about safe passage between Turk military outposts, Muhdal knew his hated oppressors were somehow involved in the plan. Bribes were most likely handed out in exchange for certain guarantees, perhaps promises to Turk authorities a bottom line would be dumped in their own laps. The commando explained how some of his own would make the trip with the Kurds to Ankara, slip them into position once inside the city, guide them through the operation, start to finish. They were to obey, not question anything, no matter how wrong they may feel about the orders.

When he heard about whom they would be up against, Muhdal wanted to smile, but kept a stone face. Iraqis, Iranians, Syrians, he thought, a chance to kill Arabs, more enemies who loathed and murdered Kurds, denying them land, their right to live in peace in those countries. Vengeance always mattered, and perhaps, he decided, there might be a chance at some point to return a favor to A. Face. Beyond that, there was another possibility he could trample their dreams altogether. With what was being demanded of them...

Muhdal tuned himself back into the moment, believing if he stayed hard and vigilant the future would take care of itself.

The commando explained the importance of teamwork, but that his men knew one another like a man and woman who had been married a hundred years. They had trained and fought together more times than he could blink. Thus the Americans were the spearhead; but the Kurds were more than welcome to join in the fun and games when the show started. And, by the way, it would get ugly; there were going to be nasty surprises, expect casualties. If he thought this would be some leisurely day at a Black Sea resort, he might as well decline now. Any wounded who couldn't walk on their own would be left behind, Muhdal certain that meant on-the-spot executions. A few more details tossed out, and Muhdal believed their real use was little more than cannon fodder and pack mules.

"If," the commando said, "you choose to go, I strongly urge you do not eat anything from this moment on, or sit in here filling up on tea. There will be no stops once you are on the way to Ankara. You will, however, be given a bucket."

Was that a grin on the commando's lips? Muhdal wondered, feeling his ire rise.

"Well, Muhdal," the commando said, "do you and your people accept our terms, without conditions, without question?"

Muhdal heard the chatter behind, turned, found Balik and Zeki deep in thought, looking at him. He didn't need their approval, aware they would go along with whatever he chose to do.

"I need an answer now."

Muhdal turned to the commando, recalling his arrogance, the casual contempt he was treated with back at the prison. He knew their lives were only worth the degree to which they performed the commando's wishes. The decision was made, but he enjoyed the impatience building in those dark, evil eyes. Smiling, he spread his arms. "I can feel the love."

Muhdal watched the anger and confusion shadow the scarred face, the man glancing up at the scowl on the black commando, then looking back.

"Is that a yes, or no?"

Muhdal stood, taking the assault rifle with him. "I do believe we can all get along."

"Maybe my Kurd isn't all that great. Yes or no?"

"When do we leave?"

Ax Face frowned, snorted. After he gave the translation in English, the black commando burst into laughter. The scarred commando chuckled next, the twin belly rippers echoing through the cave. Muhdal was more certain than ever there were, as the commando stated, going to be nasty surprises when the show began; their laughter sounded every bit as evil as he knew their hearts were. He wasn't sure what was so funny, at whom they were laughing, but Muhdal, then his fighters joined the wild chuckle session. Soon enough, he knew, no one would be laughing, least of all these insolent, evil men.

"ADAMNAN? WHAT KIND OF name is that?"

Paul Turner chuckled as he stepped into the general's quarters. Looking around at the spartan furnishings, he nodded approval. For all the rumor of the man's greed, General Ataturk Hamisi kept it simple. Nothing ostentatious, not even a chaffeur, he'd heard, tooling him around Ankara. No posh Black Sea digs, no excess he knew of, other than a mistress who came with the usual price tag of whore excess. Low profile—that was good, he decided, a man pretty much thinking only about retirement, looking ahead to golden years of comfort and leisure. The flashy ones always drew attention, Turner knew, started rumors that could have a detrimental ripple effect.

Turner held on to the black nylon bag. Closing in on the desk, he saw the Ugrak base commander staring at his tribute from behind a cloud of smoke. Greed was good, too; it motivated.

Before getting down to business, Turner helped himself to one of the strong Turk cigarettes, the lean, swarthy general frowning, leaning back in his chair. He was a handsome man, Turner decided, nearly as dark and good-looking as himself, thanks to plastic surgery, those pigmentation injections, years in the sun on a remote Seychelles island, waiting on Lazarus to come to life. Someday soon he'd return to the good life. The job first.

"Adamnan," he told the general, showing off his perfect Turk, lighting up, "was the abbot of a monastery in the Middle Ages. Seems he had horrific visions of the tortures of Hell, or so goes the story. Sinners thrashing and wailing in lakes of fire, ripped apart by wild beasts, chained to molten pillars made of snakes. Demons running around, shooting flaming arrows into their eyes, piercing various body parts with red-hot spikes."

Hamisi looked amused. "Is that so?" He smoked, grunted. "And which are you? Sinner or demon?"

"I believe each of us makes our own Heaven or Hell right here on Earth." Turner took a sheet of paper from the pocket of his black leather trench coat, flipped it on the desk. He waited while the general perused the list. "Those men had better be worth every dollar they have been paid. If they do not live up to expectations, they will suffer far worse than any torment Adamnan conjured up."

"No need to make threats. They know what to do. These radio and radar operators will perform, from here to the border, I assure you. After that, you are on your own. Is that bag for me?"

Chuckling, Turner dumped the payoff on the desk. "Count it on your own time." Moving for the curtained window, he heard the general zip open the bag anyway, grumble they were old American bills. "Inside you will find the name and phone number of a man in Switzerland we have used who will take care of it."

Turner pulled back the drape, looking out at the American fighter jets, figured twenty-some F-15s and F-16s fanned out on tarmac. Throw in near as many Black Hawks, Apaches and Hueys, jumbled up on helipads, close to massive fuel trucks, ammo depots, and he could already envision the complete obliteration of a few hundred million bucks' worth of American hardware. He smiled at the picture, then stared south toward the lit urban sprawl of northern Ankara, aware a ghastly version of 9/11 was roughly twenty-four hours away from erupting on the city.

Talk about Hell on Earth, he thought.

Turner caught the general commenting about the rest of his tribute. "You will receive it at the border, as agreed upon with the man I sent before." A grunt, a heavy pause from the general's way, then Turner looked back, tired of having to reexplain the program. He found the general smiling, Hamisi indulging a good chuckle. "You care to share the joke, General?"

"You speak of this Adamnan, the tortures of Hell." Hamisi killed his laughter. "My friend, if what I hear is true about what is down there, where you and the others will be going, you may well discover unimaginable suffering yourselves."

Now it was his turn to smile, only Turner fully intended to hold on to secret knowledge. What the general didn't know, he thought, was a lot. He almost said it, but figured, what the hell, why bother? Tomorrow night would unleash a horror, he knew, that would make many long for the simple torments of Adamnan's visions.

WHATEVER EVIL CHURNED inside this butcher, Bolan didn't much care. He felt cold anger, just the same, over the savage boasting to Geller about past work on helpless victims. Whatever source, indeed, created the monster inside the man, Moctaw could take it to hell with him. Oh, the soldier knew the arguments, the rationale, defense lawyers famous for defending clients who claimed the most heinous of actions were the result of abusive parents or molestation, mental defects, one-parent families, grinding poverty. Or maybe their brains were addled by drugs, rendering them psychotic; even too much caffeine or sugar made them do it. The list, it seemed to the Executioner, was always growing these days, until nobody was responsible for anything he or she did. Life was a never ending procession of choices, Bolan knew, believing what a man did was what a man wanted. Period, no discussion needed.

He'd heard and waited long enough, and he wasn't here to help Moctaw psychoanalyze the beast inside. Geller's pleas and Moctaw's chuckling and sadistic taunts having drawn him to the open doorway, the Executioner made his entrance. Subgun up and leading his charge into the study at the sound of Geller's scream, Bolan sighted on the black-clad figure by the bookcase. Two steps in, the Executioner hit the trigger, burped out three 9 mm rounds, tagging the butcher's comrade from the blind side. Hot subsonic lead shattered the hardman's skull, brain turned to gobs of raining mush, the CD-ROMs flying from his hand. Tracking on, Moctaw in high gear, the Beretta up and swinging around, Bolan opted for a crippling touch. He went for the gun hand first, squeezed the HK's trigger. Several rounds blasted the Beretta away, the thumb and meaty part of the butcher's palm disintegrating in a red mist, a stream of blood shooting from mangled glove edges. Going low, Bolan chopped Moctaw off at the ankles, the man screaming like the damned now, toppling to thunder on his back at Geller's loafers. Quickly, Bolan picked up the CDs, tucked them into a slot on his combat vest.

Moctaw, thrashing around in his pooling blood, bellowed curses. "Do you know who I am?" he roared as Bolan moved toward the butcher, scooped the Beretta off the floor. "Do you know what you've just done?"

The Executioner ignored Moctaw for the moment, found Geller a blubbering mess. The man responsible for drawing Price into a trap appeared so shaken with terror he might as well have been on Mars. It was decision time for one of them.

Moctaw kept on swearing, pounding out threatening noise, the butcher torn between grabbing his mutilated hand or reaching for his ankles.

"First one who talks gets a pass," Bolan told them.

Moctaw cursed, but Geller came alive with hope,

swearing he'd tell anything Bolan wanted to hear. Then Geller wanted to know about his foot.

"He missed." Geller looked set to faint, Bolan forced to bark his name to snap him out of it. "I'm only interested in the truth," the Executioner told the man. "If you can't deliver..."

"Okay, I understand, you'll get it."

"How about you?"

"Go to hell," Moctaw answered. "I won't tell you jackshit."

Bolan considered tossing the Beretta onto the floor, give Moctaw three choices. Surrender, suicide or certain execution. Considering Price's life was at stake, no time to choke Moctaw with his own poison to get answers, and knowing this monster had not a shred of a single redeeming quality...

And for all his victims, Bolan drilled him with a 3-round burst to the chest.

Geller strained at his bindings. "Don't kill me!" he wailed.

"Talk or you're next."

And Geller couldn't get it out fast enough. In fact, Bolan was forced to slow him down, pulling the man's nerves together with a shot of whiskey. He told Bolan about Alpha Deep Six, naming the players. What they were, how they had gone "under," then resurrected themselves ten years later, these masters of the global arms race. He explained his role in keeping Alpha posted just before the resurrection on NSA intercepts about the rising Red Crescent organization, which they helped create, arm, train and fund, the worst of lethal remnants of other terror groups on the way out. When he first learned they had risen from the dead, Geller took their money, giving them information on whereabouts of former employers they held accountable for their near-death experience after they cleaned out DOD slush funds.

"What is Price to them?" Bolan demanded.

Geller couldn't be sure, but Alpha's chief, Cramnon, and the late Moctaw thought she worked for a covert agency they believed illegal and off the congressional books. She was leverage of some type, a bargaining chip, maybe, the way Geller understood the kidnap. Geller didn't know where they'd taken her, what they intended to do to her, but he believed it was all part of Operation Lazarus.

"How so?"

Geller told Bolan it was Alpha and its new team of recruits who used Arab cutouts to infiltrate Red Crescent into America. He began jumping around from explanation to speculating, talking about a Bank of Islam, where hundreds of millions of dollars in terror funds were stashed. He believed the operation actually began with the destruction the other night of a Turkish military outpost in Kurd-controlled Anatolia. When Geller told him he believed Alpha was looking for an edge with its own 9/11, Bolan interrupted.

"You're telling me Alpha used what happened in this country today as a smoke screen?"

Geller bobbed his head.

"Why?"

Geller told him about the terror funds, underground

ancient cities, vaults stuffed with cash, gold, diamonds. Where, exactly, the Bank of Islam was located, Geller didn't know.

Bolan felt his blood boil as he thought about all the carnage out there after the day's mayhem. It was all he could do to keep from shooting Geller.

"This is all about a bank heist?"

Geller gave Bolan a feeble nod.

CHAPTER EIGHT

"Listen up, assholes. This is it, the hour of truth is upon us. Lazarus has risen. We are now officially into Operation Leviathan."

Marching into the room, Cramnon claimed the far end of the massive cedar table, all eyes, he found, aimed at their commander in chief. Their minds, hearts and souls were in the game of their lives, he knew, the future theirs to take, but it never hurt to shore up resolve at the final hour, go over it all once more. Beyond that he sought to separate the wheat from the chaff, and for his own benefit. Then there was his own peculiar, and at times, frightening gift to throw into the equation.

Having been around violent death close to four decades, he believed he had developed a psychic power concerning the future of a warrior. Those who didn't know him—meaning they had never gone the distance by his side in battle—might scoff at his claim as seer, mock him for a lunatic or fool. Those who knew him had become believers.

The first time it happened he wasn't sure what he saw, but half his platoon in that long-forgotten war in Southeast Asia had been wiped out the day after the event. Call it an aura, the energy of life force radiating from within, but he could see it, a sign, for better or worse, foretelling a man's fate. Granted, it didn't happen every time, but when it did it always left him shaken to the marrow, as nothing in life ever had. Sometimes, he wondered if it was even real, if he imagined or wanted to believe he saw it.

Whichever, he believed he could stare into a man's eyes, feel, almost absorb the inner life, determine whether the force within was strong, weak or straddled the fence. Often he was certain he saw the aura, a faint halo, it looked, enveloping a man's head. Red hue shimmering in white, he thought, shone for the warrior who would go all the way, and come out the other side. Then there was gray, fading to black. Pity that man's fate; it was the color of death.

Collecting his thoughts, he helped himself to one of Acheron's smokes, his right-hand man offering him a light.

They were gathered in an abandoned monastery, perched on a rocky cliff with a bird's-eye view of the blue Mediterranean waters of Lanarka Bay. This area of eastern Cyprus was controlled by Turks, since 1974 when they kicked in Greek teeth. Times changed, regimes fell and loyalties shifted allegiance, but money was still king, Cramnon knew. All part of planning Lazarus, he gobbled up a big chunk of change, greasing the right Turk officers, snapping up countryside the envy of any rich Eurotrash.

Twelve of the best commandos sat before him. He felt like a proud father, thinking these men could have been his own children, if he had a bloodline to inherit his coming new Earth. As father in spirit, he knew the hearts and minds of each and every warrior before him. He knew their pasts, their triumphs and failures. He could identify with their struggles, perhaps emphathize with the suffering and falling down that had led a few of them to this point in their destinies. Using recruiter cutouts, he had culled them, over the past several years, handpicked from Delta, Special Forces, SEALs, Marine recon. Beyond proved lethal talent on the battlefield, all of them shared one thing in common.

They were addicts.

And as such, he thought, they weren't normal—whatever normal was anyway, but he knew what it wasn't. Abnormal was going to the extreme outer limits in anything they had ever done in their sorry excuse for a life. Whatever demon they kept on loose chains, they would never know peace, happiness, joy, but he'd yet to find the son of a bitch who could define what those things were anyway. These men, his adopted sons, would, could never be satisfied, no matter what or how much they consumed. Always one more mountain to climb beyond the next hill, one more fight to win, the whole world their personal battlefield. They burned, seethed, hungered for more, and, oh, how he felt deep affection for this special, abnormal breed of human. They wanted life, on their own terms, something he could damn well appreciate. Whether substance abuse, degenerate gambling, sex of the natural or aberrant kind, whether hooked on their own anger or hunger to control and dominate, they had once been runaway trains, chasing whatever howling wild beast that drove them to the certain derailment of self-destruction. Until, of course, he had come along and saved them from themselves, shown them there was another way.

Their savior.

Before he handed the chosen the keys to the kingdom, he wanted to be clear they understood what they were up against.

Smoking, he wandered a look over each man, searching just above their heads for the first faint glow. Nothing yet. Could be the adrenaline, their bodies so charged, he could almost smell the testosterone through the clouds of smoke, the acidic bite of strong bad coffee. They had trained, drilled as a unit to the extreme just for this moment in the harshest deserts North Africa could serve up. They had killed, drank, whored together as a unit. They knew one another's thoughts, fears, moves and skill in battle so well they were one. They had studied every shred of intelligence, every computer graphic of the target and layout he had drawn up, all of it gleaned from reliable sources on the ground, and pity any poor bastard whose information wasn't on the money. With the like-minded lions on the other end they were a good platoon strength going in.

Getting out, gone and vanishing again was yet another matter.

Cramnon cleared his throat. "I'm sure I don't have to tell any of you this, but humor me. I want you to think of the worst firefight you've ever been in. I want you to recall the most vicious hand-to-hand combat you have ever engaged in. I want you to remember the most gruesome sight of the end result of violent, mutilating, eviscerating death you have ever seen. For those of you who were in Iraq I want you to see those mass graves, I want you to mull over what you heard went on in their torture chambers. Whatever you have seen, done, experienced before now will prove a happy-hour circle jerk compared to where we're going and what will happen. I won't shit you. There are going to be those among us who aren't going to make it. If you've studied, if you've listened to me and your handlers, if you've trained hard enough, as I know you have, your chances are a little better than fifty-fifty."

"Fifty-fifty?"

Cramnon caught the grumble, but couldn't pin down the source of malcontent right off. He saw Acheron lift an eyebrow his way, then found several of his troops passing one another looks. It was coming, but he knew it was inevitable. The whining faithless were about to toss in their concerns, he sensed, whatever their thoughts and fears, though, about as useful as Iraqi dinars at this stage.

It was the Marine sniper, Chambliss, who gave the dung ball a heave to get the bitch session rolling. Cramnon watched Chambliss shake his head, lips moving, but no sound coming out. There was an angry but distant look in his eyes, some madness, he thought, perhaps trapped in the soldier's head, screaming for release. He could have exploded over this display, but he had a soft spot for the Marine, aware whatever insanity raged inside was engineered by constant pain. Sometimes, though, children needed correction, not a problem, but Cramnon debated whether to go gentle or hard on the soldier.

Chambliss, he knew, had served his country with honor and courage, lost half his skull from an Iraqi land mine in the process of hunting fedayeen. Cramnon looked at the lumpy patch of purple flesh on his shaved head, where the steel plate replaced bone, searching for a glow of rising aura. They shared something in common, Cramnon knew. Chambliss was a decorated soldier, a hero among lions coming home from war, only to find his wife pregnant by another man. There was divorce, the whore remarrying, a stranger now raising the soldier's natural children. His pain didn't end there. Because of his injury, Chambliss suffered from agonizing migraines that could drop him to his knees, if not for painkillers. How long had it taken, Cramnon wondered, baby-sitting the man while he puked and sweated his way through heroin withdrawal? Two, three weeks? He'd practically held the soldier's hand, wiped his ass.

"You care to share with the rest of the class?" Cramnon asked.

"Fifty-fifty, you say, sir," Chambliss growled, getting himself worked up, glancing at the others. "With all due respect, we're going in blind as bats—sir. One, you can't tell us for certain how far down and in we'll need to go. Is it a few city blocks, a mile, what? You can't give us a fix on numbers. You say anywhere from fifty to a hundred or more. That's quite a margin for error—sir. Then we're up against maybe land mines, booby traps, you say, some nasty surprises you say may or may not be waiting for us. Stuff you hinted at they've got waiting, but can't be positive where or what it is."

Cramnon heard the Delta commando, Stevens, pipe up. "Sir, what if they… What if they even have 'it.' If we have 'it,' sir, there's a good chance they have 'it.' And all of us here know where we…got our supply. Sir."

"They don't have 'it,' as you say," Cramnon told them all. "That much I am positive about."

It was only natural, Cramnon knew, the troops, putting it all on the line, wanting to plug up the holes, contingency plans on the backburner, escape hatches at their beck and call. There was nothing he could do or say to give them anything close to one hundred percent guarantees. They all knew it. Chalk it up to pre-battle nerves, jet lag, too much coffee, restless sleep rife with bad dreams, if they slept at all the past week or so. He listened, the patient father, the concerns flying around the table, now the door was cracked.

"I mean, we signed on, free and willing, sir, we've been ready to go for months, hell, years some of us, don't get us wrong.…"

"Other than our raw talent and experience…"

"Good looks and a giant swinging pair…"

"How in the world, sir, are we going to pull this off? How are we going to do this?"

"How, you ask?" Cramnon bobbed his head, smiling into the silence, then laughed. "Ye of little faith. We're going right through the front door."

BARBARA PRICE FELT sick. Whether due to the drug's lingering grip, a creeping sense of fear and utter sense of aloneness, she couldn't be certain. She only knew she was in serious trouble. Whatever was next, she suspected it would only get worse.

She had drifted off into another deep coma during the flight, unable to fight off the effects of whatever the shot. With no sense of time, she was clueless how long they were in the air, where they had landed. Vaguely she recalled being ushered from the jet to a large stone building, high on a cliff. She'd seen, through blurred vision, the striking blue waters of an ocean. She knew it was daytime, late in the morning, she believed, wondered how many time zones they'd crossed. She thought the flora and trees—cedar and pancaked trees—looked familiar somehow, indigenous to Mediterranean islands and countries. Did it even matter where she was? What was this? she wondered. Was she losing hope?

No, she told herself, that wasn't it.

But the evil that was Cramnon had, she believed, burrowed fear into her heart. For some reason she couldn't get his voice, that sick laugh out of her head. It was as if, God help her, Cramnon lived inside her mind.

They had dumped her in a small room with four stone walls. She sat on the edge of a metal bedframe. The wooden shutters, nailed over by a thick board, kept her in the shadows. They had left the door open, light from the hall spilling into the room. Voices, Cramnon doing most of the talking, floated through the door from a distant point. She stood, listening to a minor heated exchange between Cramnon and another man. At the door, she looked out into the hallway, found a long, empty corridor, stone walls and high ceiling. No sentry? Was Cramnon testing, taunting her? Her hands and feet were now manacled together; no way could she even move double-time. And what? Walk right out of here? They'd hear the rattle of chains, anyway. Surely an armed guard was in the vicinity, at either end of the hall....

She fell back into the shadows, her head spinning, bile rising in her empty stomach.

"Nothing like a broken heart, huh?"

Laugh, laugh.

"Babs...cupcake."

Was Cramnon right? she wondered. Had she really missed out on something in life? Could it all have been different somehow? What if he was right about her former husband? Say he'd been faithful, they'd had children together, raising a family. Mother and wife, the sweet sanity, the beautiful simplicity of a normal existence. Someone to love, someone to love her. Was her commitment to one of the most important jobs in the nation worth sacrificing the kind of life—family, home, love—others had?

"*Cosmo* girl...Little Miss Independent..."

Laugh, laugh.

Could he see into the most secret corner of her heart? Was there truth in Cramnon's mockery? No, she determined, that was what he wanted her to believe. Evil, she thought, knew the human heart every bit as deep as Good. Evil, though, searched out, used whatever weakness or emptiness it found in others. Whether to break down the spirit to fill its own emptiness, use another human being like a pawn to take what it wanted, or outright destroy life simply because the very idea of life itself was both abomination and a threat to its existence....

Laugh, laugh.

Cramnon was a monster, no more, no less.

She shuffled across the room. An inch or so to spare, she raised her hands, wedged her fingers into the end of the board. Where they had driven mason nails into stone, the wall was cracked, enough so the board began to give as she tugged. She was wondering what she'd do even if she opened the shutters when his voice hit her from behind.

"Unless you're carried on wings of angels, it's about a sixty-foot drop, Babs."

She turned to Acheron. The ghoul's smile warned her this wasn't any standard check-in. Was this where they began proving themselves the savage animals she already knew they were? He took a step into the room, flipped a canteen and a sandwich onto the bedframe. He lingered, and she was positive he was reaching to close the door. Price stood her ground, ready to fight. She may be chained like a common prisoner, but she wouldn't give it up without causing the bastard real pain and grief.

Acheron took another step closer, Price steeling herself, thinking she could maybe reach his eyes when she heard Cramnon's laugh roll through the doorway.

"Hey, you! Playboy!"

She watched Acheron lose the smile, standing there, deciding. "Your master calls."

Acheron grunted. "No man is my master, lady."

He didn't budge, Price wondering if he'd defy Cramnon.

"Hey! What the hell are you doing down there?"

Acheron scowled, then backed out through the doorway.

Price let out a breath, found her hands shaking. She'd gotten lucky, she knew, but there could come a time, soon, when Cramnon wasn't around to keep the pit bulls on their chains.

"ANY QUESTIONS?"

Cramnon stared them down. The grumbling was over, reality taking hold, the clock ticking. Despite spelling it all out, all of them aware he would lead them from the front line, first one through the damn door, in fact, he found Chambliss muttering to himself, caught Acheron darting glances from the Marine to his commander. Unable to read Acheron's look, he couldn't decide if his right-hand man was amused or troubled.

It was time to dismiss the troops, he knew, having just restated the bottom line. The coming battle would settle all unresolved matters, answer any questions, clear up all doubt. This, Cramnon thought, would prove the final few hours he would ever see a number of them alive. He'd measured them, heard their gripes, seen more than enough. One last look at Chambliss, and he didn't like what he found at all where the Marine was concerned. A part of him grew heavy with foreboding knowledge. The guy had known more than enough pain in his days, shown heart and balls the width and depth of whole oceans to the world too many times to count. But who among them hadn't?

"You have a little more than four hours before we launch," Cramnon told them. "You had your last meal on the flight. I would put the coffee down from here on, but in your kits the big brown pill will thoroughly clean your systems out. I believe I can spare drawing a picture of what might happen should you not heed my advice. The white pill is optional. It is speed. Should you wish to take it, I want to know one hour in advance, and I will tell you when to take it. Clean your weapons, check your gear, rig your chutes, get some rest if you can. That's it. Good luck. Dismissed."

They gathered their intel packs, smokes, then rose as a unit and filed out of the room. Acheron was shaking his head at Chambliss, the Marine muttering on the way out the door.

"Something is definitely wrong with that guy," Acheron said.

Cramnon nodded, heavy and sad, wondered perhaps if this was how a father might feel if he was looking at a dying son.

"I know," he told Acheron. "He's not going to make it."

BOLAN FOUGHT to get himself refocused.

It was critical in helping reach the final goal, he knew, gathering intelligence, checking facts, laying out the next leg, lining up contacts in-country. But far too much time was ground up once again, before he was finally on board the Gulfstream climbing into the clouds. Thirty thousand feet above the Atlantic, and the soldier, heavy, tired and worried, shut the world out, pulling down the porthole cover.

Alone in the cabin, he tried to sweep his mind of grim thought. Thankfully, Geller had proved a gold mine of information, filling in the blanks as best he could, the soldier eventually dumping the setup artist in Brognola's capable hands. Some of what Geller told them was verified by the big Fed's own wealth of sources.

Alpha had been allegedly killed in two botched raids on terrorist strongholds, bodies burned beyond recognition. There was, according to CIA agents in Turkey, an attack on a remote military-MIT compound in eastern Anatolia, details sketchy, which left the soldier wondering who was covering what and for whom. Then there was confirmation of a breakout by forces unknown of Kurd prisoners branded terrorists by the authorities. Not a single Turk soldier or prison guard was left breathing in their butchers' wake, many of the prisoners burned alive in their cells, for reasons Bolan could only guess.

The whole murdering band, or so the assumption went, had vanished east for the mountains, into what Bolan knew was some of the most dangerous real estate on the planet. Whatever could be dug up through official channels on Crannon and his brigands was standard DOD fare, service records and so forth. Beyond that, black ops, he knew, were never left to dangle in full view of public or congressional scrutiny. As for the Bank of Islam, Geller didn't have a clue to its location. No one, for that matter, in the intelligence community could point Bolan in that direction. Even several of Brognola's sources appeared to shrug it off as wild myth more than anything else. Bolan, though, had a strong hunch it not only existed, but had a rough idea of its location.

The good news, if Bolan could call it that, was the attacks on his country appeared to be over, but who could say? Two more Red Crescent operatives had been taken down by the FBI, one in Houston, the other in Miami.

America was reeling, he knew, weeping for its dead and dying, demanding answers and revenge. He couldn't even begin to assess the fallout, backlash, how long or if America would recover from the murderous catastrophe. Whatever his part, for the warrior it was over back home.

Another bloody horizon waited.

And the Executioner knew who was responsible for cutting loose the human bombs. The question of where they were, he knew, needed solving first. No matter what it took, he would hunt down the savages, retrieve Barbara Price, safe, whole. He shoved from his mind a picture of her, alone and afraid, perhaps being tortured and abused in the most heinous ways. Bolan knew the lady well. She was tough, strong, resourceful, but if the Alpha savages wanted the truth about who she was, whom she worked for, or whatever their intent...

Whatever they did to her, the Executioner vowed

they would get it back, a hundredfold, in ways that would make them beg to die.

By now, the Farm—her friends and coworkers—knew she'd been abducted. Whatever their tasks, dealing with Phoenix Force and Able Team operations, Bolan knew they would make the time, lend him all the help he needed, the Stony Man warrior certain their hopes and prayers were riding with him.

One item Bolan was sure of, aware Brognola and the other members of the Farm likewise knew the unspoken truth. Despite the fact they stole whatever intimate moments they could, whatever deep feelings he had for her, Price was an integral, if not critical, part of the Farm. What he now did, the soldier would have done for any member of the Farm, for any friend in such dire peril.

Bolan thought about settling in for the long flight, but felt too restless. He should sleep, but doubted even a quick combat nap would come.

For the soldier, there was never any point remembering the suffering of the past, even those battles lost where loved ones were taken from him at the hands of the enemy. Still…

There was April Rose, slain during an attack on Stony Man, long ago, yet another lifetime. He wasn't the kind of man to compare notes, mental or otherwise, about any woman he'd known. He had loved April, deep, real, powerful, mourned her loss like few he ever had outside, of course, of his immediate family. Barbara Price was her own woman, in a class all by herself.

Bolan tried to shut down a grim train of thought before it began rolling, spiraled anger down to depression. Still, if something happened to Barbara...

Focus. Clear the mind, he told himself.

Somehow, some way he would get her back.

At all cost, he would make certain he wasn't haunted by more ghosts of those he cared for.

Bolan offered up a silent prayer to the Universe. He knew he would need all the help he could get, unseen or otherwise, and it never hurt, he believed, to call on some divine guidance.

The Executioner stood, went and unzipped his war bags. With time to kill before the real thing started, Bolan decided the hours ahead would be best spent stripping and cleaning his weapons before he was locked and loaded for the fight of his life.

For damn sure, someone was going down on the other end.

Hard and final.

SHE FELT the tension, the adrenaline of precombat jitters swarming her like an electric field. Shoved ahead, Acheron barking at her to face front every time she attempted to view her surroundings.

Price looked at the ride that would take them to Operation Leviathan. Parked in a stone building, gutted for service as a makeshift hangar, she presumed, the military version of the Douglas DC-3 was undergoing last-minute preflight checks. Only the two men in bomber jackets and olive-drab fatigues appeared more interested in the missiles, mounted beneath the Dakota's wings, than standard mechanical and instrument inspection.

Shuffling up on the plane's stern, she counted six pods, each one holding three warheads. With stabilizing fins, she judged the missiles six feet in length, fat, like well-fed man-eating sharks, in diameter. While Bomber Jacket fiddled with a remote box, adjusting horizontal deviation, aiming the outside pods, port and starboard to ten and two o'clock, Bomber Jacket Number Two tapped away on a computer keyboard. As they toted war bags and parachute rigs, Price counted twelve commandos in combat blacksuits climbing into the fuselage. Judging how they hustled, they couldn't wait to get in the air.

She knew exactly what this was all about.

But how could she not help hearing the details? she thought. Her door left open—on purpose, she was certain—Cramnon boasted the scheme during the final brief, letting her in on the sordid truth. She remembered Cramnon laughing about the carnage of the terror attacks they'd left behind in America, bragging to the troops how it was both a stroke of genius and sweet revenge, something about a wake-up call to former employers. To think of all the innocent lives churned up in their death machine—and for the reason as she understood it—made her both angry and sick to her stomach.

She stopped as she felt Cramnon tug her arm.

"How are we looking?" he called out.

Price watched as Bomber Jacket Number One pushed the dark aviator shades up his nose, showed Cramnon a broad smile. "Whenever you're ready, big man, she's all yours. She's topped off, packed down, ready to cruise and bruise. A few minor adjustments for the added weight on board, but your supernova package inside is hooked and ready to cook. All you have to do is punch in the code I showed you, but watch your GPS once you hit the red zone. Timer and altimeter will do all the work after you get her on-line. You and the boys just jump, wave goodbye to your shooting stars on the wings."

Cramnon chuckled. "I don't plan on being anywhere near that close to ground zero."

"The ordnance you're unloading, I would certainly hope not."

"This had better be the encore you promised."

"Let me put it this way, Chief. You drop this curtain call, and after the other night, you will not have them screaming for more. Show's over."

Price shook her head, then saw Cramnon looking at her. "And this is all about money?"

Cramnon laughed. "Well, it's not about love, Babs."

"This her?"

Bomber Jacket flashed her a grin, another lady-killer.

Cramnon scowled. "Get your mind on the job. Anything happens to her, she so much as breaks a nail, I'll hang you by your balls from the nearest tree. Just in case you can't control yourself." Cramnon produced a wad of rubber-banded American hundreds from his coat pocket, slapped it on the man's chest. "That's the last of it. Go sample the local talent when you get there. Just make damn sure you and her are there when we land."

"Oh, you don't have to worry about me being AWOL, Chief. Just make sure you don't forget me on payday."

Cramnon grunted, turned to Price. "Before I leave, how about wishing me good luck, Babs." He smiled. "Hey, you might really want to think about things while I'm gone. Next time you see me, I'll be rich enough to buy a small country, although I'm more of an island kinda guy. I may come back, looking to you the man you've always dreamed about."

Price stared at Cramnon, believing—or wanting to believe—his time was growing shorter by the minute.

"Somehow, I seriously doubt that," she told Cramnon before he laughed and pushed her away.

"We'll see about that, cupcake."

CHAPTER NINE

Gordon "Buck" Walters licked his middle finger and stuck it in the air. It wasn't Doppler radar, he thought, but a poor farm boy from Kansas could damn sure tell which way the wind was blowing with a little spit. Shuffling for the deep southwest corner, burdened with war bag, and he figured the stiff breeze wasn't shifted much by those rusted, crappy metal TV antennae sprouting on the apartment rooftop, the likes of which he'd seen in every Muslim city from Casablanca to Karachi while working CIA black ops. Old school still worked for him, by God, the wind sweeping in nice and steady from the steppe, east of old Ankara. Maybe Noah's ghost even, he chuckled to himself, up there in Mount Ararat on the border with Iran, now lent them a helping hand with good strong gusts, blowing over the vast east plains, keeping it honest for them, downright calamitous for scores of unsuspecting Turks out for a late-night stroll or cup of tea. Factor in the hills that ringed the town Kemal Ataturk, or Father Turk,

staked as the country's capital, and Walters had to believe—between high-tech and his middle finger—they
were covered from having to whiff the nasty stuff.

God help them, he thought, if Mother Nature decided to belch long and loud in their faces. Talk about
screwed and tattooed....

On the move, shuddering at the image of dying the
way he'd seen thousands of Kurds go when Saddam
got nasty after Gulf I, Walters watched two of his four-
man team hustle into position, claiming their roost. No
longer necessary to tromp around as *askeri inzibat,*
Walters knocked the white helmet of the Turkish military police, branded with As Iz, off his head. Lanyard
around his neck with pistol was dumped on the deck
next, Walters looking back as Grimm drilled the steel
plate into the doorjamb of the service stairwell. Mid-
night lovebirds or any party-crashers of the armed variety would have to blow the door, but Walters sure as
hell hoped they were long gone by then. Grimm, he
saw, then scurried to the far northeast edge, depositing four iron talons, already fastened with coiled rope,
at the base of the retaining wall.

As Judd and Gregory unzipped their hefty war bags,
hauled out and began assembling the two rocket
launchers, Walters took a few moments to get his bearings. Snugging the com link over his bristled scalp, he
crouched at the wall, the two Delta commandos erect-
ing the launcher, clamping it down, diddling with cush-
ioned recoil cradles. From his buzzard's-eye view he
found plenty of nightlife, stretching up and down the
main street. Choked with traffic, the creatures of the

night whooping it up in street side cafés and bars. The wide boulevard stretched south, ending about six klicks down before it rolled up at the gates of the presidential mansion. There were hotels, department stores, he saw, the famous Kocatepe Camii, which was the Turk version of Saks, gobbling up what he figured was a couple of blocks or so. The Haydarpasa train station was due southeast, bustling with late-arriving or departing travelers, that particular patch of real estate ripe and ready for a few bull's-eyes. Across the city, in promenades and parks, old Ataturk had raised a few statues to his war of independence, but Walters didn't see any Baghdad-style toppling of his late honor in the near future. Unless, he considered, maybe what they were about to unleash created a mass uprising, from Kurd country to the landgate between East and West that was Istanbul, anarchy lashing out at any symbol of past glory that couldn't save them from this night's horror show. What the hell, huh? What was some carnage without the fallout of rebellion after they vanished from the scene? Nothing like the collapse of a country's entire infrastructure to give new meaning to survival of the fittest.

Panning on, surprised this wasn't the atypical big, dirty, congested Muslim city, but sprinkled, of course, with the standard minarets of mosques, Walters took in what he believed were several famous Turk museums. Near under his nose, he lingered a gaze on the Museum of Anatolian Civilizations, wondering what treasures were housed inside those walls. Back to business. He wasn't here for the sights or to ogle ancient

Hittite relics. This was, however, the land of King Midas of the golden touch. Walters smiled. So far it was by the numbers. Sweet, all systems go. Sheer guts and daring from there on, maybe Lady Luck blowing them a kiss, and Walters figured to claim the throne of King Midas for himself.

Quickly, he began digging out the Russian hardware. An RPK-74 with 45-round banana clip for him, AK-47s for the younger guys, three RPGs and a fat bag of warheads, Makarov side arms, enough spare clips to tackle a small army, if it came down to shooting here to the evac site. A lot of their hardware, he knew, was custom-built from the first bolt and screw on up. There were plenty of Russian armorers, he knew, standing in the unemployment line right after the Wall came down. The big bossman, peering into their collective futures, had dropped a fat wad to buy the best weapons designers he could hunt down in the motherland. Those launchers, about to blanket a chunk of Ankara with doomsday clouds, he knew, were recoilless, self-propelled, hand and machine tooled from spec. It was the payload he stewed over.

Walters looked up, laying the weapons on the deck, Judd and Gregory setting up high-tech shop. The two Delta commandos were fresh off a war, he knew, blooded in battle and all that, fedayeen scalps on their belts maybe, but Walters figured there was at least thirty-five, could be closer to forty years in age difference between himself and the Delta specials. Judd, he saw, hacked away on his keyboard, fiddling with gyroscopic sat dish, Gregory adjusting the azimuth on both launchers. Walters began locking and loading, the two of them muttering about degrees, windage, deviations down the line of the first series of targets. Then Judd gave a weather report, wind holding steady, the Delta commando glued to the monitor as if it were a crystal ball.

"We're covered far as the wind goes, son," Walters growled.

When Judd gave him a brusque shake of the head, kept on tapping away with his space-age toy, Walters damn near cussed the insolent prick. He was about to tell him where he could stick his Medal of Honor, Judd bulling ahead, ignoring him. Walters scowled when he heard weather status confirmed for the next ninety minutes. He just told the prima donna that, Judd trusting more in his wonder gizmo than a Kansas farm boy's common sense and the tried-and-true ways of a grizzled combat vet. By God, Walters figured he was killing VC on his third leg of duty for the Green Berets when Judd's mama was little more than some schoolboy's masturbatory fantasy.

Kids these days.

Walters checked his chronometer, glimpsed the Delta hotshots hauling the first set of 10-round magazines when he heard the dull metallic thud on stone.

"Goddamn it!" he snarled, jumping back as the projectile rolled for his feet. He flashed the kids an angry look, both of them frozen on a knee, clearly anxious and aware it could all end before it got started. Bending, Walters reached out, wrapped his hand around the 85 mm projectile. There was Arab lettering on the warhead, but he already knew their origin. Carefully rolling it around, thinking he would rather hold a cobra by the hood, he grunted at the infamous mustachioed mug painted on the flip side. He was looking for cracks in the casing, wished he'd taken the time to inspect each of the hundred rounds, but was unwilling to show the kids he wasn't the man of steel as reputation preceded.

"Cute," Walters said, and held out the warhead. "Which one of you hotshits is the artist?"

Judd took the projectile, grinned. "That would be me, sir."

The Delta specialists back to prepping launchers, they snapped the first two 10-round loads home, bottoms up, near the breech. Walters then scoured the eastern skies for the comet he knew was coming. He took a knee, cradling his light machine gun, nothing to do but wait for the green light. This was either, he knew, going to be a night to remember, one for the ages...

Or all of them would be in Hell long before the next sunrise.

"HOSTILE IS DOWN. You're clear on the front end, old man."

If that hadn't been Chambliss cracking flip on the com link, Cramnon would have ripped him a new one, big enough to drive their transport truck up his semper fi sphincter. But they were on, ready to grab the spotlight. Leviathan was thrashing up from the deep, time, Cramnon knew, to go gut the beasts down below.

Thompson, he heard, relayed the order for Rodrigo to park it, the back end shuddering to a stop, nearly bucked up against the wall. It wasn't even a short reach to the top edge, Cramnon saw, picture perfect, then told himself not to get carried away.

This was as easy as it would get.

RPK-74 with fixed bayonet slung around his shoulder, combat vest and webbing weighted down with spare clips and a mixed bag of grenades, Cramnon grabbed the top of the wall, his heart thundering in his ears. This was the moment, he knew, that either marked the beginning of the rest of their lives—or the end. Well over a decade in the planning. Laying his life on the line, time and again, just to create Red Crescent, more of a diversion than any hard-nosed vengeance angle. Hiding in countries that gave a whole new version of man's inhumanity to UN do-gooders. Dreaming of the day he could make it happen, hoping, craving his one shot. Spending virtually every dime of pilfered DOD slush funds to pave the golden road, payoffs, weapons, aircraft.

The hour was upon him—all of them—to execute, and in all ways that mattered.

So far, so good. He briefly recalled jumping to the DZ where Ramses and his team were holed up with their bought-and-paid-for Company station agents in the steppe village of Kharduz. A short, almost arrow-straight flight to the outer limits of Anakara, due north from Cyprus, but a small CIA airfield just east of the target would refuel the Dakota. From there, all Lyson had to do was keep the flying supernova on autopilot, then jump to a waiting van.

Evac, Cramnon knew, was way down the road.

There was now work to do.

He was up and over the wall, swift and dropping, so jacked up on adrenaline he landed on his feet like a cat. Combat instincts sparking like severed live wires, Acheron, then Stevens with his handheld heat-and-motion sensors landing beside him, Cramnon led the charge, absorbing his surroundings. The big stone warehouse appeared deserted, a dim naked bulb hanging on both ends of the structure. The noise of the old city was a distant buzz, his sights locked solely on the prize. Whatever security their millions could buy, Cramnon knew they had opted for the ancient ways of shock and ambush instead of high-tech. Arrogance bred sloppiness to detail, hardened a false and flimsy armor of self-deluded invincibility, Cramnon thought. Arrogance could be a killer. The SOBs were paying tribute all these years to Turks who counted the most, everyone from MIT and CIA on up to Ankara movers and shakers knowing full well what was down below the warehouse proper. No problem, he decided, the wait, while they fattened their coffers, was worth every drop of blood he and the troops would shed.

Cramnon surged past wooden and metal crates, all of which he knew were empty. Head swiveling this way and that, sound-suppressed Beretta 92-F leading the way, he knew Chambliss had them covered from above, the young Marine perched on the rooftop of the next warehouse down. He hugged the line of crates, checking the third hand—timer preset for thirty-second intervals—on his chronometer. He waved his slack men to a halt, counting down the seconds. A glimpse at the heap crumpled up against the wall, and Cramnon allowed himself a smile. One neat dark hole between the mark's eyes, the guard's scrambled brains still running down the wall, and Chambliss had proved himself beautiful in his madness, showing off his rep with the sound-suppressed HK 33.

Peering around the corner of stacked crates, Cramnon found the camera in a slow roll, going left. He bolted for the steel door, crossed the patch of no-man's land, then flanked their back door entrance. He found Stevens looking up from his monitor, giving him the peace sign. Two assholes, Cramnon thought, watching as Stevens worked five fingers of his left hand, up and down, three times, before giving him the middle finger. Thirty-three yards deep in the hole, then, Cramnon finding the young Delta stud smiling as he used the middle finger flag to indicate direction.

Cramnon smiled back at Stevens, then lost the expression as Acheron gobbed the keyhole with plastique. A little dab would do it, then they were in, running and gunning.

The others, he knew, were foaming at the mouth to get the fireworks lighting up the hole. Oh, how he loved these guys, he thought; even the Kurd and fedayeen rabble were looking good to him at the moment. Get a bunch of men together who weren't afraid of death—wouldn't even blink at the thought—and the world had definite problems.

In this instance it was a pack of terror hyenas, way down below the city, guarding the kingdom.

Cramnon didn't think there was a power on Earth that could stop them now.

RAMSES HEAVED on the titanium crowbar. They weren't even down there in the dark and literal bowels, and already the stench was choking off the oxygen to his brain. The grate was a massive mother. Ramses was afraid it was so heavy, so wedged into the alley floor— and from the time of the Romans—it would take ten Samsons and Goliaths just to budge it a couple inches free. Already he was drenched in sweat, but felt confidence swell, aware Dawson was on the other side, his black mug a mask of simmering rage and determination. Silently cursing the chore, the miasma almost making him retch, he worked the bar in tandem with Dawson's huge muscled arms, those pistons the size of engine blocks, he glimpsed, rippling with each mighty angry heave.

Ramses could have cursed Cramnon for this shit detail, but the plan was mapped, nailed to specific tasks, all logistics computed. It had to go by the numbers, or the small underground city would become their tomb. So they had to wade through a sea of raw sewage, the good news—or so Cramnon told him—there were no nightmare traps waiting to spring on the way in. Just in case, Cramnon had left him with two fedayeen walking dead.

There! The SOB of all manholes was up, steel groaning as it chipped at stone edges, Ramses straining to bring the hooked end in his hand just a little higher. Dawson was grunting and snorting, he heard, like a rhino about to break into a rampage. Sensing the black commando's seething hatred of an inanimate object, Ramses was certain he would love nothing more than to blow it to smithereens with some plastique. It was giving, though, and they began inching it over in the direction already agreed on. Ramses looked up, met Dawson's flaming orbs.

"Down," he grunted at Dawson, thinking he'd be damned before he put it back. Henley would just have to back over the hole, since he was assigned to watch their rear anyway.

As Dawson hauled up his custom-Russian SAW with 200-round box magazine, Ramses snapped up his RPK-74. He looked over his shoulder, the troops poised to kick Kurds and fedayeen in gear.

"Shake a leg, ladies."

THE EXECUTIONER FELT his anger rising.

Greeted on the tarmac by an underling, two hours and forty-seven minutes ago, the soldier had been whisked to a sterile white room. Now he paced around, according to the aide who showed him in, his Spartan temporary quarters. The soldier might as well have been locked in a jail cell. Both Farm pilots, for reasons not stated by the flunky, had been steered to an undisclosed waiting area. None of them had been issued a base pass, but Bolan held on to his side arms, thinking something was wrong with the setup the longer he was left alone. There were delays, excuses, apologies handed off by the underling roughly every thirty to forty minutes. The general was busy with unspecified but urgent business. The general was in conference.

In other words, Bolan wasn't exactly feeling the spirit of cooperation.

He considered hauling the satlink from his war bag, have Brognola light a fire, then decided he'd go find the base commander. Besides, given Turk inclination to spy on American operatives, he wouldn't put it past his hosts to have the walls bugged, maybe a minicamera hidden in the light fixture.

Perhaps it was a mistake, not flying direct to the American air base at Incirlik, down to business with members of the home team. But the Geller files had encrypted messages from e-mail theft of Alpha the Farm had decoded. All indications, and if his own hunch was right, the Bank of Islam was somewhere in Ankara. Geller either knew more than he thought, or had only told Bolan what he wanted.

Slipping the war bag over his shoulder, Bolan was out the door. He looked both ways down the long narrow corridor, every bit as stark white and sterile as a hospital. No arrows or markings to point the way around the base, the soldier homed in on the chatter and low hum of instruments to his left. Marching, suspicion there was more to their stall tactics than some undeclared emergency, Bolan stopped at a thick glass partition. Looking in at the massive room, he found it choked with banks of monitors, digital wall maps and other assorted tracking and surveillance high-tech equipment. He figured it for the base command-and-control nerve center, but with floor-to-ceiling windows at the other end, fanning in a half circle around the sprawling bays, it could likewise pass as the flight tower.

Four operators in Turk uniform, he saw, manned a bank of monitors. Considering a Turkish military outpost had been reduced to a smoking crater in Kurd rebel country by what was believed some type of flying bomb, the soldier found it strange the room wasn't jumping with a platoon of alert, grim-faced control men. Instead, Bolan found them engaged in more clock-watching than anything else, sensed they were ill at ease. Or waiting? On what? Orders from the base commander?

Bolan spotted the short, lean, uniformed figure roll up on his left flank.

"Colonel Stone, I presume?"

Bolan turned, looked into the dark eyes of the base commander, the soldier not bothering to hide the anger in his stare.

"My apologies for the delay," he said, and held out his hand. "I am General Hamisi."

CRAMNON TAGGED the first armed shadow as he bolted from the office cubicle. One squeeze, one sneeze of the Beretta and the hostile was toppling to the floor, AK-47 flying from his hands. Whether the muffled bang of C-4 had alerted them or not, Cramnon couldn't be sure, but they had come to life on Stevens's monitor, three steps into the warehouse.

Cramnon found Hostile Two reaching for the red button to sound the alarm below. The terror guard was practically flying for the Klaxon, hand streaking down, when Cramnon unleashed a series of lead jackhammers to his skull. He lost track of the rounds, pouring it on, blasting apart bone and brains, driving the hostile from the alarm button in a spasmic jig. Two more to the chest, overkill, but Cramnon wasn't satisfied until the body slammed the wall, crumpled on its haunches, twitched out.

He whirled on Acheron and Stevens, who told him the warehouse was clear. As Acheron keyed his com link and gave the order for the others to fall out, Cramnon paced off the steps from the edge of the outer office wall. There was a chance they could have moved the crates, but if they were arrogant they might just be lazy, too. Thirty paces toward the middle of the warehouse, sheathing the Beretta, and Cramnon put his shoulder into the big crate that supposedly marked the spot. A heave, sliding it away, and he looked down, snapping his fingers at Acheron to put his flashlight on the floor.

And Cramnon smiled. In poor light, the naked eye would have missed it. So far, inside information was panning out. No believer in dumb luck, Cramnon knew a man made his own good fortune.

Cramnon slid free his commando dagger from the sheath on his shin, then prodded the putty they had smeared over the ring. Working the blade carefully, chipping away at the putty and probing for wires, he exposed the ring, but he wasn't going to be the one to pull it up.

Standing, Cramnon plucked the tac radio off his belt to place the first of two calls.

It was show time.

THE MORE the man's lips moved, the deeper Bolan's suspicion that Hamisi was lying.

"The incident, as I said, is still under investigation, Colonel. Understand, this is a most regrettable tragedy, an embarrassment to our government. An entire base was destroyed, officers, soldiers, men with families were killed, many of them burned alive in this savage attack. Yes, we do believe it had something to do with the simultaneous attack on the prison. What the motive, who can say how the mind of a Kurd works? Those people, they are little more than terrorists, murderers who blow themselves up in our cities, killing innocent women and children. We are at war with those people, and the incident the other night was simply another example of their barbarism."

Bolan broke the general's eye, every instinct shouting at him the man was acting, covering up. Hamisi might believe he could snow what he thought was another CIA operative, but Bolan wasn't going anywhere until he had some answers.

They were still standing in the hall, no invitation by the general for Bolan to join him in his quarters, brainstorm over tea. The Turks, even hard, by-the-book soldiers, officers or MIT agents, Bolan knew, were, as a rule, gracious and hospitable to foreigners. No, Hamisi was feeling him out, Bolan certain the general was itching for him to be on his way, the incident, as he called it, a whopping mystery yet to be solved. Sorry for the inconvenience, the waste of his time.

"And the Bank of Islam?" Bolan posed.

Hamisi smiled, shook his head, shrugged. "I am

afraid, whatever you have heard, Colonel, it is
rumor, speculation, myth. If it existed here in my
country, as you implied, do you not think, with our
vast intelligence resources, we would know?" he
said, looked to Bolan as if he was holding back the
laughter.

"You're telling me I've made a long trip for nothing."

"Perhaps not. There is a thriving terror network we
believe, right here in Ankara. The CIA, as I'm sure you
know, lends us invaluable assistance in tracking down
these criminals. We have picked up recent chatter, the
usual references to a big event, you understand, but we
believe they are planning an attack on our country that
could rival…well, we do not know what they intend,
but I was in the process of mounting an operation to
strike, what I believe, is a large cell here in the city."

"And?"

"Please, indulge me a little more time. By then I
should know more. I could use your help. Feel free to
move about the base. I can have food and whatever
beverage you like sent to you and your men while I
look further into the incident of the other night."

Bolan shook his head at the offer. "I'll stick around
until you get back to me."

"Very well, Colonel. If you will excuse me now, I
will get back to you shortly."

A curt nod and bow, then the general marched away,
Bolan watching him round the corner.

The Executioner picked up his war bag, lingered at

the glass partition a moment, then moved into the flight control room. Hamisi, he was now certain more than ever, was hiding something. Call it gut feeling, years of hard experience trampling through countless nests of vipers, but Bolan knew Hamisi was dirty.

CRAMNON SAW, beyond the hate he found aimed his way by their fedayeen booby-trap detector, the Iraqi was scared.

Mother-in-law terrified, in fact, Cramnon thought, chuckling to himself over the analogy. Just in case his Arab was rusty, Cramnon barked the order again for the dung ball to get his ass in gear or get shot where he stood.

Cramnon stayed hunkered behind a stack of crates, a good twenty yards from any ground zero, his troops and Kurd mules fanned out beside him. The Iraqi stared at the ring, muttered something Cramnon couldn't make out, but bent at the knees, grasped the ring, tugged, hesitated.

"Pull it up, damn your eyes!" Cramnon snarled.

Cramnon slid behind full cover of the crate, heard the grunting, cursing, then a groan of rusty hinges. He waited a few seconds, laughing when the blast never came. He broke into the open, flying up on the Iraqi, grabbing him by the shoulder.

Cramnon stared down into the hole, the stone steps falling for maybe twenty feet, his small army gathering around him. He didn't need Stevens to tell him there were no hostiles in the immediate area at the bottom or in the first hundred-yard vicinity of the tunnel. He could feel the absence of threat.

Shoving the Iraqi closer to the hole, Crannon laughed. "This is where you start spreading some real sunshine, asshole."

CHAPTER TEN

Bolan decided to give Hamisi another thirty minutes of jerking his chain. By then, the soldier, suspecting already the general would send in the flunky with another round of lame bullshit before the allotted time was up, would have mapped out how he was going to lean on Hamisi.

Or maybe he wouldn't get that far.

Midway across the control room, the Executioner felt it in the air.

Treason.

The members of the four-man team made a pretense of watching their screens, but Bolan felt their grinding unease. They fidgeted in their chairs, threw him hooded looks, fiddling with knobs and dials as if trying to busy themselves, watching him without watching. One of them was breaking out in a sweat.

What the hell was going on?

Instinct told Bolan to lug the war bag along. His nerves were twitching, adrenaline ready to burst at the first hint of trouble. But what trouble? He was on edge, trusting raw gut feeling, but where was the threat? It was here, somewhere on the base; he could feel it, much as, he imagined, a man bleeding in the middle of the ocean on driftwood knew a man-eater was somewhere in the water, closing, unseen, about to chomp and tear flesh.

And the soldier was positive sharks of the human variety were now circling, blood in their nose. But who? Where? How many?

Take the attack on the base in Anatolia, for starters. Turks were staunch, even rabid believers in an eye for an eye, Bolan knew. Yet beneath the surface act of sounding off about Kurd savagery, Hamisi seemed almost—what? Glib? Willing to shrug off the attack as the cost of Kurd rebellion and the Turk military's ongoing war of attrition with homegrown terrorists? Second, if the unknown attackers who freed the Kurd prisoners had one flying bomb at their disposal it stood to reason there were two, maybe more just such potential conflagrations with wings. The flight tower, the whole base, in fact, should be bristling with beefed up security, hopping with enough armed and technical manpower there wouldn't be an inch of elbow room to spare. The radar screens should be swarming with sorties, Turk fighter jets, Black Hawks practically choking the skies above Ugrak, sealing an aerial net around Ankara and well east. Moving for the observation deck, and Bolan found every radar screen clear.

Warning Number One.

Turning, he looked over his shoulder. One of the operators was up and shuffling for the exit. The soldier's combat radar began to blip, sensing there was more to the operator abandoning his post than a nature call or coffee refill.

This was all dead damn wrong.

At the window, Bolan surveyed the airfield. Every warbird was grounded. F-15s and -16s, Black Hawks and Apaches sat like ghost ships. He spotted shadows meandering near the fuel trucks, maybe a trio of silhouettes around the distant hangars. There was no discernible activity, no maintenance crews, no aircraft landing or taking off.

He looked at the vast steppe that stretched away beyond the fencing to the east. Other than the burning lights of distant villages there was nothing out there but rugged barren plain. Too empty, the night way too quiet. He scoured the northern, then eastern skies, thinking he should find at least one military bird up there.

Nothing. Warning Two?

Considering this base—though built recently and with the aid of a hefty chunk of U.S. dollars—housed the bulk of Turk soldiers, fighter pilots and flying hardware for the Ankara region, something should be rolling down the runway, mechanics at work, something…

A red light flashed in his mind, as he noted how packed in neat rows the aircraft were parked. Bolan scoured the heavens again, bells and whistles going off in his head. Then, as if sensing it coming, he felt his stare pulled east. It was a dark speck, nearly invisible to the naked eye, but the shape and bulk of a transport bird, even with lights out, was unmistakable.

And it was descending, hard, low and on a collision course with the grounded warbirds.

Bolan swore, then sensed movement from behind. He turned just as the last Turk was clearing the exit.

ONCE CALLED Angora from the time of the Hittites, going back over thirteen hundred years, the town, Cramnon knew, had seen its share of wealth, thanks in large part to its central location in a land that had changed names, people and boundaries for about ten thousand years. With north-south and east-west trade routes, the ancients primarily barbered fine goat hair, while garnering for themselves spices, gems and other exotic goods from the east. The land had also seen about as much bloodshed as the Black Sea was wide and deep. Everybody from the Mongols to Alexander the Great to the Romans, to Persians and Arabs had passed through in stampeding waves, staking their claim, grabbing up what they wanted and leaving behind their mark in various ruins and monuments throughout the country. Truth was, the Turks, diluted blood of their cousin Huns, had stayed on.

Whether the underground city was dug, and by hand, to hide treasure or spare various and sundry rulers from invading hordes, Cramnon couldn't say. Whether it was burrowed beneath what had become modern Ankara by Romans, Greeks or Arabs or even Ataturk for some reason long since gone to the grave with him, Cramnon didn't care, either.

They were going for the gold.

Where the end of the line stopped at his vault to Paradise on Earth, he had a rough idea, already counting off the paces to himself. But he knew for damn sure the hunkered hostiles of a terror organization he and his men helped bring to life had invested a lot of time, sweat and cash into a series of booby traps that, once sprung, would leave no doubt anyone brave, reckless or fool enough to venture down here would know the true meaning of horror.

Since he wasn't about to lie to himself he was some kind of Indiana Jones, Cramnon forced the fedayeen to keep moving, prodding him with a jab to the kidneys with a bayonet whenever the Iraqi hesitated or flashed back a mean face. He had been told three, four at the most, or so his inside man believed. With a vague idea of what ambushes awaited, he had come prepared to navigate through at least one of the ghastly obstacles.

Torches set inside iron flanges on the walls, the dancing light spaced and alternated on each side every thirty to forty yards or so, Cramnon shuffled ahead, looking for telltale signs the horror was about to start. It was hot, sticky, the walls reeking of mold, a faint coppery taint of spilled blood in Cramnon's nose. That particular odor brought a smile to his lips.

Getting real close now, he sensed, fisting sweat out of his eyes, the troops and Kurds strung out in single file behind him as they trailed in his steps, which followed the Iraqi. The tension behind him like an invisible steady blow to his shoulders, and Cramnon saw it.

It was so obvious, he fought to hold down the laughter. The stone pathway had been laid out in sections of three blocks, the corridor perhaps twelve feet across, sloping gently toward the first pillared corner. Imagining these blocks nearly the size of what the poor slobs humped for the pharaohs at Giza, Cramnon spotted the evidence of recent uprooting and replacement of ancient stone. It flared in his eyes, in fact, a neon sign urging him to halt. Not only that, but he saw the dark splotches of crimson, the lazy bastards too trifling to bother giving the blood pool a thorough scrubbing. Careless? Or were they making it all appear too easy? There was concrete, he then saw, plastered over what had been rows of holes on both sides of the wall, hardly blending in with the dark, ancient blocks. How fresh, impossible to say.

The Iraqi, either sensing the danger or getting a whiff of blood, stopped in his tracks. Cramnon poked the bayonet into his spine, a nice painful nudge that got him moving. Howling, cursing, the Iraqi was lurching ahead, feet landing on the middle block—

It happened so fast, Cramnon jumped back as rows of steel fangs shot out from both sides of the wall. The Iraqi was clamped in the teeth with such force, flesh erupted, bone snapped and splintered like matchsticks. Cursing, Cramnon turned away as blood and gore bathed his face.

IF EVER THERE WAS such a thing, Bolan knew he now bore witness to a smoking gun. Whether the flying bomb was manned by martyr or steered by autopilot, Bolan knew it wouldn't sway the end result of the coming holocaust.

Bolan, angered over the obvious treachery, aware there wasn't a damn thing he could do but spectate, stood his ground by the observation windows. Just before the aircraft sailed over the fenceline, the Executioner saw the shooting tongues of flame, as warheads were jettisoned from the wings of the flying wrecking ball. The rockets streaked for different points of impact, roughly nine to three o'clock, but Bolan reckoned the brunt of devastation was preset for the jumble of aircraft.

As close as he was to ground zero, he braced for a hard dash to deep cover. Then Bolan briefly wondered if he'd manage all of a few yards running, when the first wave of explosions ripped into the far end of the warbird parking lot. It was all thunder and lightning down there, the deck trembling beneath his boots, the massive windows shimmied, it appeared, from the invisible pounding of shock waves. Bolan stole a few more heartbeats of dangerous spectating, stunned by the ferocious rolling storm that seemed to blossom yet more titanic fireballs from within the bursting heart of each blast furnace of tornados. From aircaft to hangars, to what he believed were troop barracks and officers' quarters in the distant northwest quadrant, saffron lightning bolts tore across the earth. Each detonation appeared to belch forth yet more supernovas, hurling blinding jags of lightning and streaking comets in all directions. The sky strobed, the earth danced, peppered with shooting firestars that multiplied with no end in sight. Bolan knew what terrible wrath was devouring Ugrak.

Clusterbombs.

And the mother of all mayhem, he saw, had only begun to give birth to this raging hell.

The soldier couldn't even venture a guess how much superenriched, high-octane jet fuel was being ignited from that sea of marching explosions. From where he stood it looked as if the world was going up in one endless tornado of fire. He was spinning on his heels, just as the winged leviathans of wreckage began to spew out of the erupting trash heap below. The Executioner pumped his legs, the thought an incendiary blast of mammoth and all flesh consuming dimensions was only a few eye blinks away, locked in his mind as he left his feet.

It was coming, and Bolan wondered if this was the end.

The Executioner didn't need to look behind to know the SOB of all hurricanes was right then blasting through the observation windows.

THE SHOCK AND HORROR were anticipated, the other fedayeen now crystal clear on what sort of gruesome fate awaited them. Crammon heard his walking dead snarl curses at his back, their brother-in-jihad pinned upright like some grotesque, gigantic, half-splattered bug, feet sort of dancing in the air as the mangled body twitched out the last of nerve spasms. The architects of this death trap, he saw, had left no more than two to three inches between the bars, aiming any vertical impalement for the average-sized man, roughly skull to groin. The Iraqi was a shredded mess, his brain exposed where one spear had sheared off the back of his skull. That was about as pretty, Cramnon decided, as it got. Blood, guts and body waste were running off the boots, pooling on stone, shards of bone sticking out from where his right and left arms had been shot through from lances, skewering the sack from opposite directions.

The good news, he saw, was that there was a three-foot space below the last row and the floor. Plenty enough room to crawl to the other side, dragging behind their human ambush detectors, weapons and bagged ordnance. Just in case the terror bankers were making it look too simple and inviting, Cramnon grabbed the titanium rod from Chambliss. Bending, he stretched out the pole, pushed the end down on the next two rows of blocks ahead. Figure new stone was set over spring mounts, a pressure plate releasing a trip lever beneath the block. How the ghoulish engineers set it all back in place for the next poor schmuck wasn't his concern. Once safely across he'd let the Iraqi on deck take point. From the squawking he heard behind, it sounded his hand was about to be forced to address their defiance.

"I'm not going!"

Wheeling, Cramnon cursed the Iraqi. Tossing the pole back to Chambliss, he fisted a hand full of hair. "Come here, you rotten little…"

The Iraqi struggled, took a swipe at Cramnon's arms with cuffed hands. Acheron was all over him next, driving him to his knees, using the butt of his rifle like a blackjack. Cramnon didn't have the time to beat his will into them. He decided a display of his charming personality was in order.

"I won't die like that for you! You will just have to drag my dead body!"

Cramnon laughed, bobbing his head at the Iraqi. "By all means, have it your way."

Likewise he had seen the future where this kind of resistance was concerned, and summoned forth Thor. The big shadow boiled up from deep in the pack, shouldering his way through the Kurds, their own, Cramnon saw, parting for the muscled behemoth. Chad Summers, former Green Beret, was indeed a beautiful, fearsome sight, Cramnon thought, smiling at the red-white-and-blue war paint masking his face, striping bare muscled arms the envy of any Mr. Olympus.

Cramnon stepped back from the Iraqi as Thor reached behind his shoulders, then hauled out one of his two battle axes, the sound of Velcro tearing the last thing, he knew, the Iraqi would ever hear. Thor drove the ax down, buried the blade in the Iraqi's brain.

JARIC MUHDAL RETCHED, felt the bile writhing in his stomach like a nest of angry snakes. Breathing through his mouth not only didn't stem the tide of evil stench, but it also seemed to draw the poisonous fumes deeper into his lungs, ballooning his belly with yet more queasy acid.

For men who acted as if they had all the answers—and so far, he had to admit, they had slipped safe and unmolested by Turk authorities into Ankara—this leg of the operation struck him as something of an obscene joke. Up to his knees in sewage, the slimy filth even now worming into his boots, squishing between his toes, he questioned the sanity of men who would rather wade through raw human waste than use the stone walkways. Unless, of course, they knew something he didn't.

Which, he knew, was entirely possible, certain he and his brethren were on need-to-know.

Middle of the pack, Muhdal watched as the scarred monster jabbed each Iraqi in turn, bayonet between the shoulder blades, the commando cursing them to move faster. Submerged in the evil sludge almost to their shoulders, the Iraqis probed the bottom with poles. Muhdal believed the two point men were searching for mines, booby traps. Then he corrected the thought, since Scarface and the black commando near shuffled up their asses. Figure, then, they were feeling for some hole, fissure, drop-off point hidden at the bottom of this vile mud. Hanging back, most likely, waiting for one or both of the Iraqis to vanish into the soup. He hoped that happened. Maybe then they'd walk the rest of the journey to whatever final destination on dry stone ramparts.

Muhdal gagged.

"Hey, asshole! Puke on your own time."

Muhdal balked, a wave of barely suppressed rage rolling over him. The black commando was hissing back at him, his eyes framed with menace against the soft glow of hanging naked bulbs. It was all Muhdal could do to keep from cutting loose with his assault rifle. Trouble was, the other team of Americans had snapped up the bulk of his men, including his two top lieutenants. Still, even covered from behind by seven commandos, a slack man behind Scarface, glued to his GPS monitor…

No, he told himself, head swimming with nausea, holding on to every withering shred of willpower to keep from collapsing. Wait, the right moment would reveal itself.

One of the Iraqis cried out, stumbled. Muhdal watched him sort of list to one side, before whatever the hidden problem beneath dunked him, sucking him down, up to his chin in the wicked filth. He was cursing, blubbering something in Arabic, but Scarface erupted into a rage, barking for him to get up or he'd hold him under until he drowned.

Muhdal couldn't stand it anymore. "Why do we not use the walkways?" Ignored, he snapped, "Answer me!"

The scarred monster wheeled on him, the motion flinging muck in Muhdal's face. "Shut your godcamn Turd piehole!"

Wiping off his lips, Muhdal stared at the American, smiled to himself when the scarred creature turned away. Turd, huh, he thought, but already suspected the American's true bigoted nature. Just the same, it was good to hear it out loud, all that contempt and hatred serving to only fan the flames inside, keep him strong and going.

Muhdal saw the commando prod the Iraqis on, bayonet nudges to the back of the skull as they swished and clambered to a higher point. Then the commandos lifted their nylon bags and weapons over their heads, taking their sweet time, feeling their way with cautious, probing steps. The lead commandos slipped down and up to their chests in the sludge. Muhdal felt his own way in their wake, taking their cue, lifting the AK over his head. Perhaps the moment would pay off in the short term, he thought, a reward, of sorts, before the big taste of the apple, as the image leaped to mind. Follow the scarred monster, hope the commando stumbled into a fissure, swallowed down into the quicksand of sewage. Barring the commando choked to death on shit, Muhdal began scheming other options for the near future, just in case his first wish didn't come true.

"Colonel!?"

Bolan recognized the voice of his pilot, distant at first, but slowly clawing through the gonging in his skull. A noxious concoction of burning fuel and the sickly sweet bite of roasting flesh hauled him, coughing, to his senses. Buried under splintered metal and beds of glass from the demolished workstation, the soldier groaned, sweeping the garbage away, tasting blood on his lips. If a few cuts and dings, which may or may not need some sutures, were the worst of his injuries, he'd take it. Considering he'd been punched and lifted by the shock hammer and hurled through the air, a tidal wave of glass slashing his six, the sky falling...

Had one of those cluster bombs been cut loose his way, or the flying bomb itself impacted a direct hit on the control tower...

That neither happened confirmed absolutely what he already suspected. At least five snakes were meant to slither off into the night. How many other Turks onbase were bought and paid for? And what exactly did the attack mean? Was it the beginning of something far more insidious already in the works? A diversion? Bolan could venture a pretty good guess what had happened here and why. If he wasn't sitting right on top of the Bank of Islam, he was in the neighborhood.

They kept calling for him, the roar of angry flames, a far-off wail of sirens tugging him back to the moment. Rising, glass slivers falling out of his hair, banging aside the crumpled shell of what had been a table, Bolan took a moment to get his legs under him. At least two-thirds of the control room, he found, was trashed. Other than a few loose fangs, the observation windows were obliterated. Superheated wind gushed and swirled around him, debris and papers riding the air in miniature tornados. Fires were breaking out in pockets where flaming debris had torched strewed paperwork, mashed computers and other equipment jumping with sparks, pumping smoke. Bolan hacked, saw his flight crew materialize out of the thick clouds drifting to his right. They were armed with Beretta side arms, Bolan waving them off as he read the concern and questions in their eyes.

As he kicked through the glass and smashed ruins of high-tech equipment in search of his war bag, Bolan quickly put to his pilots what he wanted them to do. Moments later, retracing his steps, he tugged the war bag from the pulped shell of another workstation. Unzipping the bag, he hauled out and handed his men two miniUzis, three spare magazines each. He put it to them, clean, direct and simple, hooking a tac radio to his belt.

The three of them were on their own.

The Executioner took an M-16/M-203 combo for himself. One final look at the leaping sheet of fire beyond the observation deck, and Bolan led the way to the exit.

Time to do what he should have done when he first laid eyes on Hamisi.

Only now the Executioner had a full head of angry steam.

CRAMNON KNEW with every yard covered they were closing on the enemy lair. The fact they hadn't come charging up from the bowels, guns blazing, he took for a definite plus. That, he knew, could change at any second.

And they were still, if his sources were right, two to three city blocks from launching themselves into the real fight. He needed haste, had to pick up the pace somehow, but at this stage he couldn't risk bulling ahead, not with two or three more nasty death barriers set to spring. There was one more call left to make, but he had to time it in relation to distance shaved to goal line. So far, so good, by the numbers, but knew it could go to hell any moment.

In fact, he fully expected the shooting to start anytime.

Already passing on, in Russian, that his men were to

keep their eyes peeled for fresh stone, Cramnon kept scouring the floor and walls for telltale indicators. To compound anxiety the alarm would sound, and the Iraqis were proving uncooperative to the point of exasperating anger and defiance. Down to two Walking Dead, he had been forced to shove the severed hands of their late and unlamented squawking brother in their yaps. No problem if he ran out of live guinea pigs—he'd use the gory meat inside the body bag Thor toted to probe the way.

The light began to dim, Cramnon feeling the hair rise on the back of his neck. Just like that, the torches became spaced farther apart.

Show time again.

He stopped, gave the hand signal, three flashlights mounted on assault rifles flaring on. Acheron set down the Iraqi package, his ankles now cuffed, the fedayeen gagging on the meat lodged in his mouth, squirming to break his bonds, aware he was up next.

As they danced light over the walls and floor, Cramnon smiled at the glaring discrepancy in the stone coloring. He saw they had cut blocks in even rows down both sides of the wall. A vague idea of what was coming, Cramnon ordered in Russian for Chambliss to give him a hand. Quickly he took the tape from Chambliss. Measuring the gap across the corridor, he told Chambliss which precut pieces to attach to the end of the pole. It was going to be a snug fit, titanium the strongest known metal on earth, used to reinforce steel….

Even so, Cramnon knew it would be dicey.

A nod to Acheron, then the two of them dug their hands into the Iraqi's shoulders. They hoisted him, writhing and growling, off the floor, then tossed the fedayeen ahead, dumping him on the middle white stone.

No sooner did Bolan read the nameplate than he sent the door crashing in with a thundering boot heel. The M-16/M-203 squad killer leading the charge, he swept the quarters.

Empty. No surprise really, but Bolan had to know.

Hamisi was bailing.

Bolan was thinking the general and his four snakes already had an escape hatch, surging out the door. Senses pummeled by the wailing of the base Klaxon, Bolan saw three uniformed, armed Turks charging down the hall. He was drawing target acquisition when the Turk with the pistol threw his hands up in the air, skidding to a halt.

"Who are you?" Bolan shouted, advancing.

"I am Colonel Ghazi Tulruz."

"Where's Hamisi?"

"That is what I am attempting to find out. I was coming to arrest him."

CHAPTER ELEVEN

Up until this moment, in ugly and often nightmarish passage of close to forty years of wading through blood and mayhem, pain, misery and wailing grief—both giving and receiving, mind you—Michael Mitchell, Acheron—thought he'd seen it all.

That was then, baby-cakes, he thought, stare fixed on the pulped sack of ooze smashed before him. This was most definitely a new, eye-opening dimension in the terrifying now. Hell, even the Vietcong or the cesspool of Latin drug traffickers he'd seen while a Company man—a lot of the former and few of the latter he'd checked out of the world by his own hand—could steal a page from the manual of the mechanics of these chambers of mangling and mashing. Where the VC and narco-giants liked their pain inflicted to last, though, the terror bankers clearly enjoyed searing long after the hideous act a memory of grisly, instant death. Likewise it was a warning, meant to change the hearts and minds of greedy trespassers, send them packing, running back to the warm bosom of sweet dreams.

Not this wild bunch, Acheron knew. He walked with the last of the dinosaurs. He would live or die fighting on his feet among the lions, not, he thought, on his knees, simpering beside some pampered Hollywood punk-worm weeping at the bedside of some ten-year-old-kid collateral damage, nor shrugging off bad luck alongside some overpaid, overglorified, overindulged, overeverthinged so-called sports hero who whined for the world over hemorrhoids or stubbed pinkie. In their game of life and death, wearing the armor of the code of Bushido, every crumb, every dime was earned the hard way. He walked with iron men, into the jaws of battle, far from the limelight, where only comrades and the individual's heart knew what he was made of, the who and the what that counted the most. Oh, they— lions—had come this far, but there was never any doubt they would drive all the way for the goal line. No tail tucking between their legs, scurrying off at the first tough obstacle, no taking oneself out of the lineup to protect overinflated salary and gilded future, no, sir.

Lions.

Acheron hung back, but itched to get moving, aware they were all on the clock of the guardians of the terror bank. No point in crossing over the spattered mess on stone, though, until Cramnon gave the nod. It was a hell of a way to cashier off the planet, he thought, the fedayeen mashed between two giant slabs of pulverizing stone. He couldn't say how many pounds per square inch had left little more than muck, gristle and powdered bone at Cramnon's feet, but Mitchell knew he'd rather eat a lead sandwich slick with shit first. Sure, it was over, as fast as lightning winked. Sure, the victim, squashed like a bug, probably never felt it coming.

Not exactly his dream idea of a warrior's way to go.

In the plus column the human press had retracted, clearing the path, sort of, if he factored in the dance steps required to slip and slide past all the running slime. Barrier removal, though, had likewise been anticipated. Only Mitchell didn't think they could spare the bulk of their C-4 or the heavy artillery on blasting through what would have been in the neighborhood of ten feet of solid stone. Why imagine phantom trouble? Problems soon enough would rage up, he knew, the deeper they forged into the bowels of this hell. If nothing else, killing the opposition would be pleasant, compared to a tip-toe pace where sudden gruesome death could fly out of nowhere. However it was sliced and diced, there was no textbook solution here, or for when they met the enemy head-on.

Feeling the tension ratchet up behind him, Acheron watched Cramnon nod at Chambliss, both of them crouched on haunches on opposite sides. They wedged the titanium pole in place, four or five inches up, midway through, Acheron fearing it wouldn't be enough if the blocks sprung forth. Give Cramnon credit, he decided, the man was one hundred percent leader, unflinching, unafraid. No, the big guy wouldn't order one of the troops to tackle the most hideous, dangerous task he wouldn't dive in and do his damn self. A simple showing off of Godzilla-size balls, and men there to follow were inspired to go the distance, no questions. Point-blank, a leader led by example. But there was something about Cramnon, he knew, recalling a young Green Beret he'd seen in Southeast Asia, always willing to take point, risk life and limb over booby traps that often left a soldier facing a fate worse than death. And he knew—if so inclined to believe in what he considered the mysticism and occult of religious drivel—he would proclaim before God, Satan, all the angels and saints there were things in life far worse than death.

Whatever it was that seemed to steer Cramnon like magic through the most horrific of unseen obstacles, even feel them out and find them back then, worked every bit as well now, experience, of course, the sweet icing on this hunk of blood-and-guts cake. Not only that, the man seemed to have eyes that saw more than what was in front, behind or beyond him. Spooky, perhaps, he could damn near see the fates of men in combat. Real, imagined or bullshit, the man had something Acheron couldn't define in physical terms, at least not any that would make sense. But there were men, he knew, and liked to count himself somewhere in their ranks, who could walk through fire, not even a hair singed off. He'd seen, lived through it himself in more hellzones than he could count. It was as if Cramnon had some supernatural shield around him, bullets, shrapnel, every sort of danger imaginable, veering off course, as if these inanimate lethal objects simply couldn't, wouldn't maim. As if it were an insult or something to whatever force protected the man.

Acheron only hoped the strange blessing would hold up, since the coming firestorm would prove unlike any combat he'd ever known. What was stashed in the vault at the end of this jaunt through the ambush maze, well, the other guys weren't about to give up the store without a fight he imagined would leave Hell's angels singing in joy.

The problem at the moment was maybe the kid, Acheron thought. Chambliss, or so he believed, wasn't meant to taste the fruits of anticipated victory. No beach party, no endless nights of hedonism or fat numbered accounts reaching halfway around the globe for the young Marine. Damn shame, Acheron decided. He kind of liked the kid, even if he was FUBAR as the day was long. And the way Cramnon looked over at him, he could tell the Alpha leader viewed him as the son he wished he'd had. Had Cramnon sensed the kid was cursed? What if this was the young Marine's swan song, right here, those walls snapping together, titanium pole or not? And if Cramnon went...

Well, Acheron knew he was second in command, but for the remainder of this trip through booby-trap alley he only hoped he could display one gonad half the size of what Cramnon had.

He watched Cramnon light up a smoke, offer the kid one. While Chambliss accepted, Acheron listened for any warning groan, steel maybe buckling, the walls shuddering as they strained to blow.

Cramnon smiled, waving on the point men. "What the hell you waiting for, gentlemen? This ain't no disco. Step up to the plate—time is money."

Acheron heard a few nervous chuckles from the troops. Reaching behind, he jacked their last fedayeen to his feet. The Iraqi's face and scalp a patchwork of blood and bruises, he saw, where he was forced to beat some willingness into his brain—smart move to plug their pieholes with their comrades' fists—Acheron lifted him by the seat of his pants. No sense risking an uncooperative spirit at this late juncture, he figured, rotten SOB maybe kicking the pole out of spite.

Acheron hurled their Iraqi tripwire to the other side.

GENERAL ATATURK HAMISI knew it was impossible to cover every base, much less create a vast array of foolproof escape hatches or engineer a network of contingency plans that would see him fly, safe and unmolested, on his merry and wealthy way into the future. There was no such creature, he knew, as the perfect plan. Yet, so far it was going exactly according to how it had been laid out for him by the American cutouts. So why did that disturb him so badly? Did it all appear too good to be true? Was fate prepared to play some cruel joke?

If the magic carpet was indeed yanked out from under, he believed he would rather die first than give up the brass ring now. So close....

When this dream was first hatched, he briefly recalled, it couldn't have landed on his doorstep at a more opportune time. Years before the first of the American cutouts brought him on board the operation, he knew he'd never become a rich man, much less even reasonably comfortable, no matter how high up the chain of military command he climbed. Turkey's military, he knew, wasn't exactly famous for generously providing for those who served in all good faith and loyalty. If a man wanted to get ahead in Turk uniform, corners needed to be cut, a new course had to be charted, with a keen eye always aimed at the bottom line.

With money, naturally, certain perks and frills came attached to power, the combination of both a heady aphrodisiac alone. Thus, like any man with a normal libido, he had acquired a certain lifestyle over the years that demanded more time, attention and money. The final decision, however, was based more on an eye toward his own future than any continued romp with his young mistress. He was getting older, wondering where it was all headed, if he had wasted his life in service to politicians who were either ungrateful or corrupt, tired of chasing down Kurd guerrillas or plugging up one hole after another in the terror dyke in his country, which was bound to burst someday....

What? Had he simply thrown his hands up in disgust with the status quo? Quite possibly he had. But, he reasoned, had he not jumped on this particular gravy train, someone else would have beat him to the gates of the Bank of Islam's vault. By either force of arms or threats and intimidation, he knew of plans already on the drawing board to raid the bank. The thought of someone else with his hands out or guns drawn...

Well, that would only keep him impoverished, subjugated to wishful thinking, seething in envy of those who seized the initiative, while stealing his thunder and retirement dreams. The terror bank's very existence, he knew, was no secret to begin with. Why, a chunk of the officer corps, a cobra's basket full of MIT agents who had long since grown weary of their paltry tribute and had let the terrormongers maintain shop below the city. Whether it was greed or winking on the sly at fanatics they sheltered—slapping the face of the West while taking their money and hardware—he knew the military and political powers were becoming increasingly agitated and angry over American imperialist aggression. The mounting concern was understandable. After Iraq, for instance, who was next on the American to-do-away-with list? Syria? Iran? Arab countries right next door, what was to stop war from spilling across the Turk border? What would prevent endless seas of the displaced and homeless from swarming into Turkey if the Americans went after their neighbors next? History had proved that entire infrastructures of nations had collapsed due to starving war refugees.

Not his problem.

Geopolitics aside, it was high time now to ride his one big wave to shore. Truth be told, he didn't care what the Americans or the jihad fanatics did over here. He was in it for the money. At any rate, the law of the jungle always determined who survived when the smoke cleared. Why get chewed up in the middle of a war that couldn't be won anyway?

Bulling through the door that led out from the last main corridor of the command-and-control building,

Hamisi was thinking he was too old in more ways than one. Huffing as he sucked wind, his lungs burned, strained for oxygen, but he was tempted to halt for a quick smoke. There was no time, he knew, for such indulgence. Once he boarded his Black Hawk, in the air and putting behind a world on fire he had helped create, he could smoke up a storm, perhaps break out the good cognac.

Far from home free, he knew that Colonel Tulruz, a by-the-book team player, was looking to impale his head on a spike. Hamisi knew the dog, always lapping at the heels of officers and politicians behind his back, was bent on using him to make an impression, advance his career at someone else's expense. For days now, Hamisi recalled the man's hooded looks with every new order handed out. These days, the snake practically shadowed him to the toilet, Hamisi certain his phone was tapped, the walls of his office bugged. Yes, perhaps he'd been careless, discussing the operation with the insolent Adam Ant—or whatever his real name.

No matter, another hundred feet or so, as he found the blades spinning to life on his Black Hawk, and he'd be flying for new but golden horizons. There were other pressing matters to iron out once airborne.

Beyond the nylon bag hung from his shoulder, he was burdened with the baggage of the four-man technical team. They had been transferred from Incirlik several months back, delivered to him by another cutout, insinuated into the scheme. It had been his task to further break them in, explain the parameters of their roles, feel them out for duplicitous motives. Whoever these fellow countrymen, whatever their own reasons, all he knew right then was that it was done; it was happening as designed.

Two stops remained before he reached the border and received the remainder of his payoff. Then Hamisi would be free at last from Turks, Americans, a contentious wife. As for the pack of hounds trailing him, he would make the foursome understand, in no uncertain terms, they needed to go their own way. They might tote M-16s, but if down the road they needed additional persuading to seek out their own arrangements, Hamisi had no problem allowing his Beretta to explain the simple facts of life.

The wail of sirens seeming to chase him, Hamisi picked up the pace, crossing the hangar. The Black Hawk, parked at the deepest northwest corner of the base, was the only aircraft spared the holocaust. Surely that was another red flag for Tulruz the snake to wave in his vanishing act. The cluster-bomb shellacking alone nearly razed the entire base, and Hamisi knew no amount of the most plausible explanation would keep his scalp off the Tulruz's trophy mantel.

It was a fearsome, unexpected, even unholy sight, he thought, no matter how he justified his motives. He had been running out of his office when the first series of explosions rocked the compound, his cue to bail. On the run, he'd seen the smoking ruins of both officer and soldier barracks, a sea of wreckage and hellish destruction so vast he believed only a miracle could have spared even a few souls. It was shocking how more and greater explosions appeared to erupt and expand from the core blasts. With that kind of Hell on Earth, he was certain no one on tarmac, runway or barracks had survived. He felt no pity, no mercy, no shame. The dead or maimed were soldiers, after all, understood the risks of war long before they decided to become fighting men.

Life was tough like that.

Hamisi squinted against the brilliant sheen of firelight in the hangar doorway, nearly laughed with glee as he closed the gap to his freedom ride. Scorching winds then began gusting in his face, carrying to his nose the stink of burning fuel and cooking human flesh. Unbelievable, he thought, the awe and might of American killing ingenuity. Even at a good two thousand meters from the conflagration, he could still feel the rage of the firestorm, his face heating up, sweat breaking out on his forehead.

"Stop!"

Hamisi felt his heart lurch, recognizing the voice.

"Lose the weapons!"

He nearly stumbled, fear then hardening his limbs, adrenaline propelling him forward with sudden speed and greater urgency as he heard his startled cry flung away by rotor wash. Angry questions were boiling to mind, but Hamisi let instinct answer for him. He was digging out the Beretta, whirling toward the big shadow rolling out of the fireglow, when the first wave of bullets began tearing into his four-man tech team.

CRAMNON SENSED their time was up.

His last fedayeen a blubbering, bloody mess, Cramnon was forced to hold him upright by the scruff of his neck. After tripping the latest booby trap, the bag of bait would have to see them through from there on. Besides, he sensed the Kurds ready to burst from frayed nerves, certain they were agitated to near reckless eruption of anger, wondering where their leader was, poised to sound off 101 questions, the snarling racket of voices sure to sound the alarm.

Once more the lights faded, reducing the corridor to deep shadows. A hundred paces ahead, he saw where the walled depression forked. That would mark their final point before the planned split of his team, and the march jettisoned into juggernaut status.

They were close to the end zone. He listened for boot heels rapping on stone, the slightest breathing of men lying in ambush. Nothing down there, he sensed, searching for hunkered shadows framed in the distant dance of torchlight.

Back to work, he watched flashlights wash over the path ahead, and Cramnon found three slabs of white stone across. Not good. Whatever the hell it meant there was no time to ponder.

He shoved the Iraqi ahead, the fedayeen stumbling, pitching facedown on stone. Cramnon was lurching back when twin funnels of fire shot from both walls. The dragon's spray igniting the fedayeen, Cramnon heard the screams, muffled but growing in volume behind the bloody gag. He lifted his RPK as the flaming scarecrow pinballed, wall to wall, then shot down the corridor.

THE EXECUTIONER GAVE these vipers the option, but experience warned him they were a lost cause. Forget the fact the Turks didn't look kindly on foreign agents gunning down their own, dirty or not—Bolan needed a live one to sing the blues. Figure they were pumped on adrenaline and fear, eager to put behind their treachery and grab whatever gold was promised, but the four-man tech team went for broke.

They formed a barrier to Hamisi, the general clawing for his side arm, which presented the soldier with his potential songbird. The Executioner zipped the line of 5.56 mm flesh-manglers left to right, M-16 stuttering on full-auto. Two of four M-16s were flaming downrange, but Bolan was already creating a chorus line of jigging bleeders, wild rounds screaming off the hangar wall to his nine. He bowled two flailing Turks into their master, Hamisi's cry of either pain or outrage lost in the din of weapons fire. A glimpse of the pistol sailing from Hamisi's hand, and the Executioner raked them again, starboard to port. The last two snakes were spinning, howling out the ghost, then pitching back to take their hopes and dreams to Hell when Bolan became aware of the paper tornado swirling around Hamisi.

CRAMNON STILLED his trigger finger. He waited until his flaming comet danced over enough stone down the corridor, drumming feet sure to set off any more surprises, then cut him down with a short RPK burst up the back.

The snail's pace, he knew, just ended.

Cramnon looked at the roaring tongues. They formed a flaming X, but for whatever reason a two-foot gap would allow them to crawl under the funnels. A whiff of gasoline, and he knew napalm was the consuming fire of choice.

Cramnon spun on his troops, snapped his fingers at Dekyll, who threw him an RPG and bag of warheads. Stretching out on his belly, positive the shooting had echoed all the way down to the deepest bowels to scramble the enemy, Cramnon crabbed under the dragon fire.

This was it, he knew, squeezing by the demon tongue with inches to spare. The big ticket to paradise was just around the bend.

"THEY'RE COMING."

Farouk Tabrik was on his feet, grabbing the AK-47, spare clips and RPG rocket launcher from beside the divan as soon as the words left Hasmali's mouth. Whoever the Palestinian referred to as "they" was a matter open to debate. For months, Tabrik's paid sources inside the MIT and Turk military had floated rumors for his private mulling. Apparently there were those in the political and military hierarchy who weren't satisfied with what he viewed as overinflated tribute. No, they wanted it all. Then there was local rabble, bands of petty thieves who had shown more daring than good sense. There were whispers even the CIA, the Mossad, knew the Bank of Islam existed.

Attack on the underground city, a raid of the vault, he knew, was anticipated, well in advance of his Saudi brethren reconfiguring sections of the tunnels, installing the three ambush points. Over six years now, the fighters rotated out every four to five months for R and R, and only four locals had fallen prey to the sweat and genius of Saudi engineers. No one had yet to breach the third trap—until now. He caught the echo of brief weapons fire, then the sickly sweet aroma of cooking flesh wafted down the passageway and into his private chambers.

No question—barbarians were at the gate.

Tabrik charged through the archway. Veering for the steam billowing out of the antechambers, he began barking at his fighters to get dressed. They had war-gamed enough down here, and they knew the drill. Time to earn their keep.

And that, he thought, could prove fatal for some of them by itself.

Yes, they were seventy-eight strong, culled from various organizations to be the guardians of Muslim finances here in the netherworld beneath Ankara. Yes, they were well-trained, experienced, blooded in battle. Yes, they believed in the strict tenets of Wahhabi, what the West in its arrogance called fanaticism. They would stand their ground and fight. But for how long? And how many invaders were on the way down? Say they were facing a battalion of Turk soldiers bent on looting, an armed raid betraying the word of those who took their monthly percentage and pledged them safe haven….

Would many of his fighters throw down their weapons at the sight of overwhelming force? After all, it wasn't their cash, gemstones, gold and heroin they were about to fight for, risk death for a cause hardly fitting their notions of martyrdom.

He would see soon enough. Woe be unto this country, he thought, if they were in fact Turk soldiers coming to pilfer the store. The Turks had been warned in advance, he knew, about any armed theft. Should just such a bloody drama play out, then a wave of mass attacks, suicide and otherwise, would sweep their land until it ran deep with blood.

Since they were Muslims, Farouk Tabrik hoped to God it was anybody but Turks.

BOLAN WAS SICKENED by the sight.

Hamisi was on his knees, hands slapping at bills, the general growling and cursing as more of the god he prayed to was sucked from the tear in his bag, vacuumed up into rotor wash.

Whether Tulruz would hold to his pledge the general belonged to him for takedown and the first round of questioning Bolan wasn't banking on blind faith in the colonel. The Executioner was going to do it his way.

Advancing, Bolan spotted the armed shadows bull into the hatch. Helmeted and togged in flight suits, they took one look at Hamisi, the strewed bodies, whatever their cut of blood money being swept away in the cyclone, and swung their pistols toward the Stony Man warrior.

Bolan had his own pilots.

The Executioner hit the M-16's trigger, blew them both dancing across the floorboard and sailing out the other side. Another long burst of autofire, and he eviscerated the money bag, Hamisi lurching to his feet, howling as the paper storm burst in his face.

Bolan aimed the muzzle between Hamisi's eyes. "This is where the road forks."

CHAPTER TWELVE

"Fire at will, girls!"

With a thumbs-up, Walters flashed the Delta studs his best wry grin. He was quite pleased with himself, his delivery of the line he scripted for the moment bringing the kids to scowl, certain he'd managed a dig to their monumental Medal of Honor egos. It was something of an act, he knew, keeping up the tough front. Beyond the imagined Lee Marvin facade he felt the shakes, nothing he couldn't handle, but there was enough quiver in his old war bones to leave him wondering if the kids could feel his nerves. They looked at one another, Judd shaking his head, as if to say, "What an asshole." Walters felt like a third wheel on a bad blind date.

Screw 'em, he thought, leave 'em to their toys. Any gas blowback, cracked shells dispersing clouds over their perch, they were dead meat, too. And, by God, at some point, probably during evac, they were going to find out what he could do in the trenches when all hope looked lost. When the real feces hit the fan, he was sure their pink little sphincters would pucker up with gratitude he was along for more than just the joyride and to collect a fat payday. If they thought the Turks were going to just let them sashay out of the city after this gig, they were in for the mother of all rude awakenings.

He wasn't their spotter, their wonder gizmos and digital grids and readouts doing all the work for them, but he lifted field glasses for better viewing of the show. Right then the game beneath the city, he knew, was in full swing. The word from the big boss man was something like five to six hundred million was down there, and this was only stop number one on the way east. Since it was dirty money—blood money, to be exact, financing jihad—who, if there were any survivors, could dare cry to the proper authorities they had been robbed? Dirty money belonged to any man with balls enough to take it. Walters wished them good luck and good hunting.

That crunch-chug-pop was perhaps three times as loud as, say the standard 40 mm round from an M-203, he figured. No ear-shattering decibels, the automatic cannon was simple enough to operate, just aim and squeeze the trigger. Walters watched the first line of rounds arc over the rooftops of buildings along Ataturk Boulevard. They worked their fields of fire in opposite directions, drawing them together as the warheads began erupting in sidewalk throngs. The horror and panic was instant, clouds spewing poisonous strangleholds that began to drop victims where they walked,

stood or sat in sidewalk cafés, street corners, alley-
ways and courtyards. Within seconds flat, they were
writhing on the ground, bodies contorting in impossible positions, nervous systems set on fire before they
shut down altogether, foam streaming from the mouth.
VX nerve gas, Walters knew—or so he'd heard, visu-
alizing memories of its effects—was a bad way to go,
and it wasn't all that quick. The body burned up from
the inside, organs feeling on the verge of exploding
while victims believed they were being incinerated,
lungs starved, every gasping breath like drawing fire
into the mouth. The nervous system collapsed while
erupting into a blaze so fast, he'd heard victims often
constricted in such agony they broke their own bones.
Better, he thought, to be eaten alive by wild beasts.

Shuddering at the picture, he went back to spectating. Fender benders started banging the night next,
horns blaring as a few shells were dumped into traffic.
Panning on, Walters saw the stampede break out in full
earnest at the train station, bodies flailing on the plat-
forms, thrashing out of the boiling clouds, runners
tumbling to the tracks. Carefully, he checked those
billows of doom, watching if they were shifted by
wind. No telling how those lethal umbrellas might get
pushed in whichever direction, what with alleys,
canyons between the larger structures. From what he
could tell, as the puff adders of chemical death blew
and expanded, they held a steady course to the west.

Outstanding.

What, me worry? he thought, and smiled. He lowered the glasses while the kids did their thing, pulled

out a pack of smokes. Too bad, he considered, lighting up, easing back on the retaining wall. The only thing that would have added sugar to sweet anticipation of the reward at the end of the line would have been finding his two ex-wives down there in that hell.

CRAMNON KNEW, going in, the Kurds were a question mark. As bona fide leader, who had proved he had no problem taking point and charging the guns, he knew men of any nationality, race or creed, soldier or otherwise, needed, almost demanded to be told what to do. That, he thought, was pretty much human nature. Only the sheep needed angry, sometimes hateful refinement, taken to the extreme in combat. The trick was finding what made a man tick, what buttons to push to motivate him to levels he never dared dream himself capable. On the run, in terms they understood, Cramnon roared over his shoulder, between obscenities, for his platoon to get it in gear, switching from Russian to Kurd.

Cramnon sensed, then heard the enemy coming. A nervous last few steps, eyeing the floor and walls the whole way, he secured a firepoint at the south edge where one corridor met another. HUMINT laying out the rest of the descent, he took in his surroundings, the RPK down for the moment, the RPG in hand. Three rings had to be breached. Inside each pillared, stone-encased circle was a series of courtyards, chambers and antechambers. Everything from harem courts, sultan quarters, steam baths to narrow tunnels leading to yet more chambers. His troops knew the drill, how to play it.

Advance, drive the fight down their gullets. Hurl as many bullets, warheads and grenades as quick as they could, but keep advancing.

"Go, go, go!" Cramnon growled at his squad as they peeled off to charge down the bisecting corridor the opposite way, Dekyll and Bigelow hauling the bagged heavy artillery.

A full squad of his own plus Kurds falling in behind, Cramnon homed in on the drumming of bootsteps down the corridor. How many? Who knew? Who cared? Chambliss and Summers hunched up on his backside, likewise ready to cut loose with initial RPG volleys. Garson, Ryker and Sandival were arming frag grenades, while Cramnon whipped his rocket launcher around the corner and triggered the warhead, in sync with his rocket team. The enemy, he glimpsed, burst out of the shadows, AKs blazing, two RPGs coming up to bring the wall's edge on line. The fanatics were just in time to get scythed by the RPG blasts, two, then four frag grenades, he saw, rolling up into the first line of mauled and howling.

Cramnon lurched back for cover as an errant RPG warhead streaked past his eyes and flew on down the corridor. Close, he thought. He fixed another missile as he heard the rolling thunder peal from some point far down the tunnel.

SWEEPING AROUND the corner, Acheron held back on the trigger of his RPK-74 just as the first batch of opposition bounded into view at the far end of the tunnel. It was first come, first serve and down for the count, Acheron barely beating the enemy to the punch. A few killshots, he knew, didn't a war win. This was going the full distance The only question to be answered was which side would stack up the most corpses.

As he marched his team into open turf, Acheron kept raking the wave of dark armed shadows, snarling out the oaths for war cries, his light machine gun slicing a crimson streak, port to starboard and back. Nice to know, he thought, he still had it, King Kong grabbing point, into the guns, a leader of warriors, no question. He figured ten, maybe twelve sucked down a taste of hot lead and RPG blasts out of the gate. Acheron knew his guys would stick to the drill—the three Kurds attached to his rear were on their own—as they advanced down the wall across the corridor, driving another double RPG whammy into the boiling smoke before they filled their hands with AKs. The rest of his trailing wolf pack began unloading with AKs, RPKs and one SAW yammering in the hands of James Samson from behind. Unflinching, Acheron felt the hot slipstreams tear past his ears, now whistling from his twelve and six. Lots of space between the walls, but the racket hammered deep into his brain, the din cleaving his senses as it notched up to furious decibels where it seemed to lift him off his feet and float him forward.

Downrange, the Bank of Islam fanatics were howling and toppling, a few jigging bloody stick figures holding on and hosing away with AK autofire, even as a wall of lead punched holes through the smoke, ripped off more ragged flesh before brute impact carried them back out of sight. Acheron could tell he and the troops were dishing out all the martyrs' wishes the fanatics could handle.

The way they vanished, though, replaced in the next heartbeat by more shooters popping up over the edge, Acheron knew they were falling and coming up steps. Which meant his squad's first task was dead ahead, at the bottom of whatever hell waited beyond the edge.

And the jihad goons just kept on coming for more.

Another wave of gunmen shuddered into the smoke, blazing fingers of autofire chopping through the pall. Maybe three fanatics held their ground, Acheron marching ahead, the RPK rattling in fusillade union with his troops, another wall of lead doom falling over the enemy.

Still more shooters rose up, slammed their way through spinning bodies.

Return fire kept screaming off stone, chips flaying Acheron's face, but he had blood in his nose, advancing, a killing automaton. It was inevitable, he knew, as he heard the sharp grunts and cries of pain erupt behind. He burned out the clip, tossed the empty away, filled the LMG with another long, curved 45-round mag, decided to check who was hit. One eye on the hanging wall of smoke, he turned. One Kurd, he saw, was down, thick, rich jets of arterial scarlet pumping from his right thigh, the guy cradled by his cousin. Dekyll and Bigelow still lugged the big gun by the straps, smoking AKs fisted in one hand. He saw Samson was bleeding around the face, a muscled black arm gouged with bloody furrows. Give the man credit. Acheron could tell the pain had only fueled his anger and determination, teeth bared like a shark on his glistening black mug. Little wonder, he thought, the tough bastard was part of the Alpha parade, even if he was penciled in the number-six slot.

Acheron was about to bark for the Kurd to give up the wet-nurse routine, when he heard the commotion beyond the leading edge. They were winging spray and pray from below, wild rounds whizzing past his ears. On the roll, he armed an incendiary grenade and pitched it. Some shock and awe, he figured, when the egg blew and he torched up a few shooters, should give them a little elbow room.

CRAMNON WEAVED his hard jaunt through the strewed bodies. The smell of smoke, blood and body waste in his nose, he latched on to the rich miasma like an aphrodisiac. Whatever groaned and slithered in running muck, the order was passed on for his slack men, Jenson and Hurley, to put the mangled out of their misery. No matter what, their rear had to be secured. He wasn't sure, at least not yet, but Cramnon sensed they had the enemy on the run. Experience warned him, though, the sudden retreat may be part of some ambush in the works at the bottom of the steps, or just beyond.

Thor and Chambliss on his flanks, Cramnon hit the top of the steps. Three enemy gunners were turning tail, hopping and skipping over bodies heaped in their descent, halfway down and hauling ass. Cramnon lent them a helping hand, stitching them across the back with an RPK burst, Thor and Chambliss taking the cue, pouring on the autofire. Two rag dolls were hurled for the bottom, the third BI goon reaching level ground, gathering speed but not before a triburst shattered his spine. He spasmed into a sort of twinkle-toes lurch, Cramnon thinking that was the damnedest dance step he'd ever seen as he hit the steps and gave the order for his rocket men to arm their RPGs, the slack men be ready with frags.

IT WAS WORSE than he first feared.

Farouk Tabrik was hearing how they were either Americans, Russians or Kurds, but none of his surviving front-line fighters could say for certain. Determining who the enemy was seemed the least of his woes. His suspicion many of his fighters weren't terribly eager to go to Paradise for other men's money was becoming more evident with each downed comrade, each scream of pain flaying echoes to those still standing. He wanted to blow up with rage, curse several of them for blatant cowardice, but wasn't he, too, falling back?

Yes, the enemy had seized the initial advantage, loosing rockets, tearing apart the front line as if those fighters were little more than zebras devoured by giant crocodiles in a river orgy of voracious feeding. But this moment had been anticipated, a few of them even boasting prowess as seasoned cave fighters from Afghanistan, how no one, no army would dare tread these stone floors unless they rolled in howitzers, tanks.

Braggarts. Fools.

Time for Plan B, he decided, shouting the orders as the next round of explosions began rocking the corridor, more waves of bullets eating up a few of his fighters in flight. Whoever their adversaries, they weren't only professionals, he feared, but they were also committed to full buzzard plunder, or die in the attempt. In other words, their hearts and souls were steeled one hundred percent to the grim task. Nothing and no one would stand in their way. It looked as if, he thought, some of the more foolish braggarts had gotten their howitzers and tanks, after all. Only he was sure they hadn't bargained for this sort of rolling human armor.

Tabrik felt the first claw of despair digging in his gut as he yelled at two of his three suicide bombers to follow.

THE PACE of the feeding frenzy tapered to a few choice bites. Acheron wasn't sure what the enemy was up to as he navigated through the litter of bodies. A few twitching limbs and a moan here and there in the mess, stole some coffin-nailers from his slack troops, as he kept cranking out the LMG rounds. The looping corridor was pocked with archways, dark holes leading to whatever network of chambers, rooms, tunnels. Return fire still swarmed their drive, Acheron sweeping a headclothed rabbit off his feet, Sellers and Christian hosing down a trio of fanatics to his one o'clock. Hard to count how many armed shadows had already vanished into cubbyholes as he jogged past two burning corpses, his nose swollen with the stink of cooking flesh. But Acheron still had contenders in the tunnel to deal with, as enemy lead whined off the floor, walls and ceiling, a raging hornet's nest of autofire snapping around his scalp with inches to spare.

Another sharp grunt, a wicked curse against someone's mother, then, feeling the hot splash on his neck, Acheron stole a look back. Stone was down, he discovered, teeth gnashed as he thundered out the swearing against God, the human race and the dung-eating-jihad-son-of-a-whore bitch who'd tagged him. He'd taken two, maybe three rounds high in the chest, Acheron noting the jagged shards of collarbone jutting through the crimson rip in his vest. Acheron appreciated the Army Ranger's mettle, stretched out on his back, soaking up his life's juices, but waving them on, shouting, "Go! I'll catch up!"

They knew the deal here when they signed on. Every man pulled his own weight. If he took a hit and he couldn't carry on, he was left behind. That standing order included the hierarchy.

Stone shed his booty bag, slapped it onto Samson's leg, his fellow Ranger stealing a second to snatch and fix the folded nylon to his belt.

Plucking a flash-stun, Acheron felt the tug of lead as it tore over the booty bag hung from his hip. The archway, he saw, had some Arab markings that Cramnon had drawn from the memory of their inside boy. Not much by way of light in that hole leading, he hoped, to the amphitheater, but flames began leaping beneath and just inside the arch. The RPK jumping around in his one-handed grasp, Acheron was forced to dart to his left, yet more grunts and howls of pain adding to the racket of weapons fire. On the fly, he lobbed the steel Russian baseball into the hole.

CRAMNON BELLOWED the order to start clearing each room, chamber and hall he swept by. Autofire roaring as he surged past each hole, nailing two runners dead ahead on the fly, he felt a few rounds punch through his flowing mane. He knew he'd already lost two men—Chalmers and Jenson down, blood and brains pooling beneath shattered skulls, their loot bags already seized by troops still in the mix—but they were eating up turf faster than he expected.

Risking a dangerous moment to halt, pluck and arm a frag bomb, Cramnon heard the thunderclaps on his six, the designated troops hurling their own Russian baseballs into rooms they had to clean up. The echoes of all-out sound and fury of Acheron and his jihadeaters reaching his ears like the songs of angels, Cramnon flipped the steel apple through the archway. He counted off two seconds, charged ahead, triggering his LMG into the hole as return fire erupted for a heartbeat before it was silenced by thunder and fire.

Getting closer with every bloody yard gained, every felled BI hardman, he knew, spotting armed silhouettes as they wheeled around the bend for Ring Number Two. Slack men and Kurds on his heels, he cursed the runners. It was clear to him more than a few of the fanatic security force didn't have the stomach to stand and fight. Even if it was some other guy's riches, it was still, technically, their cash cow. He was thinking perhaps the lack of balls was something else more insidious, they might be luring them ahead, when a tremendous explosion from behind nearly bowled him off his feet.

ACHERON BULLED FIRST into the churning pall, his RPK stammering to nail the deaf and blind fanatics, ending their dance as he drove them, tumbling down the stone rows.

"Move, goddamn it, move!" he yelled at Dekyll and Bigelow, Samson peeling off to his left flank, the black commando's SAW fanning the amphitheater. "What the fuck! You girls need a dolly to haul that load? You want a wheelchair to roll your asses in?"

Whether or not they were clear in the amphitheater, Acheron couldn't tell, the hellish racket from all points beyond the archway bursting through in relentless waves. The circle of stone, sloping down to the ringed floor, wasn't much in terms of size, Acheron figuring it all best left to the imagination later what sort of entertainment transpired down through the centuries here. He slid off into deeper shadows, using the minimal glow of a single hanging torch to search the archways around the ring for live ones. The bulk of his troops split on his order to start sweeping chambers down the tunnel, Acheron caught the grunting and cursing. One finger poised to key his com link, check to find if Omega One was where they were supposed to be, Acheron wheeled, snarling, "What now?"

Cursing, Samson flung one of the small, battery-powered lights down the aisle. Acheron glimpsed the mangled orb in flight. Obviously Samson didn't care the useless piece of junk had probably spared him a round through the hip. While Samson flared on the backup miniglobe, bolted a few yards deeper into shadows as the spotlight illuminated the arena, Acheron cursed Dekyll and Bigelow for more speed. Then he glimpsed the blood trail in Dekyll's shuffle. He'd taken a few rounds through the ribs, the young Ranger straining, grunting as he started lugging the heavy artillery down the aisle.

"You gonna be able to manage that big gun all shot up, Junior?"

"What the fuck do you think, old man? I look like some slack nuts six-pack of asskick to you?"

Acheron smiled. He always liked his warriors with a little attitude. Shine on, son, he thought, then went back to searching for fresh game.

He was sliding along the upper tier, Samson watching the rocket men's backs, when he spotted the poster on the far side of the arena. Acheron chuckled at the sight of the infamous mustache and potbelly an entire war had been fought over. Their stooge pulling through with his own version of X marking the spot was all he needed to know.

Time to dial up the sewer rats.

ARTEMUS DAWSON CHOKED down the bile, stifled the rage. At least they were out of the shit, on dry platform, waiting for the wall around the corner, down in the cul-de-sac, to come apart in smoke and thunder. The way Cramnon explained it, they needed the sewer as a secondary escape hatch in the event the first escape route was nowhere to be found. That, and it was the near picture-perfect linking point to the rest of the team, close to the gold mine. Whatever the logic, he didn't relish the prospect of hiking back this way, knee-deep in raw sewage and with hundreds, maybe even a few thousand pounds of booty weighing them down.

The more he sat, breathing in the stink, the longer

they waited for the big bang to set them free, the hotter his rage burned. It was the rats, as big as small dogs, he was having ugly thoughts toward at the moment. Them and the Iraqis.

He wasn't sure but he thought he heard the wail of sirens filter down the tunnel. With all the racket being created underground he wondered if some beat cop hadn't stumbled across all the sound and fury. Either way, Cramnon warned them to be ready for more problems when they climbed up top and hit the streets.

He looked at the Iraqis at the edge of the platform, both of them babbling in their own tongue at one another, gripping the poles. Dawson didn't understand Arabic but he was a master at reading faces and body language. The fedayeen, he believed, were going to take a swing at one of them. Ramses, crouched at the edge of the platform, hugging the slimy wall, snarled at them to shut up.

"Hey, boss. We need these assholes anymore?"

He watched Ramses considering, then the man shook his head.

Dawson rose from his haunches and hit the trigger of his Russian SAW. He blew them off the platform with a quick burst, their startled cries drowned as they splashed down into the soup.

THE SUICIDE BOMBER FLARED to his mind's eye images of fallen comrades from two wars and close to a half-dozen special ops in nearly as many countries. Now, like then, he recalled brothers-in-arms who had been charged from their blind side by some fanatic hell-bent on setting himself off, taking out as many as he could in what he considered a chickenshit way to do battle. Figure adrenaline, memories of fellow warriors killed or maimed for life, two tablets of speed jacking him up, but Chad Summers was going for the gusto, believing he was in this man's war—and checking out of the world—for the glory and revenge.

Take the money and shove it.

This, he thought, was for the pride of fallen lions.

Somehow he had been spared the brunt of ground zero when the SOB had lit himself up. Others fell while he was still standing, in the fight. Whoever sounded the alarm he didn't know, but he wasn't only grateful, he intended to dish out some sweet, heavy payback.

A huge chunk of the wall, he found, had been blown down. At least five of the team was bleeding out, writhing and moaning in the smoke and rubble. The racket of battle seemed to lash the painful chiming in his ears from so many directions, the speed burning up his system, heart pounding so hard it felt ready to blow out his chest. He felt disembodied, as light as the wind.

Good. Ready as ever.

He wasn't entirely unscathed this time around. Shrapnel, nails or whatever the bastard packed along for the suicide charge had torn off his left eyebrow to the bone. Blinded and burning in one eye, the blood streaming all the way down into his pants, Summers flew into the churning smoke. Bellowing out a war cry laced with vicious cursing, he unsheathed one of his double-edged battle-axes. The Axeman cometh, he thought. He was the god of Thunder and woe be unto any living creature that stepped into his path.

He spotted the first of several armed shadows boil from holes across the wide chamber, squeezed the LMG's trigger and charged to take it up close and personal.

CHAPTER THIRTEEN

"I did not know they would use chemical weapons! I do not know, I swear, where the Bank of Islam is located! I only know it is somewhere in the city!"

Bolan had Hamisi, cuffed and on his knees, the soldier holding him in the hatchway, a wad of the general's fatigue blouse in hand. If not for minarets and mosques, the wide promenades and parks with statues honoring Father Turk, the museums that housed ancient treasures of Hittites, Greeks, Romans and Arabs, Bolan thought it could have been Baltimore déjà vu. Mass panic swarmed, a few hundred feet below, the soldier finding terrified throngs darting pell-mell, stampeding one another or toppling still, even as the clouds of death dissipated. Corpses littered square yardage for whole blocks up and down Ataturk Boulevard and beyond, the bedlam reaching from the train station all the way to the presidential palace. So much human and vehicular congestion, myriad flashing lights of emergency medical vehicles were stalled, blocks from the heart of this open-air abattoir. A look moments ago through binocs, and the way the victims were contorted in death poses, foam bubbling from the mouth, Bolan knew the effects of VX nerve gas when he saw it.

"Kill me if you wish! I have told you everything."

Bolan had a damn good mind to toss the snake out of the Black Hawk, a swan-dive into the mass murder in the streets of Ankara he had helped engineer on the sly. His dream trampled, the general was faced with rough justice at the hands of fellow Turks, and it would prove punishment worse than a quick death by the Executioner's hand. Knowing the Turk reputation for brutality when it came to retribution, Bolan saw a fair amount of pain in the general's near future before he was hanged or beheaded. Sure, he had snatched Hamisi away from Tulruz, the colonel, he recalled, reluctant to let the warrior have his way. But Tulruz had calamity on a scale never seen in his country to contend with, cutting both of them loose, vowing Bolan whatever assistance he could lend. Instinct warning him no one—American or Turk, CIA or MIT—could be trusted, the Executioner knew he and his flight crew were hung out here by themselves for the duration.

Nothing new.

Alpha Six preyed on Bolan's angry thoughts. They were in the process of cleaning out the Bank of Islam. But where? And was Price with the enemy? Was she a human shield? Or something else? How did they plan to evac? Figure more inside help than he knew about, the nightmare scourge of nerve gas unleashed a diversionary tactic....

The Executioner would get answers soon enough. However much enemy blood he needed to spill, whatever degree of pain required to inflict on the vipers and jackals to get the truth and recover Price, he would take this war, without limit, without fear of consequences to himself or the government he ostensibly worked for, without concession or compromise.

Without mercy.

Bolan flung Hamisi back, toward his copilot, who was monitoring military and police frequencies, all of which were either jammed or crackling with barely suppressed rage or panic as the enormity of the disaster reached the authorities.

M-16/M-203 in hand, the Executioner searched the rooftops of old Ankara. Wind, elevation and distance to the death zone spoke the facts to Bolan. Scanning on, he knew their firepoint would be high up, wind at their backs...

Bingo.

The Executioner shouted the sighting into the cockpit, heard his pilot call back, "I see them!"

ACHERON SAW Dekyll paint the gunnery sight, figured the soldier drawing a bead to put the first HE 85 mm wallop square up the bastard's mustachioed snout. Bigelow locking home the 10-round mag, they were ready to fire at will. Protective ear muffs and goggles all around, Acheron still braced himself for the coming HE tempest, hunching in the shadows, attention split between his rocket team and the ring of arches above their firepoint. Bigelow picked up arms, covering Dekyll as he squeezed the autocannon's trigger. The first round vaporized the deposed madman of Iraq in a thundering eruption of smoke and fire.

BELLOWING CURSES and shouting the names of fallen Green Beret lions from the past and teammates in the present, Summers swept three jihad demons off their feet with a raking burst of flesh-eaters. Likewise, he knew it wouldn't slow him any to fan the flames with bitter memories of every Lieutenant Colonel Asshole who tried to Section Eight his brawling hide from the service. Same seething deal with the bitch he'd married and sent him a "Dear Chad" letter when he was combing the caves of Afghanistan for Osama and flunkies. But those who ever believed, he thought, life should be fair—a word so frivolously bandied about in the world of spineless political correctness—could never walk ten minutes in his boots.

"For Megalodon! Bring it on, you sons of whores! For Blackwell! For Chuckster!"

He laughed at the fear he found popping out of their eyes. Two of them—maybe still shell-shocked by what the puddle of goo splashed all over the floor had just done—were shuffling in a sort of comical duckwalk toward him, uncertain to the point of near paralysis. Summers believed he could almost read their thoughts. Oh, yes, he was the leviathan that had just sprung from the bowels of Hell.

Keep moving, he knew, into the heart of the enemy.

All the grueling hours of training with the battle-axes possessed mind, spirit and body, it felt, rage, absence of fear and perhaps a death wish shielding him with all the armor he needed before the inevitable lead hurricane dropped him. Look for gaps, use rifle and ax to create an impervious strike zone around himself, redouble the attack with each skull splitter, every amputating blow. One miss, and he was screwed, but he knew he was dead on his feet anyway. No sweet mama of all paydays for him, why not take two eyes for every eye for every comrade slain by jihad militants.

"Come to Papa Great Satan, you donkey-dung assholes!"

Sweeping back the RPK, rounds chopping into an armed shadow vaulting what appeared a stone block for an altar and kicking him out of sight, Summers felt the first few bullets tear into his ribs. His charge faltered a half step, mouth and nose filling with more blood, the first jolt of fire searing through his limbs. It was lag time enough for an extremist on his two o'clock to sound the Islamic war cry. Grunting and snarling out the curses, Summers bulled ahead, into the militant's surge and drove the razor-sharp edge down through his skull, blood and brains exploding in his face. Beyond the speed and adrenaline jetting through his veins, the killing took on a life of its own. He felt another round or two slice over his shoulders, winged the RPK back around, sighting them out of his one good eye. Holding down on the trigger, hosing another militant and slamming him into a wall dribbling already with blood, Summers wriggled the ax around in the split melon. Cursing the embedded blade, losing a critical second, as more shooters tore out of the gate and closed, a vicious kick to the lifeless sack's guts provided the final impetus to free the blade.

They were shouting, but stumbling over rubble, slipping in blood and guts. His cue, his edge to double, even triple his onslaught.

Whatever hell raged beyond this arena, Summers only heard the sound of his own stammering weapon, the bellows and curses that swelled the smoky ring enveloping him. Laughing as a militant hauled himself from a bed of stone and human flesh, Summers drove the blade through his arm, just beneath the shoulder. The fanatic's scream like rock-and-roll thunder he loved so much blasting into his ears, the limb dropped, AK still clutched in useless grip. The militant's shrieks rocketed to hysterical notes at the sight of the blood geyser from the ragged hole of his shoulder, but Summers was already past him, surging and swinging the blade.

A clean swipe, and he sent a head flying away, flinching as his good eye was stung by spurting blood. Thinking he was most definitely all out of love, the god of thunder drove the blade back and chopped through another arm.

CHAMBLISS KNEW he was dying, and he was scared. In fact, he was terrified, the long-sleeping Catholic rising now, floating out of the cold inside, a bleating, even whimpering voice in his head telling him he was moments away from meeting his Maker.

Small comfort he wasn't alone in this final act before the curtain fell, the bloody drama of full-bore battle raging around him. The howls of pain and animal-like grunts of men, dying where they stood their ground and shot each other up, were a reminder that only heartbeats ago he was in the thick of it.

No guardian angels here.

He didn't know whether to laugh or weep, recalling a short two decades and change on the planet that made very little sense to him, but a life, steamrollered by pain, anger and disappointment, the shreds of which were now running away from him. And telling him, pretty much, he could look forward to a quick drop straight into Hell, where at least he knew he would never have to be alone ever again. Or maybe there really was such a divine all-beautiful, all-merciful, all-forgiving God. That concept alone didn't make much sense to him, considering the evil he'd seen and committed in his life. How could he possibly explain, rationalize, justify to his Creator all the hurt and suffering he had inflicted on others over the years? How could he possibly be forgiven, considering just the blood on his hands alone? Without punishment for human transgression, eternal reward meant less than nothing for virtue. The litany of his sins, offenses and transgressions against God and humankind was so long, in fact, he had to believe he wouldn't even get the chance to grovel before Saint Peter at the gates.

There was, he feared, now no escaping the coming judgment. It was time to pay.

The blood was streaming down the side of his face.

Afraid to know, he managed to reach up, feeling around. Half his scalp was gone, but the horror didn't stop there as he gingerly touched the soft mush of exposed brain. The steel plate, he discovered, was sticking up like an obscene crown, a sick joke played on him by fate.

He gagged, the bitter laugh strangled by blood and vomit trapped in his throat. All he ever wanted to be was a singer in a rock-and-roll band.

Chambliss felt his lips move, unsure if he uttered or thought the words.

"Our Father, who art in Heaven…"

The noise of men slaughtering one another kept fading away, Chambliss thinking how warm it suddenly felt to die when he sensed a presence. Before he looked up he knew who it was, as the tall shadow of Cramnon parted the pall of smoke and stood over him, the man appearing to him, a calm in the storm.

"Hey…Captain…"

Was that pity in the man's eyes? he wondered. Anger? Disappointment? If so, then over what? That he'd lost some more cannon fodder, robbed of another pack mule? He strangled on bitter laughter, as it slammed him, a bolt of lightning, that's all he was to the man. And this was the pillar of strength he had bartered his soul to see him carried through all this?

"You're not going to make it, son."

Gurgling on slime rolling back down his throat, Chambliss shut his eyes, as Cramnon lifted the RPK. "I never was."

CRAMNON COULDN'T LET his favored son die, bleeding out, brains dribbling down the ground-up burger of his face, guts pooling in his crotch. Beyond the fleeting moment of rare compassion he was, however, puzzled, even annoyed at what he saw take hold of the young Marine's face. What the hell, was the kid sorry about something other than getting taken out of the game before he tasted the sweet fruit at the end of the ride? he wondered. Was that remorse he found? Contrition? What had he been mumbling a few moments ago? No, he hadn't been praying. Or had he? He was a warrior, after all, had known the risks of his own free will, signed on for the mother of all bank heists. Beyond shocking, it was appalling, if what he spotted was real. Say it wasn't so, son, oh, please, say the kid hadn't been praying. Only something told him that's exactly what Chambliss had been doing. And it hit Cramnon next, a sick anger that maybe he hadn't known Chambliss as well as he thought. That maybe he had never deserved special consideration.

Screw him.

A 3-round mercy burst to the chest put the kid out of misery and mind. Cramnon knew he had to jump back into the tempest. Up to then they had the momentum, but he sensed the tide was not only about to turn, but it could also drown them in their own blood. With the threat of suicide bombers hunkered in countless chambers, holes and whatever other hiding places, ready to charge and plaster them all to stone already awash in muck and with wet rain still pattering his skull, Cramnon knew the stakes had just shot through the ozone.

Hard to tell how many of his shock troops and Kurds were down from the martyr's blast, but Cramnon figured at least a half dozen around Chambliss were laid out beneath the hanging smoke. He caught a couple of groans, glimpsed shredded limbs, pincushioned with embedded nails, twitching in the rubble. They would bleed out soon enough, he knew, so turned away, cracking home a fresh 45-round mag into his RPK. A quick strip of spare clips and grenades from Chambliss, and Cramnon turned his attention to the berserker inside the jagged maw leading to a wide chamber.

And he was, indeed, a fearsome, beautiful sight to behold, Cramnon thought, something most definitely wrong with that guy, as Acheron would put it.

Cramnon found Thor with a BI lackey impaled in the air, a trophy whose twisted mask of shock and agony he bellowed curses at, his battle-ax wedged so deep into another militant's brain, the slaughtered but spasming carcass was held upright on his knees. The man, Cramnon decided, stealing another risky moment to view the show, was without a doubt his top candidate for the Alpha Medal of Honor. That was Godzilla, Terminator, that twenty-five-foot white shark where everyone cried for a bigger boat, all majestically packaged into a one-man army, going all the way while racking up a body count of Koranic proportions.

Oh, the beauty.

Still holding up his prize, he heard Thor thunder,

"Guess you didn't hear, dung breath, a guest is considered God's gift in Turkey!

Whatever stories he'd heard from others about Summers—and in the beginning he'd sloughed them off as too much beer and whiskey doing more talking than walking—he was now a believer. The only handicaps about to topple that mountain, Cramnon knew, were the blood blinding him in both eyes and the trio of shooters closing the lead net from his six.

Stepping up, Cramnon closed the threesome—unworthy of such a quick waxing to say the least in that kind of gladiator arena—with a long scything burst. Firing on, he flung them back, but not before Thor toppled from a half-dozen AK rounds chopping into his backside.

Cramnon spotted the bloody snake next, sans arm, crawling out of the smoke, sliding over rubble, AK in one hand, the fanatic near lapping muck at his boots. He found the amputee's yap, bubbling with crimson froth, wide open as if to vent rage or beg for mercy. Cramnon speared that piehole with fourteen inches of steel deep throat.

A quick tug to free the blade, then Cramnon wheeled and strode toward the series of pitched battles raging in other offshooting cubbyholes. He saw the Kurds firing from crouched positions by archways, cursed. Aware they were something of a liability in a firefight, he still wouldn't tolerate the Kurds hanging back while his guys did all the dirty work. He began bellowing at them in their native tongue to move inside and take the fight to the bastards, aware his own troops were embroiled in toe-to-toe, hand-to-hand evisceration. Snugging his com link back in place, Cramnon decided to lead again by example, telling them which way and how to split off, but choose targets with extreme care and precision. And woe be unto any of them who even accidentally winged one of his troops.

"GOD...DAMN!"

The rest of the cursing was whipped away, driftwood in a tempest, as Ramses shouldered into Dawson, the black commando snarling out his own vicious oaths and passing the same bull treatmeat to the next guy in line. Ramses pressed his face into the slick wall, the platform shuddering beneath his knees, a picture of a two-ton rhino thundering over savanna and charging his way branded to mind. The ferocious pounding of the HE bombardment in the process of knocking down the wall cleaved shock waves through his body, from scalp to the hair on his feces-coated toes. Even the rats, he glimpsed, bounced into the air as the hits kept on coming. He feared the roof would come down on their heads as smoke boiled over the platform, then rubble started pelting the cesspool in a meteor shower. Another dousing of filth became the least of his concerns, considering the bath he'd already taken, as a shell erupted somewhere down the tunnel, the back blast hammering the lot of them with flying stone comets.

He was on his com link before they were buried in a shit-and-piss tomb, bellowing at Acheron to cease fire. Clear to him the hole was pounded out, but he was sure the rocket boys couldn't see what the hell they'd done with all the smoke, back blast and whirlwinds of debris in their gunnery sights.

"What?"

Ramses heard the trouble on the other end, Acheron shouting through the deafening racket of autofire. And yet another HE pulverizer rocked the sewer, pieces of loose stone bouncing off his head, as he roared, "Stop that goddamn cannon before you pound us into rat shit!"

Ramses had to strain to hear the problem spot, his eardrums split with lancing fiery pain. A line of enemy shooters, Acheron shouted, would be to his immediate left, nine o'clock when they came through the hole.

"We're on the way!"

He turned on the troops, passed on their orders, which was simply to barrel through the hole and come out firing.

"You!" he shouted at Muhdal. "Stay on my ass wherever I go! I go through a door, you and your people go left and direct fire only in that direction." What was that look he spotted on Muhdal's face? "Flip me the bird if you understand me, asshole!"

Ramses peered through the smoke. He watched the smile form on the Kurd leader's lips, then saw the little bastard actually shoot him the middle finger. He would have blown him off the deck, into the soup, but Ramses knew he'd need all the Kurd cannon fodder at his disposal before this was over.

THE EXECUTIONER needed only one of them, kicking and screaming. He discovered his timing was perfect, hope alive and burning he could reel in a live one, as he hopped off the Black Hawk, spotted his four spiders rappelling down the stone backdrop. As the gunship lifted off, his Farm blacksuits climbing up the canyon of apartment buildings to provide cover and tracking, the Executioner hit the edge of a courtyard wall at the end of the alley. Two 3-round bursts from his M-16, raking the outer left hardmen across the back, and they were in free fall, arms windmilling as they dropped a good fifty feet before they cracked and splintered on stone paving.

He was adjusting his aim when the last two mass murderers twisted on their ropes, glanced down, then flung themselves away from the wall, one of them triggering a wild burst of LMG fire on the flight down. Two lucky rounds chipped off stone above Bolan's head, the soldier's aim thrown off as the bee stings jabbed him just below the eye. Bolan tracked back on their fall, hurling four or five rounds at the dark blurs before they thundered into the roof of a van. Every sheet of glass exploded as the shell caved with their hard landing. If they were injured by the impact they showed no signs of slowing, rolling up and over their warped cushion, firing as they dropped and hit the alley floor.

Bullets snapping past Bolan's ears, the soldier decided Plan B was his best option. It was a rare oversight, indulging a whim and a prayer he could bag one, as they cranked up the heat of AK and LMG fire. Bolan went

low around the corner, stammered out a few 5.56 mm
rounds, tagging one of them to the belly, when he
glimpsed the small dark sphere arcing through the shadows.

ACHERON KNEW if he didn't plug the holes, and
quick, the dam of shooters would burst, drowning
them all in their own blood and guts. Forget the gold,
if they didn't nail this down, they wouldn't even
limp out of here, dragging their sorry bullet-chewed
tails to the vault.

It was going to hell faster than a whore took a soldier's money, but Acheron would do his part to roll
back the tide or die trying. He armed an incendiary
grenade, then poured LMG fire into the next hole.
Rounds scorching the air, near in his face, he was sure
he scored flesh, one of the flaming lances arcing
rounds up and into the archway, before the dark
shadow flew back into the chamber. He'd be damned,
though, if he could hear anything, the amphitheater
trapping every round fired, every scream of pain until
the upper tier's floor seemed to tremble under boot.

He scanned the arena on the move, trying to find
an instant solution to this mess. Whether succumbing
to blood loss or waxed by this sudden renewed onslaught of terror jackals, it didn't matter, since Dekyll
was slumped over the autocannon, out of play. Luck-
ily Dekyll hadn't given up the ghost until he blasted
out a hole big enough to drive a Humvee through, but
the way for the link-up team was hardly paved. A lot
of smoke boiled that way, but Acheron still sighted

Ramses and his Omega team slip onto the back of the upper tier. In twos and threes, they began hurling murderous play to what was already near eye-to-eye slaughter. Shooting from the hip, Ramses and shock troops began splitting up into two- and three-man teams. Lobbing frag bombs through three separate archways, they made their bullrush into those chambers. Experienced professionals, no question, but Acheron knew the manual on urban warfare was down the toilet on this one.

It was every wild beast for himself.

Acheron hosed the hole again, pitched the WP bomb inside, then jumped back as an RPG warhead streaked out of the dark. Cursing, he made out the crunching retorts of two explosions. Flames leaped from the maw, the wail of a few human torches right in his ears. It was a sweet, tantalizing aroma, just the same, human flesh being cooked to and off the bone in there, but Acheron was turning toward the arena pit, sensing a problem down there.

He cursed at the sight of Samson's inert and shredded form draped over the upper section of seats. He'd never really known the man, no real comrade sentiment welling up at the loss, but they could use every gun they had now. The thought flickered through his head, though, that with every one of the team biting the dust, his cut kept growing. That was assuming, of course, he made it out of this hell in one standing piece.

A plan began shaping up, somewhere in the ripping noise in his brain as he looked at Bigelow, the soldier hanging in there by the autocannon, spraying arches with his AK.

Acheron was turning his RPK back toward the fire-light dancing in the hole, when Cramnon patched through and began shouting in his ear. The Alpha leader, he heard, was near on top of the last series of chambers before the vault. He demanded a sitrep, wanted this wrapped, ten minutes ago. Acheron gave him the bloody score. Then Cramnon barked out the solution to their woes.

Acheron smiled. Why didn't he think of that himself?

CHAPTER FOURTEEN

The retaining wall just inside the courtyard absorbed the blast and shrapnel. No time to spare gratitude to fast feet or a little help from the unseen spirit of war, Bolan jumped up, rolled over the wall. M-16 parting smoke and leading the way, he hit the alley running. So jacked up on adrenaline and electrified combat senses, Bolan had tuned out his environment to all but his enemies. Now the shrill racket of sirens, the babble of vast multitudes spectating from balconies or the angry murmur of shadows wandering pockets of the alley filtered through the ringing chime in his ears. Turk cops or bystanders, he hoped, would turn out the least of his concerns. It was time, he knew, to pick it up another heated notch.

Whether the crushed shell was their getaway wheels or not, Bolan only knew he wasn't about to let the last mass butcher slip away. He heard, then spotted the next target. Where the alley widened to the north, a sheet of flames engulfed a box-shape vehicle. Whoever the murdering savage, Bolan found the enemy spraying a threesome of downed figures in blue—Turk police, he realized—with his Russian RPK. The murderous interruption, however, lent the Executioner a slim chance he could still bag a prisoner. As he closed on the enemy's rear, judging the mindless rage in eyes lit up by the fiery destruction, instinct shouted back to Bolan the bastard was bent on going out with a roar.

Still he had to try. Bolan needed answers, a solid lead to put him on the scent of the Alpha jackals.

The Executioner cut his rapid advance to a march, lifted his M-16. He was taking up slack on the trigger when his Black Hawk soared past the leading edge of northern towers, hovered, then bathed alley and enemy in floodlight. The savage framed in the beam for a heartbeat, Bolan caressed the trigger. Downrange, he glimpsed the dark spurt inside the glowing halo as he scored thigh, the angry howl flung away by rotor wash. The soldier was a heartbeat from following up with a crippling takedown round to the knee when the savage bolted out of the light. The enemy hobbled a few steps, screaming curses all the way, then barreled through a door and vanished.

RAMSES MOWED DOWN a mauled and staggering line of five enemy shooters, his RPK jumping and hammering out rounds, but he was tagging armed shadows as fast as he could. His troops, he knew, were spread out and down in the sprawling chambers cut by pillars, crumbled ancient ruins and sinkholes, alternating frag wallops with relentless AK and LMG autofire. Breath-

ing any number of vile fumes—from the human fu-
neral pyres eaten up by WP to running blood and the
waste coating him, neck to feet—he thought heard a
voice, buzzing with anger on his com link. He triggered the RPK, sweeping the arch ahead a few more
seconds before he was aware it was Acheron bellowing for them to fall back. Shooting from the hip and
kicking a pair of runners through drifting smoke and
raining gore, he slid behind a pillar. They were all on
the same frequency to Acheron, but he found his shock
force caught up in the frenzy of the slaughter, oblivious to everything but blood in their noses. Copying the
order, he shouted, caught Dawson's eyes. He was
forced to keep roaring above the ear-splitting racket of
return fire for everyone to bail for the amphitheater.
While his squad blanketed archways in a fighting withdrawal, Ramses wheeled on the Kurds—lagging behind, the gutless sacks, and he damn well intended to
let Cramnon know about this—screaming at them to
get out, neglecting to inform them the roof was about
to cave in. As far as he was concerned, he could carry
whatever booty they were meant to haul out, he'd
earned his cut, and theirs.

Apparently they understood the order, as they
melted back, enemy fire rising to new ear-shattering
levels. He focused on covering his own squad of real
fighters, the RPK yammering out a long burst that
raked the line of arches all the way down, zipping the
stream of lead over a few crawlers and bleeders along
the way.

Ramses armed and lobbed a frag bomb toward a

hunkered group of shadows to his twelve o'clock. As
the thunderclap cleared his own six, he turned—

And nearly walked straight into Muhdal's AK-47.

Ramses read the intent in the Kurd's stare, crystal
clear. It was funny, he thought, how he was paralyzed
by the moment, whatever anxiety and concern he'd felt
toward Muhdal or Kurd treachery strangely enough
sparking anger only toward himself. He hadn't
watched his own six, the Kurd hanging back, forcing
him into a mistake. And now it would cost him.

Ramses was bringing his LMG on-line when he
felt the first of many AK rounds tear into his flesh. He
was falling, tasting the life's juices on his lips, when
he heard another familiar rattle of weapons fire. There
was a howl of pain that seemed to echo through the
antechamber but from a great distance, as he felt his
body going cold and rigid no pain at all, which signaled to him he was checking out. The lights fading,
he looked up and thought he saw a big dark shadow
lugging a Russian SAW and looming over the rotten
Kurd bastard who'd punched his ticket.

Small comfort he'd see Muhdal in Hell, Ramses
thought as he laughed at the picture of himself burning for eternity alongside the Kurd, as the blackness
thickened.

JUST WHEN Acheron didn't think it could unravel any
worse, it did.

With angry attention split in several directions, what
seemed like a hundred tasks to complete in seconds
flat, with Cramnon bellowing in his ear he wanted that
cannon and in his lap now, Acheron spotted Dawson

rolling through one of the far north arches. He wasn't sure what disturbed him so about the black commando right then, but something warned him he was about to find out. In fact, the black commando's eyes looked set to pop from their sockets, his rage aimed square at the fleeing Kurds. Since there was no response from Ramses, Acheron assumed the worst for the Omega Team leader. He could venture a good guess what had happened and why Dawson looked furious enough to chew uranium-depleted bullets and spit them up someone's sphincter.

Acheron had the order on the tip of his tongue for Dawson to beat feet out of there, glimpsed a batch of armed shadows regrouping in the antechambers, then he froze, stunned by what happened next. He watched as the black commando shouted curses at the retreating Kurds, chasing them down the stone rows, unloading his SAW. And Dawson seemed to gather steam and fury with each kill, every row of descent. The black commando bowled them down with long sweeping strokes, left to right and back, human pins ripped to shreds and screaming on the tumble down. The last of the Kurds was airborne when the hunkered reinforcements cut loose on Dawson, three, maybe four dark holes blazing in sync with autofire.

"Son of a bitch!" Acheron roared, cracking home a full 10-round magazine of 85 mm HE projectiles, Bigelow manning the autocannon, ready to yank and crank, flinching as wild rounds whined off stone around their roost.

"Light 'em up, son!" Acheron shouted, grabbing his RPK and spraying archways with a heavy dose of what he hoped was 5.45 mm poison.

Only Acheron found he was too little too late to cover for Dawson. As the black commando was ventilated by the AK tempest, jerking and twitching, but firing back until his skull puked apart in fat chunks, the first HE shell was streaking for paydirt. Acheron was turning away as the explosion blew down half the wall beyond the upper tier in a whirlwind of smoke and shooting rubble.

AND THUS, proclaimed Abbadon, lord of the pit, the netherworld rocked the onslaught to yet another level of carnage. They screamed, bled, died. They ran, but there was nowhere to hide from the wrath of the lord of the pit. No prisoners taken, all the fleeing sacks of human feces gathered and hurled into the abyss.

How sweet it was.

On the fly, he saw smoke pluming down the far north corridor, heard screams lancing on and on from the sonic booms of HE bombardment. Acheron and company shoving another batch of meat through the grinder was just more sweet music to his ears.

So Cramnon kept chugging ahead, RPK sweeping his flanks, sights set on the archway at the bottom of what was the last flight of steps. It wasn't the home-stretch—he cautioned himself about getting too happy—but fresh adrenaline pumped fire through his veins, just the same, heart pounding with joy. So beautifully close, he laughed, could almost smell the cash, taste the gemstones. A little more mop-up, as he heard autofire and thunderclaps reverberate up the tunnel, and his rear should be secure.

Up to then he hadn't thought about the money, aware, though, he was flat stinking broke. Every dime of plundered slush funds was sunk into this operation. The cash cow from the sale of a few hundred kilos of cocaine and heroin—which Samson, Dawson and a late and unlamented CIA black-ops team in Colombia had seized and delivered to him—had stretched the payoffs to the limit for hardware, intel, pilots, grease and refuge. All the years of bloody hard nerve-racking work, but the reward was now in sight.

A time check, and Cramnon cursed, his mood deflating, then swelling back with rage and anxiety. The bubbled glass shattered, he read the frozen minute hand. "Damn it!" He reached for his radio, aware his flight crew was en route or already parked on the roof. Plucking up a handful of mangled high-tech junk from his belt, he snarled another oath, flung it away, began handing out the next round of orders. With the hefty cut his Company pilots would carve for themselves, he didn't think they'd leave them stranded...

Worse things, he knew, could and had already happened.

A quick head count, and he found he was down to squad strength, plus five Kurds, all of them looking mean and angry, in tow. He was sure Acheron had taken casualties, which meant all of them would be hauling out double loads, at least. And there were still suicide bombers, he feared, on the prowl.

Cramnon took point down the steps, ready to blast away at the first hint of a shadow, Garson and Ryker, his slack men and demo team, ready with RPGs. Half-

way down, he sensed the utter stillness, smelled the
faint coppery taint of blood. They'd made it this far;
what could stop them now? The stutter of autofire, the
crunch of frags and HE shelling trailing him, he hit the
archway—

And froze at the sight.

At the deep corner of what he assumed was a sultan's sprawling chambers rose his private stairway to
heaven. A quick scan for enemy life, ordering Wooly
Mammoth and Tiny Tim to watch the beaded arch to
his ten o'clock, and he found whoever the Bank of
Islam's president had managed to while away his underground stint in relative comfort. There was a giant-
screen TV, videos and DVDs stacked beside it. A
glance down the pile, he found they were addicted to
American movies, mostly action flicks and porn. Further breaking with Muslim tradition, he spotted a fully
stocked wet bar, most of the bottles half-empty, a fridge
he was sure was stuffed to the gills with meat fit for
royalty. Divans, massive bed with frilly curtains, as he
panned on, and Cramnon left it to the imagination the
orgies that carried them through the lonely nights here.

The party was over.

No time to dawdle, he ordered Garson and Ryker
to get busy. They shot for the vault. The door wasn't
much in terms of size, wide enough for two men to
squeeze through at the same time, he figured, but there
were four inches of steel to contend with. His safe-
crackers sliding over a divan, Cramnon took a moment to watch as they began fixing and priming
plastique to the hinges, the bottom and top corners.

Pretty sure a few dabs of C-4 wouldn't bring down the door—since the bulk of plastique would be spared to shred whatever loot they couldn't mule out and to seal their own exit—he needed that cannon to finish blasting through. No crank-combination handle, dial or any sign of a keyhole, his HUMINT told him there was a remote-control lock, midway down.

Patching through to Acheron, who told him they were on the way, Cramnon found a Kurd audience gathered behind, barked at them to get outside and stand watch. The SOBs didn't move too fast, and Cramnon didn't like what he read in their eyes. He was sure they were steamed they'd lost some of their cousins, forced by him to leave their mangled bodies behind under his threatening weapon. To hell with them—he had their futures already mapped out.

Weapons fire withering, the shelling fading to an echo, Cramnon caught the scuffling just inside the beaded curtain of the antechamber. RPK up, reaching for a frag grenade, he heard the groan, sniffed blood. Homed in on the direction of the sound, he surged through the curtain.

And smiled.

Nothing but two corpses, belts of C-4 dumped in blood pools, AKs clutched in dead hands. The good news didn't end with the suicide bombers opting to cut and run, shoot it out in a fit of panic and rage. A section of floor was up, Cramnon chuckling as he followed the crimson trail toward a swarthy figure now pulling down a carpet, revealing, lo and behold, their exit. AK-47 hung around his shoulder, the BI president, he assumed, was riddled with holes leaking red fluid.

It was the nylon bag, six feet long and bursting at the zipper, that commanded Cramnon's undivided attention.

He had the picture here: the going got too tough for these three. They had turned on one another, figured to bail with a piece of the action, the fighting and dying best left to lackeys. Oh, the love of money, he thought, had risen higher on the scales than any commitment to jihad or loyalty to blood. Funny how that happened.

A peek into the hole, finding it empty, and Cramnon laughed. The BI president, he saw, braced himself against the door, shuddered in a one-eighty, AK slowly rising.

"Allow me to lighten your load, friend," Cramnon said, and drilled him with a long burst to the chest.

"CLEAR A PATH! I'm walking out of here!"

Bolan hit the second-floor landing, veered and took cover behind a stone pillar. The enemy's instincts were strictly animal, wound tight for self-preservation. The Executioner knew the type all too well. Driven by greed and blood lust, they would take as many innocents with them as they could when they feared the end had come, no way out, their dreams vanishing like smoke in the wind.

Whoever the savage, Bolan determined to call his final act on earth.

Bolan figured the enemy knew he was being hunted on the way in, so grabbed the first available human shield. It was only a glimpse of the setup on the run, but the soldier heard the elderly woman cry something in Turk. Bolan locked the picture in his mind, adrenalized to make his play. The enemy had an arm wrapped around her throat, the heavy RPK aimed in the Executioner's direction while he dragged her down the hall, backpedaling. He was growling at her to shut up, shouting at other tenants to get back into their apartments.

"Lose the sixteen! Step out and grab some air, hands up! Two seconds, or the old hag here dies and I start blasting everybody up here!"

Unleathering the Beretta, Bolan tossed the M-16 away from the pillar. He heard the woman scream, a man's voice snarling in Turk, the sounds of a scuffle. The Executioner whipped around the corner, Beretta tracking and locked on the savage. He was cursing, dancing with his hostage as she tried to grind the ball of his foot into powder with vicious stomps.

One tap of the Beretta's trigger, and Bolan painted a dark splotch between his eyes. No sooner did the body hit the deck than the woman was screaming, working her kicks up the length of the corpse's tag. He left her to vent, scooping up his assault rifle, then keyed his com link for a sitrep from Eagle One. Two military police and several Turk medevac helicopters, he was informed, were now swarming Ataturk Boulevard. And Colonel Tulruz had, for unknown reasons, changed his tune of cooperation, demanding Hamisi return to him at once, without delay. The way it sounded, Bolan figured Tulruz was ready to cast the Turk version of an all-points net around the city.

Bolan had other plans. In fact, he believed he had a solution to his Alpha problem.

THE FLOOR SEEMED to ripple beneath Cramnon with each roaring blast. At roughly eighty feet from impact, not even the padded earmuffs stymied the din from spiking his eardrums. With smoke billowing over their firepoint, blotting out the world beyond his goggles, he hugged the floor as back blast pounded stacked divans and mattress, chunks of steel and stone ripped open fabric with gale force. When a piece of shrapnel winged off his skull, he shut his eyes, covered his head with his arms and kissed stone.

Cramnon coughed, batting his hand through the smoke. He looked over, found Bigelow slumped over the autocannon. A shove and Bigelow slid away, revealing a jagged steel fang speared through his left eye, the inside of his goggles splattered with blood. So much for giving the kid a confidence boost, riding out the storm right beside him.

LMG in hand, stripping off his protective gear, he saw his troops shuffling into the chamber. It took several moments for the smoke to clear enough for inspection, Cramnon ready to laugh, launch himself into a victory dance straight for the vault. Instead he felt sick.

The door was still standing.

Sure, the hinges were blown, plenty of jagged gaps around the edges. Yes, the area where the main lock was housed was nothing but a smoking hole from a direct hit. But the gate to heaven was still shut!

Cramnon shook with rage, grimly aware he'd have to man the cannon and keep on pounding until he brought the door down. He heard the grumbling, felt the tension mount, then he caught the faint groan of steel yielding to physics.

And then his song from heaven filled his ears with

loud scraping before the door toppled in a slow-motion sweep through the cloud. They were laughing now, as the barrier thundered to the floor.

While Acheron assigned sentries, Cramnon slowly walked over the door. He was almost afraid to walk into the vault; it was too good to be true. No booby traps according to his HUMINT, but he half expected to find a small army of shooters or a thousand vipers come charging out of nowhere. Worse still, he was scared to death the vault was empty.

Phantom fears aside, he entered the domain of gods, and filled their vault with laughter.

The huge room spun in his eyes. He felt weak, giddy. The LMG slipped from his fingers. He felt the others moving in behind, a stillness and silence bursting apart with so much joy Cramnon believed it was palpable, about to bring him to his knees, weeping.

It was all unbelievably, fantastically true.

Cramnon couldn't move as he absorbed the sight.

There were too many pallets heaped with American Franklins to bother counting. They would need anywhere from four to six transport trucks, he calculated, to haul all of it out. It was a sickening shame, so much wealth, so few mules.

He saw Acheron, Garson and Ryker dip their hands into giant urns. Their eyes shone against the glitter of cut diamonds, drool forming on Acheron's lips. There were rubies, sapphires, emeralds, the whole range of gemstones, Cramnon knowing the Red Crescent organization had gobbled up these precious stones from

Brazil to Sri Lanka to Myanmar as collateral in the event all bank accounts were frozen by the West. There was decorative gold leaf, he found, diamond necklaces, all of it useless junk as far as he was concerned. He wasn't planning on getting engaged.

A second later it was back to cold reality. Acheron held up a white brick. Cramnon was no drug peddler. Too much risk for too little profit. Nor did he want to waste time traipsing all over Europe to unload the stones. Cash was god.

"You want it," Cramnon told Acheron, "you hump it out of here. Let's start packing up, people."

"WHAT THE HELL kind of handle is Adamnan?"

Paul Turner showed the two CIA men his big winning smile. "What kind of Company outpost is called King Midas Station?"

"The kind with the golden touch."

Turner chuckled. "Well since this is the land of Helen of Troy, I suppose that's better than Trojan Horse. We all know what happened there."

"Cut the crap. I assume that's it?"

Turner kept smiling, hefting the fat war bag. He took a moment, looking around the shabby accommodations, the two CIA agents scowling, huffy and impatient for their money. They were out in the middle of the steppe, nowhere to be exact. Just the three of them, hidden in the night, the stone hovel nestled in the maw of some foothills. The walls were festooned with maps, printouts of Kurd faces on Turkey's most-wanted list. Computer station, he saw, tucked into one corner, radar and tracking equipment in the other cubbyhole.

"We're alone, friend. And daydream on your own time. You and your boys are a little too hot for us to get all cozy and drag this out."

"Radioactive hot."

"In other words, the sooner you put Turkey behind the better."

"We can only hold off the wolves for so long."

"The quicker we get you and your people out of our lives the better."

"In other words, we'd rather not get chewed up in the feeding frenzy of this."

Turner smiled at their singsong routine. He was tired but anxious to get on with it after his long drive in the Humvee, barely fleeing the Armageddon that had dropped on Ankara. He checked his watch. Hamisi was late.

One of them was standing, holding a black leather bag, the other buzz cut leaning back behind his desk in a swivel chair, smoking up a cloud. Turner waved his hand for the bag. With a scowl the CIA man tossed it to him.

"It's all there. Flight charts, frequencies to stations you wanted, refueling stops, passwords. You've got a real narrow window past Incirlik, but you're covered by my people there. Beyond your next stop a couple thousand miles down the road, we can't guarantee you don't find some F-16s, AWACs or Big Brother's eyes in the sky dogging you."

Bending, Turner rifled through the paperwork. Satisfied it was all there, he unzipped the war bag. He looked to the doorway as the whap of rotor blades reached his ears. Perfect timing.

"That would be the general," Turner said.

The smoker was cursing. "C'mon, c'mon."

Turner wrapped his hands around the Mossberg 500 Special Purpose shotgun. "I apologize for all the inconvenience."

And Turner rose up, blasting away. The first 12-gauge pulverizer hit the smoker square in the chest, blew him out of his seat. The second agent was clawing for his shouldered Beretta, snarling oaths at either his imminent doom or the blood in his eyes or both. Turner took no chances, decapitated him with a near point-blank eruption.

Another shell jacked into place, he strode for the door. He would summon Hamisi into the room, alone, his pilots able to finish off the other four inside the Black Hawk.

Standing in the doorway, a smile ready to greet the general, he peered into the swirling dust. He saw the lean figure materialize in the hatch, recognized Hamisi but—

Why were his hands cuffed? And why, no, more importantly, who just kicked him in the seat and sent him flying out the door?

Turner sensed a presence behind. He was turning toward the threat, glimpsed a tall dark man with an M-16/M-203 combo when he felt the first rounds tear into his legs.

CHAPTER FIFTEEN

Cramnon tried to focus on the good news.

The storm of weapons fire he heard beyond the stairwell door signaled him their chopper ride was on the roof. The questions begged themselves, but he'd know in a few moments what sort of shape their Chinook ferry was in, how many gunships were swarming the skies. In short, if they'd even make it off the roof.

The Alpha leader heaved himself the final few steps, shouting at his slack men to ready their RPGs. Behind, they were swearing and grunting in single file, pissing and moaning about the waiting crisis. Hell, he couldn't believe it himself, damn near laughed out loud how he wasn't surprised. A six-story climb, at the least, from the bowels of the subterranean slaughterhouse to the roof of the warehouse. Close to two hundred pounds of loot hung around his shoulders. A body count of epic proportions in their wake, ascending in belief they'd walked out of the fire. Now this. If he was drenched in running sweat, every muscle and joint on fire and screaming back at him, lungs burning and starved for oxygen, adrenaline and energy reserves on redline—

"Suck it up, all of you!" he shouted over his shoulder. "Anybody falls and can't make the chopper they're on their own! And you will be relieved of your cut!"

And Cramnon sprayed the lock with a burst of RPK fire. Following up with a thundering boot heel, he burst onto the roof. A glimpse of the black-clad Company shooter firing his Squad Automatic Weapon over the body draped in the chopper's doorway at his feet, and Cramnon swung around the stairwell housing. Holding back on the LMG's trigger, he hurled 5.45 mm rounds at the Black Hawk, homing in on the M-60 door gunner, two hundred feet up, twelve o'clock and holding. Only one gunship, for the moment, but where there was one flying shark he feared a small armada of warbirds was in the neighborhood.

"Go, go, go!" Cramnon bellowed over his shoulder as the first wave of troops broke across the roof, stumbling and cursing a path through a meteor shower of lead, the SAW-man screaming and swearing at them for greater speed.

Cramnon thought he scored, the M-60 gunner jerking in the hatch, the big gun swinging away, but he'd never know.

It didn't make any difference. Cramnon watched his rocket men knock the Black Hawk out of the park. On the tail end of smoke and flames, the first warhead slammed into the nose of the hovering shark. It erupted a microsecond before a second fireball blew inside the fuselage. At that angle, shooting up, Cramnon figured the missile hit the ceiling. Fuel then ignited, a saffron mushroom cloud sweeping the shattered hull away, where it seemed to then float toward an apartment building. There were shadows, Cramnon saw, an audience jumping up and down on balconies across the way, flapping their arms as they turned tail and shot through curtains. He was mesmerized by the sight, laughing as he half pivoted toward the Chinook. He knew what was coming, had to view the sight, taking it as a sign their luck would hold.

The fireball appeared drawn to the building, as if pulled by a giant magnet. Given this was old Ankara, he thought, a little urban face-lift couldn't hurt. The flaming comet hammered into the structure, the fireball blasting apart as it ripped off balconies, sheared away wall, slicing through any Turks with slow feet.

Laughing, a sky check around the compass showing it clear of roving gunships, Cramnon had to believe the worst was over.

"He dead?" the Alpha leader shouted, pointing at the body in the doorway with his LMG. Acheron nodded, reaching out and snatching the last Kurd by the shoulder, up and through the door.

"So why the hell's he still in my way?" Cramnon snarled, "What, you think this sorry sack was destined for Arlington National Cemetery?" he added, and dumped the body on the deck.

HADN'T THEY HEARD, he thought, the love of money was the root of all evil?

The Executioner aware of the answer to his question, it was what he didn't know that the enemy was about to give up. One look at his downed songbird, though, and Bolan didn't see the art of gentle persuasion in his future. Why cast pearls when pain and bullets worked magic?

The sight of the bleeding savage heaped on the floor sickened Bolan. He'd sold his soul for a slice of the pie, looking out for number one, killing, directly or indirectly, guilty or innocent, a whole bunch of people. Bolan was about to find out if he was only a bit player. Even so, he was sure this wounded animal knew something.

Looking into the war bag, the Executioner figured the payoff for the two CIA traitors was about three, four million in U.S. currency. He wondered how far and wide the treason spread its tentacles. There was a good chance, if experience panned out, he may never discover the whole truth. It happened. The ones at the top were usually insulated by their power, status, money. Yes, he believed in cosmic justice; if they didn't get it now, it would find them soon enough. In the unfathomable span of eternity, the alpha and the omega, a man's time on the planet was less than an eye blink.

The savage, he heard, made his sales pitch. "Hey, look, take half. Just let me walk out of here. Never saw you, forgive and forget."

"You'll never walk again, but that's about to become the least of your problems."

"Two-thirds of what's in the bag, then, it's yours."

"You won't need the money where you're going."

That sparked enough angry life that Turner forgot about his pain and shot-up legs. "What's that supposed to mean?"

"It means there's not enough here to buy your way out of Hell."

"You're taking it all? Son of a mother… Did Cramnon send you? You're ripping me off?"

"I'm not with Cramnon."

"Then who?"

"I'm with me," Bolan said, and opened the black bag. One quick examination of the paperwork, and he knew exactly what he had.

"How did you— Don't tell me—you're just a thief."

Bolan chuckled. He didn't get it, but the soldier knew he never would. "Let's just call what I'm taking a donation to charity," he said, and wanted to leave it at that.

Mr. Compassion, though, pressed the matter. "Charity? What charity? What the—?"

"Funds for the families of all the victims you Alpha heroes butchered in two countries," Bolan said.

And the Executioner dragged him by the shoulder, away from rotor wash flaying the door. He slid him across the floor, dumped him up against the desk.

"Hamisi talked. It's your turn. The woman. Where is she and what is she to Cramnon?" Bolan read the defiance. He glanced at mangled legs no doctor could ever put back together.

Something happened to the soldier next. Perhaps he was contaminated, changed somehow by the most vicious, ruthless acts he'd ever seen—from the terror holocaust stateside, to Moctaw, to unprecedented mass murder with nerve gas—but Bolan felt a cold wall drop over the warrior inside. It washed away whatever shred of humanity he'd clung to up to that point. That long-held, ironclad rule that stilled his hand from inflicting pain on downed enemies walked with the ghosts of all the victims he'd left behind on this campaign. It was time to deal with these animals in terms they understood. And Bolan, who normally detested torture, drilled the savage in the leg with a kick, lashing the air with screams.

"The woman."

He cursed Bolan, the soldier not sure if he laughed or choked back tears. "Sure…I'll tell you…why not? This thing is bigger than you, bigger than Uncle Sam, bigger than all of us. Go after 'em, I'll send you, sure, you're just extra blue cheese on their salad."

"Your buddy, the late Moctaw," he said, and read through the flicker of fear and confusion, "said something like that. But here I am."

A hard pause, then he said, "I talk, what's in it for me?"

"A little less pain."

"Stick your pain. I want cash, I want my legs fixed up on your dime, I want—"

Two swift kicks loosened his tongue.

And Bolan listened to the details. It was pretty much what he suspected. Price, according to the savage, was meat on the hoof, human barter in the event a special ops force came hunting. Cramnon and company heard rumors for years about a supercovert agency—right under, they believed, the nose of the White House—that sanctioned the missions of these black ops supermen. Since Cramnon didn't like not knowing who potential enemies could be, he wanted to know what off-the-congressional-books agency she worked for. Alpha intended to hold her up, a trophy of sorts, for an American public, already shocked and outraged by 9/11 part two. They banked a perceived conspiracy among voting masses would make them rise up against a government lying about the attacks, infrastructure coming unglued, anarchy in the streets. They envisioned a toppling of the White House, a palace coup by the common man, the haves—those with guns, the power and money—slaughtering the have-nots. Reduce America to, say, a living hell like Liberia, Sierra Leone, pick an African country that was a step from plunging into the abyss. Why do that? The savage thought it was to cover their tracks, put the fear of Armageddon in their wake, take immediate heat off them. Long enough so they could vanish again, but who knew how Cramnon's sick mind really worked? As far as he believed, they were in it for the money. Maybe one or two exceptions, blood grudges, some statement they had a bigger package than the combined might of the U.S. military-intelligence powers, better not come after them or worse than what just happened in the States was on the way.

He was fading, the soldier knew, shock about to set in, the more blood that pumped from his legs. "Where is the woman?"

He shook his head. "I don't know. Thailand. Indonesia. In the bag…encrypted…"

"Where's Cramnon's next pit stop?"

"Jordan…another Bank of Islam…"

Bolan sensed he'd gotten all he could here, his thoughts locked on a plan of attack.

"Go on…."

Bolan drew a bead on his chest with the M-16. "Ten seconds, if you're a praying man."

The savage laughed. "I did…I prayed for money. It's walking out of here with you…just do it."

And Bolan did.

CRAMNON ANTICIPATED the next round of problems, but there was always a solution where there was will. He knew whatever deceit, violence, greed, lust, schemes and so forth beat in the human heart or churned in the darkest corner of the mind always revealed themselves in due course. With few exceptions, most human beings were weak, lacking in self-control and discipline, demanding their way, Sinatra without the song to back the balls. All that was required to uncover the secret heart was patience, observation, listening. That, and being tuned in to what made him tick.

Obviously they didn't think he could hear them. Both Kurds and a few of his guys were mumbling among themselves as he stood in the doorway, rotor wash in his ears, staring out at the night blurring past the Chinook. His crew sailed them, nap of the earth, below radar, the lights of distant villages all he wanted to see until they hit the border with Iraq.

It was galling enough, forced to blast the vault to shreds, bring it down on all the booty they couldn't carry, and the simmering anger he felt was burning a fast fuse toward wrath. Going in, luck holding, he figured to walk away with at least one-third. Twenty-two bags piled around the floor, and he was now hoping for one-quarter, though feared it was more like a fifth, if that. He was lopping a third of the haul off the top for himself and his surviving Alpha comrades. With Ramses, Samson and Dawson a memory, he figured his end fattened by another five to seven million. Problem was he still had buzzards to pay from the border to the Far East, SOBs with claws out, praying, he was sure, to whatever god they believed in he was still among the living.

He turned to the malcontents, grateful, if nothing else, for the wind sweeping away the stink of blood, sweat and the raw waste plastered all over the sewer rats. To the Kurds, in their tongue, he barked, "Shut your holes! I'll deal with you in a moment." To Garson, Wooly Mammoth and Tiny Tim he held his arms out, and switching to Russian said, "What?"

The huge, long-haired, bearded mammoth cleared his throat. "With all due respect, sir, we've been thinking…"

"Speak up, son, you're among friends here."

"We walked away with what, maybe a hundred mil?"

"More like half of that number, soldier, if we're lucky. And a few of you, despite my gentle rebuke, must have a bunch of whores waiting somewhere, since about four of these bags are stuffed with a whore's best friend. I got one bag alone half-loaded with heroin for Superfly there," he growled, nodding at Acheron.

They broke his stare, looking to each other, waiting for the other guy to pick up the ball.

"Say it," Cramnon rasped.

Garson showed a pair, sat up straight on his bag, squaring his shoulders. "Sir, we're down to seventeen shooters. We lost half our force. Do we, sir, really need the next round?"

Cramnon bobbed his head, laughing. "You guys, I love you like sons. So I'll state the obvious, let you figure it out and decide. First, the next job will not be near the total fuckup we put behind us. It's just us and them. No booby traps, half the numbers of guns, but the same amount of bread, all cash. We're backed on this round by in-country forces. It should be in and out. But you already know that.

"Second, I'm a whole lot older, been around this world long enough to know whatever you think you have now isn't enough. Sure, your cut looks sweet at the moment, now that you came through the fire. Now you're all nice and relaxed, big dreams just around the corner from becoming reality, time to party. But three, five years down the road, after you've pissed half or more of it away on a good time—which you have earned— then maybe sink the other half in cars, beachhouses, boats, you'll be kicking yourself in the ass, wishing you'd listened to the old man here and gone the distance. I don't want guys who bunt or hit-and-run on my team. I only want the home-run hitters, guys swinging to drop that five-hundred-footer in the upper deck. In other words, this is the ninth inning, bases loaded, two outs, down by three, two strikes."

Cramnon gave Acheron the nod. As his second in command made the move from behind the Kurds, Cramnon drew his Beretta. It was beautifully choreographed, details already worked out. Head shots down the line. Cramnon drilled a 9 mm bull's-eye through the first Kurd, launching him off his bag, Acheron pumping two lightning rounds into the backs of the skulls of Kurd Two and Three before they knew what was happening. Four and Five were leaping to their feet, bringing up the AKs when their brains were ventilated two ways.

Cramnon let his troops chew on their shock for a few moments, Garson and Wooly smeared in fresh blood, a Kurd twitching out at their feet, then told Acheron, "Throw that garbage off my chopper." He leathered the Beretta, looked at his rebellious sons as they fidgeted, glancing at each other, and said, "Now. Where were we?"

BOLAN HAD JUMPED into this war pretty much on his own, and he would finish it, however the outcome, solo. But even he knew he would need allies to guide him toward the finish line. He would need hardware, transportation, intel, some firepower from above while he hit the enemy from the ground.

On the satlink, while the Black Hawk was en route for the American air base at Incirlik, Bolan finished giving the news to Brognola. In short order, he laid out his plan to the big Fed, the Farm already working on the encrypted papers he'd faxed along, while his crew chief examined the flight charts. The Executioner told Brognola what he needed. He already knew it would take time to iron out logistics, hours that could maybe stretch into a full day. Beyond getting Colonel Stone armed with a presidential directive, there would be official feathers getting ruffled along the way, Brognola forced to play the game, but only up to a point before he spelled out the facts of life to whatever brass desk jockey didn't like getting bumped to second string. He didn't like the coming delay, but the soldier knew he had to ride out some time in limbo. There could be no mistakes from there on.

He was so close now, right on the enemy's bumper. He could feel them, out there, heading for Jordan, laughing all the way to the next Bank of Islam, middle finger to the world. He wasn't sure how he knew, but Cramnon and his Alpha brigands had made it out of Ankara. Figure a chopper ride, but they were in the wind.

Time, though, was a luxury neither Bolan nor Price had. The good news was Alpha would keep her breathing until they broke her. He didn't think the lady would cave quick, but everyone had a breaking point, a horror, some deep sleeping fear that, once discovered by a torture ghoul, would snap them. Forget the Hollywood nonsense, matinee idols up there, laughing off every kind of pain that could be inflicted while delivering the one-liners: everyone had a point of no return.

The Executioner may go to some extraordinary distance himself under torture, but Bolan knew he was no exception. In the flesh, there were no supermen.

The Executioner weighed the long silence on Brognola's end. Finally, the big Fed told him, "Make it happen."

And he was gone.

Bolan felt the miles pressing down, but there was time enough to get a second wind.

He would need it, he knew.

The worst was yet to come.

THEY WERE special ops, seasoned terminators he'd worked with before. Now they were loosely attached to the coalition forces across the border in Iraq, in charge of their own operations, carte blanche to hunt any snakes that had slithered away during Gulf II. Problem was, as he spotted the armed shadows hunkered in roosts up the dark foothills of Ararat, they knew how he operated.

Cramnon watched his troops, all heads back in the game, file for their jet ride. The Alpha leader looked at what he was about to finish paying for, as five bags were dumped at the feet of the big shadow he knew as Brick. The sleek bird was an ultra-long-haul executive jet, the Gulfstream V good for six thousand nautical miles. It was a record holder for distance without refueling, two BMW Rolls-Royce BR 710 engines, each good for 14,750 pounds of thrust, cruising altitude of forty-one-thousand feet. For their purposes, the cabin had been gutted with the exception of a wet bar, which had damn well, he thought, better be fully stocked.

Cramnon fired up a smoke, nodded up the slope. "Is that necessary?"

"I don't know, you tell me. You made it, but no Turner or Hamisi, and there's radio silence from King Midas."

Cramnon knew that, and he took it for a red flag, anxious to get out of Turkey. He'd known Turner since Vietnam, didn't think or didn't want to believe after cleaning up a loose end he would just skip off with four million of the payoff money. Stranger things had happened.

"I take a ride over to King Midas, what do you think I'll find there?"

Cramnon smiled, blew smoke in his face. "A couple of dead CIA ops."

"Then you answered your own question."

"You bring my hardware?" Cramnon asked.

"It's on the bird. Your satlink, too. Six bottles of Scotch whiskey I threw in."

Cramnon didn't have time for a pissing contest. "You're a good man, but I get the feeling the booze isn't on the house." He stared at the shadow, reading the eyes. "You want another bag."

"Like you, I have my own retirement plans."

Cramnon was tempted to start blasting away, but smiled, aware the homestretch was one sunrise away. "What the hell. I'm in a generous mood."

CHAPTER SIXTEEN

General Karim Fahwani was having a great day, but the greatest of all blessings was yet to come.

The sun was barely up over the Royal Military Palace on Hashmi Street in downtown Amman, but he was a habitual early riser these days. Beating the sunrise by two, three hours wasn't owed to virtue of clean living. Rather, it was the personal fortune he had amassed—about to multiply twentyfold or, with luck, good planning and cunning, skyrocket him to multibillionaire stature by day's end—that swelled him with invigoration to greet the morning, a song in his heart. Thinking of the future, he decided the electric tingle was more euphoria akin to divine and eternal ecstasy, power, invincibility than to any mortal savoring of good fortune.

Paradise on Earth belonged to him, his flesh made immortal by his own hand, his own wealth.

He settled back in the deep cushion of his leather chair, lightly scraped his salt-and-pepper goatee with the blade of his rhino-horn dagger. Life hadn't always been so blissful, but the son of a poor carpet weaver had early on understood the value of money, fleecing Western tourists with cheap trinkets costume jewelry, potions he hawked on the sly as aphrodisiac elixirs, the goods always stolen from local merchants. Even when he'd been a boy he suspected he was destined for greatness, the answer as simple as the willingness to follow through with ambition. Those who toiled with hand and followed the rules—and the tenets of Islam— stayed mired in poverty. Those who used their intelligence, knew how to maneuver even the most stubborn of human mules to do the dirty work, rose to the top, never looking back, stewing in regret. And these elite few among mere mortals were always destined, in the truth of the strong, to create, live and impose their own laws on others not as fortunate to be part of God's bigger plan.

He chuckled, staring beyond the enormous mass of his polished cedar desk, itching to share all this joy bubbling inside with one of his wives. Instead of a quick romp, waiting for the infidels to march through the massive gold-edged double doors, he settled on admiring the white marble floor, frescoed with birds, flowers and those white sandy beaches he no longer had to merely dream of. His Omani banker, in fact, had just informed him the cash down payment was delivered to the Saudi contractor, who would gladly begin construction for his palace compound in the Seychelles. Thinking he was blessed, Fahwani smiled at the murals of harems with their sultry vixens of light skin and blond hair—a personal but minor indulgence that had cost him a small fortune at the hands of a greedy Kuwaiti painter—on walls sheened by hand-carved Brazilian mahogany.

Life was surely heaven, he decided, not even the sky the limit, no end to how high he could soar.

Indeed, his service in the Jordanian military-intelligence power base had, at long last, perched him on a gilded throne. All that was left was to simply wade through the coming hours, deciding it best handled by suffering fools and barbarians gladly.

With the tip of his *jambiya* he carefully flicked a piece of lint off the white Thai silk of his military blouse. The motion jangled the medals and gold-plated ribbons festooning his chest. Never mind he'd never fired a shot in anger on the battlefield—it was the shooting he'd done behind closed doors, in the cellars of prisons after extracting information on enemies, that assured him power by the rule of fear. With so many willing to die martyrs, why risk the future he had worked so hard to pave?

He stared at the blueprints to the Bashad citadel compound, but his thoughts turned to the Seychelles. Perhaps marble flooring could be gilded with gold around the edges. Maybe the concrete at the bottom of the pool, on the drawing board to be about half the size of a neighborhood block, could be laced with embedded diamonds, perhaps some sapphire, rubies. Women loved their glittering gemstones. How large should he have his yacht built? Two hundred, three hundred feet? How many decks? Teak or mahogany? What to name it? Something simple, but majestic....

His daydreaming was abruptly shut down as seven mercenaries bulled through the doors. They bore M-16s with fixed grenade launchers, webbing, belts and pouches stuffed with grenades, extra clips. He was about to smile at the two massive nylon bags, the tribute that would surely take the sting out of their insulting entrance, then saw the filth they tracked and smeared as they marched over gleaming marble. They were drenched in sweat, lips cut in snarls. Their eyes were burning and angry, like wild beasts', and the black fabric of their combat suits was ripped and torn in spots, darker shreds revealing wounds. As they closed, he sheathed his dagger, then rose, wondering which of these animals would dare breach his domain, reeking of human waste. Had they dipped themselves or rolled around in dung on purpose to further offend? Anger stirring, he focused instead on the bottom line, aware of the fate that awaited them anyway.

He recognized only two mercenaries, and even then Fahwani had to stare hard at Abbadon and Acheron. It had been years since he'd first arranged the operation with the infidels, when Red Crescent and the Bank of Islam were but a dream. He was amazed how much the mercenary leader had changed. Abbadon was darker than he remembered, the hair, slick with sweat, flowing, a knotted mane, the picture in his mind of some ancient, wrathful Semite warrior rolling for his desk. In Russian he barked something at the creature, Acheron, with his bony ridges for eyebrows. They looked up at his soldiers, twelve M-16s aimed on them from the circular balcony.

Fahwani, as supreme leader, forced himself to remain a calm in the storm, waved a hand at the balcony. Two mercenaries brushed past Abbadon and dumped the bags on his desk. He smiled, kept his composure as they fanned out, flanking their leader. Carefully he considered his opening, perhaps an inquiry as to why there were only two bags, but these were dangerous beasts, and their assault rifles were shifting a noticeable few inches his way.

In Arabic, Abbadon told him, "Three conditions, nonnegotiable. One, you keep your toy soldiers clear of my plane—in fact, you keep them all bunkered in the command post out there. Twenty guns does not, in my mind, comprise a skeleton force as you put it, but you can call and fix that. Two, my guy flies the Apache, my guy drives the truck. Three, you will accompany one of my men and wait for our return at my jet. You will be free to go once we are ready to fly out. Any questions?"

Fahwani took his time, folding his hands behind his back, a stoic in the tempest. He bobbed his head, weighing the dilemma. They were a brazen lot, but they were also insane. Unless he agreed to their terms, they would start shooting, the knot in his belly warning him he would be the first. Trouble was, he needed, wanted them to storm the citadel as planned. He needed to hold back his own soldiers, aware every available gun under his command would be required if his scheme was to succeed. Let the mercenaries do all the dirty work, certain most of them would make it out and to the Abadda compound in the desert. Once he dealt with them out there, he could make his grand entrance into the rubble when the smoke cleared, proclaim victory against a major terror cell in Jordan. Add another medal to his blouse, a hero to both his country and the West, then quietly retire, vanish to the Seychelles.

Fahwani smiled. "And if I do not agree?"

"We walk. If you had stones as big as your greed, you would have done it yourself long before now."

He lost the smile. Beyond the rising anger he felt fear. They wanted to force his hand, eager to start a shooting war under his roof, if just to kill. He corrected his earlier judgment. These men were evil.

Pulling his stare off Abbadon's weapon, he called out and ordered one of his soldiers standing by a palm tree to take the bags from his desk, place them in the corner, put them through the money counters. While the order was being carried out, he was thinking how hot and uncomfortable the wait would be in their jet, wondering if they had air-conditioning when Abbadon, as if reading his mind, said, "You won't be there long enough to break a sweat. If it makes you feel safer, bring a few of your flunkies to keep you company. Help yourself to the wet bar."

"Most generous of you."

"It stops there. Maybe you caught some al-Jazeera this morning?"

"I heard something about a terrorist attack in Ankara. Hundreds dead in the streets, nerve gas. A military base leveled by an aircraft loaded with explosives. Nasty business."

"That would be us."

"But, of course."

"Your answer."

Fahwani spread his arms, smiling. "Why all the hostility? I accept." He watched as Abbadon began perusing the blueprints. "Oh, one thing you should be aware of. There is a possibility they may have mined the inner sanctum."

"That's nice," Abbadon said, appearing unfazed as he scanned the prints. "So's my plane."

ABDULLAH RAGHIB COULDN'T take his eyes off the hole in the floor. The more he dwelled on the numbers, what he could do with all that cash, the deeper his anger burned. Close to seven hundred million down there after the recent truck delivery, with a single bulb illuminating the opening like a beacon, and the dream seemed to speak to him, as if God called his name.

Commanding him to take it.

He hefted the block of C-4, then carefully placed it on his desk. Another hundred pounds, all of which could be primed to activate with the radio remote at his fingertips, but the decision to disobey the order from his lieutenant to mine the cash was made weeks ago. Besides, the man was in Damascus, counting yet more cash, he was sure, for deposit here under his watchful eye. Naturally, he trooped in his money counters to check the store, but they always arrived, same time every month, creatures of habit. Just in case they broke with protocol he was armed with a few reasonable excuses why the pallets and the short tunnel weren't primed to blow in the event of a raid.

Decision time. Ambition and dreams were useless, he thought, unless the holy warrior, who believed in a destiny far more glorious than the one outlined by his Syrian sponsors, cut loose the lion inside, seized initiative to unite all Muslims in total jihad. Armies needed weapons, the more—and the bigger the punch—the better. And martyrs had families to be compensated when they went to Paradise.

No more floundering about then, waiting on whatever the marching orders, sitting on other men's riches, watching his own dreams evaporate like dew in the morning sun. Not only that, with each monthly and growing tribute the general scarfed up for himself...

No more.

Whatever his decision, he knew his men were behind him. They were Jordanians, Syrians, a smattering of fedayeen bounty hunters with American blood on their hands, but they all agreed they were the ones, qualified by courage and commitment, who should put the money to use for the glory of Islam. Better than sitting around, sipping tea all day, dreaming of jihad while guarding all that wealth from vultures in uniform or armed thieves with greater ambition and greed than good sense.

He picked up his AK-47, then stood. He was looking at Jabel and Habib, two of his best soldiers, Syrians who had helped fedayeen ambush American occupiers, when the first explosion rocked the walls of the inner sanctum so hard he thought the floor was heaving beneath his feet. The Syrians looked silly to him all of a sudden, paralyzed by fear, dust showering them from the ramparts above. He was barking orders for them to go help secure the perimeter, vaguely aware how absurd that sounded since they were already under attack, then the cedar doors vanished before his eyes in smoke and flames.

Raghib was hitting the deck, rubble plowing through the Syrians, their screams spiking the air as the fireball roiled over them, when something blurred out of the smoke. It was less than a fraction of a glimpse of the slender object, but he pressed his nose to stone, wrapping his arms around his head. He screamed as the missile impacted on the far wall, the blast sucking the air out of his lungs in its fiery vacuum.

THE WAIT WAS ABOUT to pay off, far better than he could have hoped for. If nothing else, it might spare Bolan precious ammo when the time came to strike, depending on who and how many were grouped in the vicinity.

Crouched at the rear on the port side of the tanker truck, the Executioner waited for the lone demo man to make his way toward the last fuel leviathan in line. M-16/M-203 in hand, he gave his surroundings a final check, quickly reviewed and assessed.

His six was clear to the east, the direction where he'd hustled in from an undulating pocket of broken earth and thorny brush he'd claimed for a firepoint, the rising sun at his back to help shield his advance from wandering eyes. Considering that roughly two-thirds of Jordan was nothing but barren desert, there wasn't much in way of cover all around the compass. And other than a few Bedouins riding around in Toyotas, the soldier could have been the last man on Earth.

Only he wasn't. Cramnon and his Alpha brigands had been made from above. As far as satellites and spy-birds went, it was a plus the compound—on the west end of the Jordan panhandle, known to American intelligence as a notorious way station in the past for fleeing Iraqi fedayeen on the Baghdad highway—was plopped down on open terrain. Backed by White House clout, Brognola had moved all the red-tape mountains, parted all the right intelligence seas, nearly putting his own Gulfstream right into the fumes trailing Cramnon's executive jet. Using a special-ops coalition base at the Iraqi border, Bolan had been choppered in by Black Hawk and dropped off. A two klick or so hike at predawn using a handheld GPS, and he found he'd been just in time to watch the enemy depart the premises in a Humvee caravan, one transport truck in tow.

Gone for their second bank job.

In the only sensible way he could imagine, he wished them good luck, an expeditious and safe return to base. It was search and destroy from there on to the finish line, but Bolan was also fighting a war of attrition at the moment. Hoping to shave down the numbers here, he needed Cramnon breathing long enough to lead him to Price.

From what he could tell, Cramnon had left two goons behind to watch their jet, the logical assumption being that was where their loot from the Ankara job was stored. Reasonable conclusion number two was that Cramnon intended to stab his Jordanian sponsors in the back. Enter a demo man, mining the tankers, the ammo depot, two Black Hawks, a dab at the corner of the C-and-C building his first stop. While he wandered and fixed the charges, Bolan had spotted his comrade rolling toward the squat C-and-C station with its sat dishes and antennae, the hardman waving a cell phone at uniformed Jordanian soldiers. They were still arguing in Arabic when Bolan made his move.

The demo man was squatting, humming a tune, all smiles, pasting a fat gob of plastique under the rear wheel flap, checking the red light on his radio remote, when he either sensed the threatening presence or wondered about the shadow falling over him. Bolan allowed him to rise, the demo man clawing for his side arm, just enough height to lend the soldier extra wallop to the fist he hammered straight into that hawkish beak. Thrown with the impetus of cold anger, Bolan mashed his nose to pulp. There was nothing like that kind of pain, he knew, that would drop an enemy flat on his back, stunned to hell and sure to get his attention. The demo man began to moan, crimson streaming off his chin. Before he could scream, the Executioner reached down, squeezed his throat in a viselike grip.

"Nod if you can hear me."

He made strangled gagging sounds, his eyes popping with agony Bolan could only compare to grenades going off in his skull, but managed to bob his head.

Bolan kept the message simple. "Tell Cramnon I'm coming for the woman. Tell him if he harms her to take a look at you. A nose job will be as painless as it will get for Cramnon. Repeat that." Bolan loosened his hold, but the demo man had trouble pulling his thoughts together through the pain. "Your life depends on your memory." It took some effort, but the demo man gave it back to Bolan near verbatim. The Executioner took the radio remote, stood and drilled a kick off the demo man's jaw.

Tuned to the distant bickering, the Executioner began retracing his steps, his retreat blocked by the line of tankers. When the demo man came back to painful reality, realized the keys to the fireworks were in the hands of his assailant, Bolan knew there was a chance he would simply disarm the charges or remove them.

If it appeared that would happen, Bolan might just start the show without Cramnon. However the coming wait played out, the Executioner banked on Cramnon's greed and savage nature to get him back here in one piece.

There was any number of possibilities, Bolan decided, all of them worst-case for the enemy.

THREE HELLFIRES APPEARED to Cramnon to have eviscerated the guts of the citadel. The tower and ramparts were now being laid to waste by two more missiles, the heavy-metal thunder of the 30 mm chain gun raking the roof. Up there, he heard them scream, glimpsed the shredded doomed on the run, their arms windmilling as they were launched away from the boiling line of smoke. With luck, two-thirds of the standing force was taken out with the opening Hellfire shockers. Alpha

Two had the task of mopping up from the front, closing their end of the vise on the inner sanctum.

Almost home, getting closer with each yard, every bullet-riddled corpse.

Cramnon led the charge across the rear courtyard, punched through the smoking maw, tuned in to moaning, scuffling, hacking. And there he heard, then spotted the reeling armed shadows, fanned out in a neat line, human bowling pins just begging to get dropped. His M-16 spitting left to right, he swept the stream of 5.56 mm flesh-eaters in sync with his squad, all of them nailing maybe ten mauled as they staggered around the rubble that led to the inner sanctum.

Again, like the Ankara job, this hit had been in the planning for years. Every nook and cranny was known to Cramnon, his shock troops briefed so thoroughly they could have lived here with the terrorists all this time. The enemy inside—what was left—didn't know it, but Alpha had created them from the beginning, from the shadows, using cutouts, preying on the greed of their own Muslim blood. Even their weapons, whatever C-4 at their disposal, were most likely courtesy of Alpha.

The shooting began to wither on all points as Cramnon led the surge into the inner sanctum. He keyed his com link, taking a sitrep on Wooly Mammoth's end. Henley was down, but otherwise no casualties. He checked with Loco and White Lightning, his Apache crew informing him they had the fort under control from up top. As he stepped through the drifting smoke, he listened to sporadic bursts of weapons fire, but knew, thanks to his tank killer, or in this instance, his citadel-crushing collosus, it was over. Weeping for the enemy, laughter for the victor.

As he passed out the standing orders to secure the perimeter, then called in his bulldozer, the same queasy feeling of anxiety he'd experienced in Ankara churned his gut. He found the C-4 in the rubble, kicked around the pulped sack at his feet and found, lo and behold, the radio remote. He doubted its range would reach all the way out into the desert, but he was sure it was enough to keep the Jordanian wolves at bay until their truck was stuffed and they were on the joyride out of Amman.

The stone slab, leading to the tunnel, he found, was already up, inviting them to come down. It felt too easy, too good to be true, but believed he read the score here. They were either warned in advance of the attack or they were cleaning out the store for themselves, looking to chase their own dreams.

Well, dung happened.

Arming two frag grenades, he pitched them into the hole, pulled back. Just as they crunched, Cramnon heard the thunder rolling their way, the floor shuddering. The shovelhead burst through smoke first, then the fanged remains of the entrance exploded as Acheron barreled the length of the transport into the sanctum. Cramnon barked for Ryker and Garson to start arming the C-4, bring it down, the others racing to snatch the body bags from the back of the rig. Acheron was out the door, snarling for them to hustle up, but Cramnon was already descending the short flight of steps. M-16 parting the smoke, he found himself alone in the tunnel. He stared at dozens of pallets, wire bands holding down stacks of U.S. hundred-dollar bills that reached chest high. It would take a closer inspection, but something told him there were no booby traps to fear.

Laughing, he took the wire clippers from his hip.

CHAPTER SEVENTEEN

Bolan was reasonably sure if Crammon and brigands knew of the story they would most likely scoff at it as so much mythical nonsense. As far as the legend went, the Executioner was of another mind.

Perhaps two hundred klicks or so as the buzzard flies to the southwest, near the southern shores of the Dead Sea, archaelogists had discovered shaft tombs, vast cemeteries, ruins and countless human remains. According to that elite among the scientific community and Bible scholars who spent entire lifetimes dissecting fact, fiction and the supernatural, there was strong and indisputable evidence of sudden, violent mass death on the plains there, dating back some twenty-three-hundred years. Whether the Amorites, the ancient peoples of the plains, fell victim to an earthquake that spewed forth bitumen and other natural gases, igniting an explosion of nuclear dimensions, was open to debate among the wise men. What they knew was that a mysterious calamity had wiped the sister cities of Numeira and Bab edh-Dhra off the face of the Earth, with hardly a trace they ever existed.

Today's world knew them as Sodom and Gomorrah.

For his purposes, Bolan found the past and the present had something in common. One, he was poised to rain down fire and brimstone, a catastrophe of epic proportions. Two, and this sealed their fate, he was one hundred percent certain he wouldn't find one righteous man down there in the open compound.

Stretched out on his stomach, M-16/M-203 at his fingertips, he weighed the setup, gauging range to targets as the four Hummers and transport truck lumbered into view. A flick of the switch on the handheld detonator, and the red light flashed on. All systems go. Beside the Stony Man warrior, mounted on bipod and ready to be pulled from the flimsy cover of thorny brush, was the multiround projectile launcher. Factory made and handtooled at the Farm by John Kissinger, the stainless-steel weapon, nicknamed Little Dragon, could pump out seven 81 mm warheads in seconds flat. In this age of high tech, with warriors looking for every conceivable edge on the battlefield, Kissinger had added laser sight, warheads with microchips that could home in on the beam, guide themselves to target, with but a few inches as margin of error. All Bolan had to do was line it up, adjust the azimuth to distance, the digital readout box on the side computing the math for him.

The soldier fisted sweat out of his eyes. A little discomfort the least of his concerns, he still felt buff-colored fatigues pasted to flesh, the length of him broiling

in 110-degree heat, heard flies he knew were the size
of golfballs and black as night buzzing in his ears. The
three hours and change wait since the demo man had
scraped himself off the ground had been agonizing, to
say the least, Bolan ready the whole time to light up
the compound, start the blitz without Cramnon on
stage.

It didn't appear he would have to strike up the band
without his lead savage.

For whatever reason. Demo Man had shuffled back
to the executive jet with comrade in tow, both of them
seeming to forget about the charges, the Jordanians retreating inside the C-and-C post, staying put. No sign
of those two since, but now they reemerged. They
lugged along a smallish figure in a white uniform by
the elbow, a chest of medals on his blouse sparkling
against the harsh sunlight, two armed soldiers in Jordanian colors falling in behind.

Game time.

Frantic commotion began in shouting earnest,
Bolan taking a rough head count as the Hummers
braked, spooling dust over the C and C, two big men
disgorging from the transport's cab. With his field
glasses, the warrior framed the long-haired dark man
first, since he was bellowing out all the orders.

It was Bolan's first look at Cramnon in the flesh.
The Alpha leader didn't look anything like the photo
in his Special Forces jacket, the few intel shots the
Farm had managed to scrounge up through various
sources, but Bolan himself was familiar with the magic
of plastic surgery. Beyond the facial alterations, the

eyes—cold, reptilian but savage—gave Cramnon away. No question that was the animal who had betrayed uniform and country. Committed mass murder. Ruined untold lives. And changed whole nations forever while intending to vanish and live it up with his stolen millions, and perhaps torture Price into revealing the truth about herself and Stony Man Farm.

Bolan decided to wait to see how the drama played out. Sensing the mounting tension, he hoped the cannibals, in their greed and anger, began eating one another. It would make his butcher's work that much easier when he waded in, began cutting them down from the blindside.

He watched as black body bags were tossed from the transport, dumped on the ground. Cramnon's cutthroats hefted them up, hustling off, best they could, strapped down as they were with what he figured was two to three hundred pounds of loot in each load. Bolan began to further assess the situation. The fact Cramnon had left his jet far to the south, turbofans now whining to life and spewing dust, told Bolan the Alpha leader was expecting trouble from his Jordanian inside help, poised to turn the grounds into a raging inferno any second. Why his beasts of burden were made to haul the body bags about the length of a football field was a question mark. Bolan's hunch was Cramnon didn't want the sleek bird anywhere near the line of fire and coming conflagration. Putting himself in Cramnon's head, that made sense. Nice clean getaway, leave behind another mess, laughing all the way.

Before Mr. Clean wrenched his arms free of the escort, Bolan had a good idea who he was, but looked anyway. General Fahwani, Bolan knew, had been under the microscope of American intelligence for some time. Somehow he doubted the general was as virgin pure as his pressed dress whites. Before the dust settled, though, the soldier intended to take the man off the CIA's rumor list as a supporter, arms dealer and strategist for various Muslim extremist groups. Whatever his cut of the bank job, he could take it to Hell.

Nose Job, Bolan then saw, got the avalanche rolling. The soldier didn't need to be a lip reader to see his message was delivered. He watched as Cramnon bared his teeth, eyes widening with rage, the Alpha leader looking set to shoot the messenger when Fahwani began flapping his arms, railing about something, cutting into the act.

Bolan was reaching for the multiround launcher when he heard the heavy bleat of rotor blades to the west. A small caravan of Humvees, he found, flying the Jordanian flag, barreled onto the grounds. As the Apache warbird soared past the caravan, the Executioner hugged the ground, aware his cover was flimsy, at best. If they painted him on their screens, if they forced him to unload Little Dragon, bring it down with a warhead or two to the rotor blades, thus tip his hand...

Suddenly the Apache went into a hover, the pilot spinning it around, the one-eighty aiming chain gun and Hellfires at the new arrivals. The pilot dipped the warbird down to near ground level. Bolan spotted Fahwani breaking away from Cramnon, waving his arms and shouting at the Humvees.

The Executioner looked back at Cramnon, bent on keeping him painted on his own screen, just in time to find the Alpha leader's M-16 flaming a short burst, Nose Job hitting the ground. The savages, he knew, were breaking under the strain.

Bolan turned his sights on the Apache. The flyboy had settled the warbird nearly on top of the tankers.

Picture perfect, it couldn't get any better than that, the Executioner decided, and picked up the hell box.

ANGER AND PANIC MOUNTED into a whirlwind of babble and confusion, his ears buzzing with the noise of men on the edge of erupting into blind violence.

And even Cramnon suddenly felt a twinge of deepening anxiety, corkscrewing to fear the more he stood in front of the transport, chewed on the message, scoured the desert.

Cramnon then stared down at Tupler, formerly of NEST— Nuclear Emergency Search Team—when the warning bells clanged even louder. He was forgetting something critical, racking his thoughts, wondering what he was overlooking at the moment. What was it? he thought, angry with himself but not knowing why. Aware only that all it took was one mistake at this juncture, and all of them were eighty-sixed from a world of dreams they had forged through blood, guts, balls and sheer iron warrior will. Oh, but he nearly sounded a bitter laugh, recalling how the second heist had been easy as swatting a fly. Now this hemorrhoid, no, this potential unknown human aneurysm about to blow the gasket on his world.

He held his ground, strange how he found it all intriguing, hanging there, waiting for the hammer to drop. They were humping bags as fast as they could, Fahwani bleating at his own soldiers to stand fast, everything was under control, but Cramnon could feel the storm coming. Impossible, he thought, searching the endless desert, north, south and east. One guy, or so the late and unlamented Tupler claimed, had breached the perimeter. Which, by itself, was no great feat, since any bedouin could wander in with his camel. Had to be a whole frigging strike team out there, but where? The sea of baking sand and grit was broken up in spots by brush, rocky tables, little dips and gullies carved out by Ma Nature. Then there was heat shimmer obscuring any clean surveillance. He could stand there all day and never know who or how many phantom gunmen were out there, hunkered down until they announced themselves, of course, by cutting loose with automatic weapons and whatever other hardware at their disposal. He felt the hackles rise on the back of his neck, wondering if a ghost sniper had him framed right then in crosshairs.

Whoever the SOB, he'd mashed his man's nose in and sent Tupler on bended knee with a message that still galled him, sparking anger to his bones as he ran the words back through his head. Whoever the mystery man, he knew the woman, wanted her back, not a scratch on her beautiful ivory model's hide. Take a look at Tupler? As painless as his punishment would get if the woman was harmed?

Oh, but who was this ballsy rotten...

Friend? Lover? Co-worker? Which, if his suspicions panned out on the latter about the woman, he was some sort of black ops. Under different circumstances Cramnon knew he'd eagerly accept the challenge, but there was something sinister, an angry justice perhaps meant to be handed out to him, express delivery by Mr. Balls.

The warning bell slammed into a gong as he wandered his stare over the Apache, the warbird tucked up against the tankers. Fear shooting toward panic, Cramnon moved like a bullet, frisking Tupler, head to toe. Heart thundering in his ears, he spotted Blackbeard, the second half of his troops hustling back for another load. Cramnon rolled up to him, rasped, "The detonator box, where is it?" Cramnon nearly shot him when he pulled out the cell phone. "That's for the jet, you stupid—"

Cramnon felt his legs buckle. The world seemed to spin in his eyes, as he sensed the SOB watching, perhaps even enjoying the show, the terror he'd created. Now he knew what he'd forgotten—or rather what his watchdogs had neglected to tell him.

The roaring curse was rising in his throat as he locked eyes on the Apache, flickered his stare to the tankers. He was about to scream for someone to get the truck out of there when the world blew up before him.

EVEN THOUGH HE WAS a good three hundred feet from ground zero, Bolan was forced to turn away from the holocaust as the supernova flashed and roared. The noise alone, a peal of a thousand thunderclaps booming in sonic unison, ripped through his senses. The superheated wind was on the way, but he risked a glimpse as the firestorm meshed into one squall that swept rolling waves of fire across the compound. He hung in there another second, squinting, watching as the Apache was hurled in the direction of the Jordanian motor pool. Like flimsy cracker boxes the Hummers were crushed, lifted and tossed into the air. Those boiling titans kept washing on, stem to stern over the Jordanians, incinerating flesh and metal, melting everything down, Bolan could be sure, to steaming goo. As the fiery hull of the Apache broke apart inside the storm, two, maybe three Hellfires were launched into the Jordanian hell downrange. Whether dead or wrathful finger already on the button fired the load, it didn't matter to Bolan. The more death and horror unleashed, the better to serve what lightning fast became a vengeful calamity he intended to wade into shortly.

Bolan saw the sky raining fire and brimstone all over the compass, and hugged the earth. He heard wreckage, whistling with the flames, pelt the ground before him. Through the roar he caught the chorus of hideous shrieks. Earth shaking, sky blazing, Bolan hauled over Little Dragon. Searching the burning wasteland for Cramnon, the soldier found the brigand's bank on wheels taking hits from flaming bats of various size. Canvas, baked bone-dry by heat and sun, ignited like fire leaping from a propane grill. Flaming human comets—maybe three in all—were zigzagging, thrashing on the ground down there, then Bolan spotted another torch job as he leaped from the transport's bed. Incredibly, that fiery human meteor was clutching a booty bag as he hit the ground, thrashing, wailing. Bolan was disgusted, angered by the sight, but he wasn't the least surprised.

The Executioner readied Little Dragon to add yet more grief to all that wailing and gnashing of teeth.

"THE BAGS! Get the Goddamn bags!"

Cramnon saw Acheron hesitate, smoke boiling over his craggy mug, flames licking at him from the bed. The shrieking of those torched already by raining fire a lancing din in his ears, Cramnon elevated the decibels, roaring, higher and higher, to get the bags.

It was unbelievable, he thought, sickened by more than just the stink of roasted flesh. It was beyond all comprehension, beyond all horror, his wrath shooting to new meteoric heights not even he imagined himself capable of feeling. They'd walked with the mother lode, fifty bags altogether. A conservative guess put each individual load between seven to ten million. He was thinking—hoping, with what was already muled to the jet—at least fifteen to twenty loads could be saved before the truck blew, or the SOB responsible for this disaster decided to throw another fastball aimed for his face.

The Alpha leader was rolling toward four bags, smoldering and dumped on smoking earth, Acheron's curse trailing him as he threw himself up and into the roiling caldron, when the warning bells Klaxoned in his skull, louder than ever. The truck's topped-out fuel tank, for one thing, was sure to blow. On the march to grab whatever he could off the ground, he witnessed flames engulfing the rig, top to bottom, stem to stern in a racing dance that seemed to have angry life all by itself.

Two, three bags, he saw, came hurtling from the bed. Acheron was bellowing curses, flying out of the smoke next. He hit the ground rolling, slapping at his shoulders where minibonfires were eating fabric. Cramnon decided to leave his comrade to smother the fire his own damn self, as he got busy stomping out flames trying to devour their way through the closest bag. Demons were still screaming from nearby when he hefted up his load, turned to bolt, shouting at his men to grab some loot. Maybe three or four fiery things, he then saw, gyroscoped before collapsing beneath smoke so black and thick Cramnon didn't think he could find a cruise ship inside those palls. He heard a pitiful moan reaching him from somewhere, thought he recognized Garson's voice, pleading to him for help. Looking over his shoulder, he spotted the kid—or what was left of him. No arm, legs chewed to crimson ruins and half his face sheared to the bone; with Garson pumping out blood by the quart, Cramnon left him to bleed out. At that point, whatever plunder could be salvaged far outweighed the lives of whoever was left standing.

M-16 in one hand, grappling to hold the load on his shoulder and fanning the sea of fire in search of the bastard who dropped the sky on him, Cramnon weaved a path, little better than a snail's pace, through raining debris. With a lumbering one-eighty he took a head—

or, rather, a bag count. Ten fat ones, including his own, that was it. There weren't enough human beings under the sky, he knew, to take the fury burning him up and stay on their feet. In fact, he decided if he had his finger on the doomsday button right then he'd just as soon vaporize the whole sorry lot of six billion on the planet. Just who was the stupid sack of walking feces who claimed no man was an island anyway?

He was about to face front when he glimpsed the streaking blur, a slender meteor homed in on the transport. Even as it cut an arrow-straight line through the smoke, he cursed, braced himself. He heard the blast, but the shock wave was bowling him down to eat dirt before he knew it. For several moments, as unforgiving objects banged off his shoulders, he feared he would pass out, his troops sure at that point to pass him by, worried only about their own hides and whatever cut of loot they could carve out of his end. With no help from the others, he staggered to his feet, took another quick bag count. Blood and sweat in his eyes, Cramnon saw Blackbeard reeling from out of yet another firestorm, his head engulfed in a flaming halo. Roaring, Acheron bulled into Blackbeard, somehow wrestled the bag off his shoulder, then moved on with his twin burden.

And Cramnon felt his shuffle grind to a halt.

Watching the sky rain down flaming confetti, Cramnon felt his rage melt to sickening frustration. He turned away just as the transport's fuel ignited, the fireball puking out a few geysers sure to vaporize whatever was left in the bed.

Son of a…

Then the answer hit him as he found his jet ride, waiting and unscathed. One last angry search down that ocean of fire, thinking he spotted an armed and upright figure rolling behind the flames, Cramnon knew he'd make it out of here.

He knew why.

And he knew exactly what he had to do.

GENERAL FAHWANI HEARD himself sobbing, the pain so intense he vomited again. On his elbows, his legs trailing him like two blocks of wood, he dragged himself ahead. Two feet of crawling, and he began retching at the overpowering fumes of his own vomit, the ripe stench of cooking meat and the stink of loosed bowels sliming around inside the seat of his trousers, trickling down useless deadweight. Through stinging tears, he looked at the gnarled flesh before him, his hands little more than charred stubs, the flesh on his fingers seeming to melt off bone before his eyes. Even worse, if that was possible, his face and head were burning up against a squalling wind that felt as if it washed and seared him with all the heat from a blast furnace. He was terrified that whatever hideous injuries he now found, far worse disfigurement awaited his eyes, if and when he ever looked into a mirror again.

He buried his face and wept.

Another round of bile squirting up his throat, he looked up, hoping someone was still alive somewhere, close enough so they could help him. He would pay whoever came to save him all the money they wanted.

What was that? With one clubbed mitt, he slapped at blood and sweat in his eyes, straining to focus on something that appeared to float on heat shimmer just beyond the next barrier of flames. No, not something, but someone!

"Help me. Please!"

Whoever it was, the general watched him drift through the smoke and flames, the tall dark figure seeming to part the fire with his very presence. Impossible, he thought—it was trauma, perhaps shock setting in, thrusting a mirage in his eyes.

But he sensed a presence closing on him. He heard himself bleat some warped noise between a laugh and sob. He saw the boots next, slowly panned up the figure. He felt his eyes widen at the sight of the M-16 with fixed grenade launcher. For some reason—perhaps it was the way in which the figure stopped, not calling to him or reaching down to help—he felt hope fading. One of his own soldiers would have surely helped him, at least spoken by now. Abbadon? One of his jackals? No, if they were still alive, they wouldn't bother with any course of action but escape.

"Please, I have money…. Name your price…. Help me…. Save me…."

He felt the muscles in his neck twist in pain, as he fought to lift his head. Why didn't he speak? Why did he just stand there?

"Please…."

Another inch or so, raising his chin…there. He wanted to bring the face into view, but felt his stare freeze on the dark stranger's eyes. They were two orbs, ice blue, he believed, but burning down with some unspoken thought. Or what? Judgment?

The offer of money was nearly out of his mouth when he saw the M-16 rise up.

Fahwani heard himself scream just as the muzzle flamed.

CHAPTER EIGHTEEN

Unless they changed plans, Acheron knew they were sunk. And he wasn't in any big hurry to cut the world's population by one by stepping off the planet, making a little more elbow room for the poor starving unwashed masses that comprised more than eighty percent of humankind, and that he would never have to trouble with. Not when there were the spoils of the heist of the ages to spend, his cut of the job sure to land him in the exclusive company of high-price-tagged prostitutes. And there would be a sea of booze, every rich man's toy he could dream of owning and then some he was sure he didn't even know existed.

Later.

The pressing dread question at the moment was where it all went from here. Land, air or sea, he feared the end was coming. Next question, then, was how to stave off the inevitable, get his kicks while the getting was still good.

But do what exactly? he wondered. Chart a new

course? Buy their own Third World dungheap some-where along the way to the Far East? Follow through with Cramnon's blackmail ace of spades? Purchase a couple of nukes instead of a cache of VX? Maybe bar-gain for an ICBM or two, warheads packed with an-thrax, smallpox or botulin? Think the North Koreans they were supposed to meet when they landed in Ma-laysia would throw in a little extra something for old times' sake, seeing as Alpha had sweetened their own WMD pot in the past?

Fat chance, he thought. Pyongyang was greedier, more power hungry and every bit as vicious as the lot of them put together.

Hell, no, he didn't have the answer, and it sure looked to him as if Cramnon didn't, either. Sucking down another fat swallow, straight from the whiskey bottle, Acheron stared ahead, wondering where it was all headed, but feared he knew the answer in that re-gard already.

It was going to hell. It was just a question of when and where the hammer would fall.

Another one down the hatch to take some more sting out of the burns on his shoulders and back of the neck, he started wondering where the smack was stashed. Cramnon, he knew, might have liked pain as the great motivator, but he was no fan of that concept. Let the SOB stew in his boots for a while, fire racing all over every pummeled, sore inch, no matter how soused he got. He needed a heavy dose of some good stuff, heroin sure to do the trick, drift away, forget the pain and the nerve-racking uncertainty of the future.

Before him, his back to the cockpit door, he looked at the bags stuffed into the cabin, knowing it was buried somewhere. Wedged into the bulkheads, port to starboard, the pile nearly touched the ceiling, just about standing room only. Deciding he didn't have the energy to start tearing through the loads, he shifted his weight on the bag he used for a stool. He fired up a smoke, the soft whine of the turbofans filling the silence, but seeming somehow to hurl his anger and fear back in his face. The longer Cramnon stood, bent over, hands to bulkhead, staring out the porthole at the shadows lengthening over the Indian Ocean, the more he drank, the deeper his anger burned.

How many hours now had they been in the air? How many time zones crossed? Since refueling at the prearranged pitstop in Sri Lanka, two bags handed over to some greasy general from Colombo, reality took on a shadowy blur. Hell, they weren't even ten minutes in the air, zipping across Iraq, when they picked up the first fighters. The jets might be long gone now, but they were the biggest damn red flag he'd ever seen. So much for all their inside help on the ground, Turner either dead or talking, a few others who'd taken their money nowhere to be found in crunch time. Big Brother knew, and he would shadow them to the ends of the earth. Worse, he was sure they'd be waiting when they touched down on the other end.

Then what? Go down in some last-stand blaze? All that dying-on-their-feet-like-lions crap Cramnon threw at them no longer cut it.

It all boggled his mind now. They had started out

with thirty-four guns, a lot of them young guys, kids in comparison to the original Alpha Six. Not quite wet behind the ears, but enough putty around the edges to have molded them for the job. Sure, the civilian world had snubbed them, branding them losers, misfits, good for nothing except when the civs needed someone else to walk into the lion's den on foreign battlefields in lieu of their quaking tails and puckering sphincters. Still, those guys had been part of the team, gone the distance. They had been warriors. Now they were down to nine—excuse him—eight shooters, just in case Cramnon had any more dreams on tap, what would prove fatal delusions of grandeur.

Speaking of lethal bottom lines, Acheron looked at Tiny Tim. The former Army Ranger had just groaned his death rattle, limp weight sliding down a few bags, jaw slack, eyes wide, kid looked to him as if he was amused or relieved. Wherever he was now, Acheron wondered if Tiny was laughing at all of them, anxious for the rest of his comrades to join him in Hell.

He pulled his M-16, cocked and locked, an inch closer to his leg. Cramnon was losing it, no shrink needed to tell him that. Acheron watched his eyes flicker, back and forth, like pinballs, nose to glass, that thousand-yard stare searching for phantoms in the clouds.

And Acheron never thought he'd see the day, but one SOB had rattled the man's cage. Thinking back to the carnage in the Jordanian desert, he was positive, as hard as it was to stomach, that only one man had sent them running, tails tucked for the first—and for him—

the last time. Beyond the money, he still had his pride. Too late for hindsight, whoever the nameless faceless shooter, he had a bad gut feeling they would see him again.

The one-man wrecking crew wanted the woman back. Somehow, Acheron doubted it was that simple, would appease the bastard. Besides, Cramnon had been obsessed with her long before they grabbed her in the garage. One hundred and one "if's" shot to mind. The biggest of which was would they even be in such dire straits if they'd left the woman alone in the first place.

In that spooky way he had of making others think he could, in fact, read minds, Acheron found the Alpha leader suddenly looking at him, measuring. He turned to the others, pinning them with a look Acheron read, loud and clear: "You're on with me, or you're gone."

As battered, beat, unwashed and with more than a few nasty cuts and dings still running blood, the others came alive, some fear in their eyes before they broke Cramnon's penetrating stare. They went back to smoking, hitting their bottles with renewed vigor, probably, Acheron figured, hoping they lived long enough to spend some hard-earned money.

Cramnon, he knew, was clinging to other plans. Or maybe not. Perhaps the man was hatching his own scheme. All Acheron had to do was look at what was churning through his own mind right then to know there was no such thing as dark secrets among them.

He found Cramnon back at his staring duties, but he saw something change in his expression. Was it fear? Terror? Don't tell him, there was a squadron of fighters on the wing right then, fingers on the button, ready to blow them out of the sky.

Acheron was about to say something, then it hit him what was happening. With the overhead lights striking the porthole and against the thick veil of darkness outside, there was nothing out there to look at, other than stars, if he could even see those if they were running under thick cloud banks. What the hell, Cramnon, he was now sure, was staring at his own reflection. The Devil only knew what the man was thinking. Acheron shook his head, took another long pull from the bottle.

This game was dead.

If he was thinking about going for number one, he could be sure every gun under that roof was plotting the same thing.

Maybe not the kids, too young to know any better, but Acheron had been with Cramnon from the beginning. He knew better than to turn his back on the man.

It was time to bail, he decided, take the money and run.

It COULD HAVE BEEN anywhere from one to two days she'd been shoved into the darkness of a corner room in the bamboo-and-thatch hut. With no light, she thought she could measure time by the ebb and flow of wild birds cawing, the howls and screams of monkeys, the chitter of insects beyond the wall. But the racket of the rain forest outside, she discovered, didn't hold to any single pattern, all the eerie noise filtering into the room near unabated, with brief periods of diminished crescendo. Night or day, what difference did it make? No idea where on Earth she was, but her mind was set to make a move.

To do something.

Even still Barbara Price clung to hope that help was on the way, but she figured to help herself in the meantime. It was a jungle out there—that was about all she knew—but the animals were right under the roof. Three of them, to be exact, a dark bearded man in a silk suit jacket she took for Middle Eastern. Then the two pilots, the cocky one with the perpetual leer who fancied himself a swordsman, no doubt, checking in on her two, sometimes three times a day. He'd bring her a canteen, mangos and broth laced with fish meat, then hover around. She could almost read his mind. Whatever restraint kept him chained—Cramnon most likely—was cracking with each swaggering entrance, every one of those "hey, baby," smiles. Sick bastard, he kind of reminded her of her ex-husband, another wandering wanna-be swordsman. To her, men like that fell way short in more departments than whatever they deluded themselves as carnal prowess. Always on the prowl, looking to prove something, but proving they were really nothing at all, flaming assholes, all show. Beyond no balls, there was no heart, no honor, no man inside.

Well, she was no damsel in distress, no fawn frozen in the headlights. Next time Swordsman wanted to lay on the charm...

She heard a voice beyond the door. She stood,

listening, stretching a moment to work out the kinks in her legs and arms. It sounded like Swordsman out there. Talking to himself? He was going on and on, alternating tones between beseeching and praise. That meant the other two were outside, perhaps sitting in the jet. Or maybe taking one of the four jeeps she'd seen near the dirt runway slashed through the jungle out for a spin.

She didn't trust whatever sounds she heard Swordsman make, thinking he was on the verge of snapping, ready to bull into the room. Alone, in the jungle, she sensed the pilot would just as soon let dark animal impulses take over, despite the fear of Cramnon.

She tried the wooden handle. It lifted from the catch, the door parting an inch or so. Her heart raced, sure they were setting her up, making any possible escape look too easy, daring her to try. Or perhaps not, in their arrogance thinking her too scared, too weak, too female.

She pinned the direction of Swordsman's voice. To her immediate right then, parting the door a few more inches, hope, desperation and anger coiling her limbs into a giant spring.

Then she caught a few words out there in the hut. And couldn't believe what she heard, though somehow wasn't really all that surprised. Swordsman was praying for the safe return of Cramnon, imploring whatever god he thought he believed in for delivery of his money.

She went through the door, found him on his knees, back turned. He was unclasping his hands, head swiveling as Price gathered steam, cut the six-foot distance in two shakes. She saw Swordsman smile, start to rise, reaching for the shoulder-holstered Beretta, expression and slow-motion move telling her this was nothing he couldn't handle. Propelled by anger and disgust, she drilled him a kick, square up under his jaw. Whether weakened by exhaustion or the blow delivered with such unthinking savage force, Price lost her balance. She was on her back, scrambling to her feet, Swordsman snarling curses, when she felt the arm sweep through her ankle.

She was down again, lashing out with a kick when he fell on her like an enraged wild beast, blood and spittle spraying her face. She met his snarls with a growl that unleashed all the raw fury and desperation she felt pent up for days. As he straddled and pinned her to the floor, Price thrust her bound hands up. She dug her fingers into eyes lit with savage intent, the spear job rewarding her with screams. He grabbed one hand, tearing it away, shrieking and cursing, but she was sure the other eye was all but plucked. The open-hand slap flew out of nowhere, slammed her flush on the cheek, blasting bells in her eyes. She held on, digging, twisting, his bellows cleaving her brain, blood spattering her face. A hand was wrapped around her throat next, the bastard squeezing the life out of her, the air seeming to vacuum back into her lungs.

She threw her hands up, clawing for the other eye, determined if she was going to die, like this, at this bastard's hand, he would rue the moment in seething hate, trapped in a dark world the rest of his miserable life.

She was fading, dying quick, she knew, the world fading to a shimmering blur when she heard the crack of a pistol, nearly on top of her. She felt the hot spray of blood on her face, deadweight collapsing on her. Gasping, rolling the body off her, Price looked up, and found half of Swordsman's prayers had been answered.

THE MOUNTAIN HAD been moved.

Whether it was simple arrogance, a feeling of supreme invincibility or a subconscious death wish on their part, Bolan didn't know or care, but the enemy had practically drawn a map, complete with signs pointing the way. Between the Farm breaking Cramnon's coded flight charts, Brognola and the Man marshaling every available military and intelligence resource in Southeast Asia, the Executioner had nearly dropped in on their back door at the end of a six-hundred-foot combat jump from the C-130, landing at the edge of a mangrove swamp near the Perak River. With clear skies the past eighteen to twenty hours over the Perak State of Malaysia, satellite imagery had painted the way, layout of the enemy lair and numbers.

Whatever local authorities they'd greased to carve out their base here in the jungle, Bolan thought, their money wouldn't save them. Whatever their dreams they'd never see them become reality. With the long ride from Jordan to get it here over, the end was upon his enemies. Now, maybe two-thirds around the planet from where the campaign began for him, the Executioner was in an element so familiar it felt as old as the jungle itself.

With two-thirds of the Malayan peninsula shrouded in jungle, it was believed to be the oldest rain forest known to man, dating back some 130 million years. A Methesulah in the span of aeons against South America and Africa, this was where Bolan determined to lay waste to the rest of the most evil SOBs he'd come up against in recent, or even distant memory.

The Executioner had come to bring lamentation enough to spare the damned who'd gone before them.

His first target came wandering toward the motor pool, M-16 leading his stroll. A crouching lion in thick prehistoric vegetation, Bolan went utterly still. M-16/M-203 piece on the ground, the commando dagger in hand, the soldier knew he was invisible at the edge of the jungle, a ghost in black war paint, one with the night. Brigand One's comrades were out there on the dirt runway, barking at him to get over to the jet and help them hump some bags. Four shadows were outlined in cabin light, a string of flares going down the runway toward the Quonset hut, and Bolan already had his next move mapped out.

Brigand One ignored his pals, two of them lumbering off with double loads, hurling soft curses his way in response to his middle finger. Bolan read the face, knew the hardman's animal instincts warned him he wasn't alone. It had been close, mining the four jeeps with a gob each of C-4, silently melting back into the jungle before Brigand One decided to come to seal his doom.

He started on the far side of the motor pool, peeking and bobbing, weapon fanning, this way and that. The hardman was working his way down the line when

Bolan pitched a stone about the size of his hand, bouncing it off the rear end of the jeep closest to his ambush point. Sure, he knew it was an old ploy, but there was never anything cute or tricky about killing the enemy.

And death was never pretty.

There was a slim chance the mark was playing him, maybe having thought he spotted him in the brush, ready to pivot and sweep the jungle with a long spray of autofire. He didn't think so, Bolan a master at making himself invisible to the enemy. But he was ready, just the same, the slightest stiffening of shoulders, a flicker of eyes his way.

Bolan waited until he wheeled around the front end, staring at empty space, then lunged at him from behind. Slamming an open hand under his jaw, knee speared into his lower back and jerking his head up, the Executioner drove razor-sharp steel across his throat. There was a predictable instinctive reaction, his victim losing the assault rifle, grabbing at the hand that locked his jaw. By then he was dead on his feet, legs kicking around in a convulsing dance step, blood gushing from the yawn slashed deep, ear to ear.

The Executioner set him down, wiped off the blade on the pant leg twitching out the final spasms. Blade tucked back in shin sheath, sights set on the next batch, Bolan retrieved his M-16 and slung it. Drawing the sound-suppressed Beretta 93-R, he walked away from the motor pool. No hurry, one of the boys.

The arguing he had heard minutes ago, lashing out

from the open doorway at the hut, was reaching new angry levels. He didn't need to know Cramnon's voice to read between the lines of the squalling tones he heard. Greed was about to set the savages at one another's throats.

Why not give them a good shove to start the avalanche?

One of Cramnon's cutthroats, he saw, was crouched in the jet's cabin hatch, taking a smoke break while the others trudged on with their burden. Bolan watched the goldbricker look his way, shaking his head, scowling, muttering something how he was there to fly the plane, not play wetnurse to guys who didn't want to pull their weight when it came to a little manual labor. He went back to smoking, then opened his mouth again when Bolan brought the Beretta up, squeezed the trigger. Whatever gripe was next on the tip of his tongue was blown out the back of his skull, as the 9 mm subsonic round streaked through his open yap.

One eye on the lit entrance to the hut, Bolan angled toward the three mules. The trailing beast of burden was turning, another one with a mouth going wide to piss and moan when the Executioner pumped a round through his skull. Four and Five on the hit parade obviously heard the crunch of deadweight behind. They were dropping their loads, in the act of either grabbing for side arms or shouting a warning when Bolan doused their lights.

Two clean head shots, five down.

Quickly Bolan retreated to the jet. There was another sleek bird parked just beyond the motor pool to mine, but decided to leave that one alone. Too far, the doomsday numbers ticking. If they came out now and discovered the bodies…

He hoped the enemy held their ground inside the hut. Maybe another a minute or so of the savages stating their case to one another, and Bolan would end all heated discussion.

PRICE DIDN'T NEED to be out there in the hut to know they were on the verge of killing one another. Tossed back into her dark cage by Cramnon, who cuffed her feet together and vowed a coming lengthy discussion, she listened to the angry exchange. She counted five voices going back and forth. Say they did start shooting, then what? Greed, anger and something about a plan with North Koreans falling through were pushing them fast and hard toward the breaking point. Could she get so lucky they'd all kill one another? If there were any prayers to be said, that's what she'd ask some divine intervention for.

"It's over, Cramnon."

The creature with the deformed face.

"It's over when I say it's over. Why don't you just go suck down some more whiskey and leave the North Korean problem to me."

"Oh, you're a beauty. There is no North Korean problem, Chief, because the gooks were turned away by a squadron of American fighters. No VX card for you to play, Cramnon, no more showing off who's got the biggest pair on the block."

"Sir, with all due respect, I have to agree—"

"Shut your face, soldier! If I want your opinion, I'll squeeze some shit out of your head! And why aren't you outside helping your teammates!"

"Sir—"

"One more word out of you I think you know who's going to end up with your cut and how."

"Gentlemen, gentlemen, please."

The Arab, she thought, playing peacemaker. Then the fifth wheel, chiming in. "Hey, I got paid to fly your jet, Cramnon. I don't need the circle jerk. I want my money, and I'll take his cut since he obviously won't need it."

"Please, enough already. Why do we not just divide the money—?"

"I'm taking my share, Cramnon. I'm walking. You have a nice life. Do not get in my way, do not lift that rifle the first inch."

"Mr. Cramnon, if it's VX you desire, I can procure some for you. I have contacts in Syria. If that fails, it can be made from scratch. You need, what? Basic ingredients are simple pesticide for starters…"

"No, he wants the blond cupcake he's got caged up over there."

She heard Cramnon roar an obscenity, braced for the sound of autofire, ready to hit the floor if stray bullets came tearing through the wall.

Then the jungle beyond the walls thundered with a series of explosions. They were shouting next, a picture of panicked animals, cornered and staring at one another, framed in her mind. She didn't need to see the bedlam, the blasts or the coming slaughter to know the identity of the night slayer there to drop the hammer on her captors.

For the first time in days, Barbara Price smiled.

AFTER HE HEARD everything he needed to know, the Executioner lit up the motor pool, the radio signal to the primed charges likewise blowing one wheel off the bird that still stored a fat load of their bank, the starboard side drooping to burrow wing into runway.

Bolan threw himself around the edge of the doorway, holding back on the M-16's trigger. Nothing tricky, nothing fancy, just blaze away, chop them down. Rolling thunder warning them their world was all but going up in flames, no hope of escape, there was enough paralysis by shock and fear to grant Bolan two heartbeats of an edge. Five targets altogether, Cramnon hesitating another moment, bellowing curses at the sight of the armed invader, before he cut loose with his M-16. Problem was, the big Alpha hardman with ridges for eyebrows was in the line of fire. But Cramnon didn't bother to shoot around him, mowing him down instead, a flimsy human wall that toppled in spurting blood and flying shredded cloth.

A dark guy in silk was hopping in retreat, Bolan glimpsed, the soldier shuffling to the other side of the doorway as rounds chewed up the jamb he'd vacated. The fancy dancer's arms up, he was screaming for the invader to not kill him. Whoever he was—some of Cramnon's inside help—the Executioner had his number. The screaming dancer was taking blood in the face, expensive threads splashed with the life's juices of two sacks of red ruins already going down to his right flank when Bolan swept the burst of flesh-eaters over his chest.

Tracking on, he saw Cramnon's comrade rise up,

the M-16 flaming in his hands. They were bellowing and cursing each other, shooting it out at near point-blank range when Bolan gave them a helping hand out of the world. Washing a few rounds over the back of the skull in the path of his own line of fire, Bolan kept pouring out the lead tempest. Cramnon was jerking back, taking hits high in the chest. The Alpha leader was still cursing, his autofire spraying the room and ceiling as the hits kept on pounding him, then he exploded through the wall, tumbled on for a vanishing act into the night.

A fresh clip slapped home, Bolan decided to leave no doubt. The Executioner walked to each body, pumped a round into each head. Something told him they were now well on their way to a horror and a torment no human being could possibly fathom the first scintilla of their waiting nightmare.

CRAMNON FELT the fire racing down the length of his body. Pain was good, though; pain told him he was still alive, in the game.

There was hope yet he could make it out of here. If that meant crawling along through the jungle with one bag to a village, he could buy all the help he needed. With the others dead he could come back for the rest.

Hope.

All he had to do was reach his weapon, loose a 40 mm round from the M-203 and bring down the hut. Specifically blast the area dead ahead where the woman was caged. Whoever the big dark bastard, it was clear his crusade was all about the woman. No problem, he could have her. The nameless adversary didn't know it, but he'd actually done him a huge favor by taking out the rest of the buzzards.

Cramnon laughed, even enjoyed the taste of the blood in his mouth, the sound of the wheezing in his ears. A lung was punctured, but he'd been shot worse before. He was gifted like that.

He reached out, wrapped his hand around the M-16. He was bringing it on-line, finger inching up to slip around the M-203's trigger when he sensed the presence rolling up behind. He snarled, lurched the weapon up to blow down the hut anyway. The thought he could deny the bastard, even in his own death, was obliterated by a stammer of weapons fire before the lights were punched out.

EPILOGUE

Bolan wouldn't deny the money did matter.

It had taken time, retrieving his satlink, placing all the right calls, but the night passed, a new day dawning over the jungle. They were on the runway, choppers and twin-engined Cessnas choking the landing strip, Brognola's handpicked team securing the bags. Bolan had already counted them. The big Fed had put him in charge of watching the final money tally when they reached the DEA-CIA base of operations in Thailand. When that was done, it would be shipped back to the Justice Department. And woe unto any man who thought he could pull off another Alpha act.

The soldier didn't know how much cash, gems, jewels and heroin Alpha had seized, but the message on Brognola's end was clear. There would be no Cramnons on his team. As for the narcotics, they would either be incinerated or dumped into the DEA's lap for future stings.

It was blood money, the warrior knew, but it would

now be put to other uses than engineering mass murder. Small comfort for the families of victims, on the home front and Turkey, but a good portion of the cash would go toward a victims' fund Brognola was setting up.

Funny how things worked out.

The soldier left them to their chore. There was a brave lady waiting for him on the late enemy's undamaged Gulfstream.

As he walked to the jet, Bolan wondered where the world was headed. Times had changed, and he couldn't but think the worst. The list of ills consuming the human race was too long to contemplate right then, weary as he was, but relieved, looking forward to an idyllic stretch of paradise himself along the Sea of China, with someone he cared about.

Yes, he decided, there was always hope it could turn around, as long as there were a few good men and women left who wanted more than the fleeting temptations of the world. Indeed, those seven deadly sins he had seen on this campaign taken to new extremes. Or was it all just a fool's wish?

Maybe. Maybe not.

Someone had to try. Someone had to keep going, fight to make a difference.

If not, then it all meant nothing. Man was just an animal.

He boarded the jet, found her sitting, thinking her own thoughts. She looked up, and smiled. It came from the heart, and Bolan thought the look was worth far more than all the money in the world.